Th

"*Rolling Thunder* is
and a solid moral.
ment from Mark M

DAVIS BUNN, best-selling author of *Heartland*

"Drawing upon his real-life experience as a police detective, Mark Mynheir has given us a realistic story and characters to care for. Mark presents us with a fresh new voice and writes from a unique perspective."

ANGELA HUNT, best-selling author of *Uncharted*

"Mynheir is a talented storyteller… In both of his novels he dedicates creating tension and suspense by including family in the plot. This is brilliant. Most cop novels have the detective working to solve a crime because that's what detectives do. By having the storyline revolve around family members, the built-in anxiety is already revved up and ready to go. Well-defined characters fill the pages, while scene and setting perfectly pepper the chapters to make it all like watching a movie inside your imagination. Clever and relevant, *From the Belly of the Dragon* is Mark Mynheir's best novel to

—In the Library Revi

D1057254

Praise for
The Void

"*The Void* is nothing short of a page-turner. Mark Mynheir is truly hitting his stride as one of our industry's most notable Christian novelists. This latest book has it all: suspense, humor, intrigue, realistic police action, and one thought-provoking storyline."

—CRESTON MAPES, author of *Nobody*

"*The Void* was my first book from talented storyteller Mynheir, but it won't be my last. He brought the heat and danger of Florida to life in a remarkable way. His real-life job as a police detective infused authenticity into this suspenseful novel. Highly recommended!"

—COLLEEN COBLE, best-selling author of
Abomination

"When the pursuit of power ushers in evil, man is helpless to continue alone. A magnificent story that teeters between reality and the bizarre."

—DIANN MILLS, award-winning author of The
Texas Legacy Series and *When the Nile Runs Red*

THE VOID

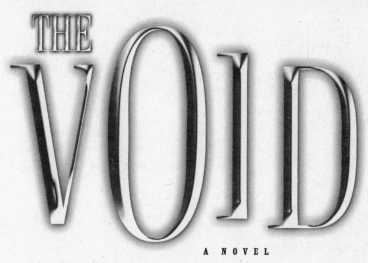

THE VOID

A NOVEL

MARK MYNHEIR

MULTNOMAH
BOOKS

THE VOID
PUBLISHED BY MULTNOMAH BOOKS
12265 Oracle Boulevard, Suite 200
Colorado Springs, Colorado 80921
A division of Random House Inc.

All Scripture quotations or paraphrases are taken from the Holy Bible, New International Version®. NIV®. Copyright © 1973, 1978, 1984 by International Bible Society. Used by permission of Zondervan Publishing House. All rights reserved.

The characters and events in this book are fictional, and any resemblance to actual persons or events is coincidental.

ISBN 978-1-59052-400-8

MULTNOMAH is a trademark of Multnomah Books and is registered in the U.S. Patent and Trademark Office. The colophon is a trademark of Multnomah Books.

Library of Congress Cataloging-in-Publication Data
Mynheir, Mark.
    The void / [Mark Mynheir].
        p. cm. — (The truth chasers series ; bk. 3)
    ISBN 978-1-59052-400-8
    I. Title. II. Series: Mynheir, Mark. Truth chasers series ; bk. 3.
PS3613.Y58V65 2007
813'.6—dc22

                                        2007015422

Printed in the United States of America
2007—First Edition

10 9 8 7 6 5 4 3 2 1

To my dad.
Thank you for your steadfast,
unconditional love and support.

ACKNOWLEDGMENTS

Writing a novel isn't the solitary process I had first assumed when I began this venture. Before a story is ever committed to paper, it requires a certain level of research and immersion into an altogether different world. During the course of this project, I have been amazed by the selflessness and kindness of so many people who allow me to pick and prod their lives with my questions and curiosities.

I would like to express my appreciation to Florida Department of Law Enforcement agent and criminal profiler Tom Davis for his advice and insights. I've not only had the pleasure of working criminal cases with him and learning much along the way, but also have the privilege to call him my friend.

I'd also like to thank Rachel Savage for her keen eye and willing spirit, and I'd be lost without my wonderful and gracious editor Julee Schwarzburg and the tremendous staff at Multnomah Books. A special thanks to fellow police officer Cynthia Williams for sharing her experiences in the Cuban-American culture.

And to my precious wife, whose patience and encouragement are without measure, and to my children, who inspire me daily. Thank you for your time, support, and love.

PROLOGUE

Lifetex Labs, Palm Bay, Florida

Clear!" Dr. Neal Meyer slapped the defibrillator paddles onto the man's bare chest. Another jolt ripped through the body as his muscles seized, then relaxed back on the gurney.

The heart monitor flatlined again, and a high-pitched alarm echoed through the laboratory. Dr. Silverstein squeezed the oxygen bag over the patient's nose and mouth with rhythmic precision as Neal pumped out chest compressions in time. Sweat tumbled off his face and onto the man's well-muscled torso. Nearly an hour of frantic effort without the least sign of vitals. Teetering on the edge of exhaustion, Neal didn't know how much longer he could continue.

"It's no use." Dr. Silverstein lifted the rescue breathing mask from the lifeless form on the table. He pulled a handkerchief from the top pocket of his white lab coat and dabbed his moist forehead. His gray hair frizzed in all directions, his glasses hung crooked on his face, and his portly belly sucked in and out at a worrisome pace. At nearly seventy years old, the doctor appeared as if he might need CPR next.

"I'm calling it now." Dr. Silverstein waved the hanky in the air like a flag of surrender. "He's gone, if he was even here to begin with."

Neal's arms quaked with fatigue from the impromptu workout. He had anticipated a much different result. Why did this keep happening?

"Dr. Silverstein." Warren Finstead stepped out of the darkness and up to the edge of the table. Dressed in his usual dark suit and red power tie, Warren had accomplished more in his forty years than most men dreamed of doing in ten lifetimes. "What in the world is going on? Each time you've called me here I've expected to see a breakthrough, but I only get more disappointment. I don't like disappointment, Doctor. It's bad for business."

Warren's sigh hissed from his nostrils like steam releasing from a geyser about to erupt. His handsome face reddened as he gazed back at the physical specimen splayed out on the table. Tall, muscular, and without physical defect, the body before them lacked nothing—except life. That four-letter word proved more elusive than anyone anticipated.

Steve Glick, Warren's personal assistant, loomed just behind him like a hulking shadow. In a drab suit that barely restrained his monstrous frame, Steve had a square jaw with a chin dimple large enough to store a cell phone in and a flattop that could double as a landing strip. A man of Warren Finstead's stature and financial means required a high level of security, and Glick filled that role as well as he filled a doorway.

Dr. Silverstein pushed up his glasses and took a step back, drawing exaggerated breaths. "When asked about his more than one thousand failures in inventing the light bulb, Thomas Edison said they weren't failures—he'd just learned a thousand ways not to make a light bulb. With each failure, we are just that much closer to our dream, Warren. Science can be arduous, meticulous work."

"I didn't dump millions of dollars and my time and effort into this project for a thousand failures." Warren gripped the edge of the gurney, gazing down at the still body before him. "I want success, and I don't care how you do it. We're on a timetable here, gentlemen. I don't think you appreciate the enormous pressures I'm under."

Dr. Silverstein slipped his hands into his coat pockets and lowered his head. "I'm as frustrated as you are, but we must review the data again. Every time we get to this point, we lose them. We're missing something, but we are so very close."

"Close isn't good enough." Warren pierced them both with his steely blue eyes. "I need the Genesis Project moving forward. *Now.*"

Warren glanced over his shoulder at Steve and then down at the body on the table. "Make this go away…again."

1

Nothing in life is quite as exhilarating as hunting people.
Agent Robbie Sanchez's mind flickered with the remembrance of her college days at the University of Miami when she and her girlfriends' idea of fun and excitement was to hit the bars and go dancing. Now, with nearly ten years of experience as a homicide investigator, she'd long since amended her naive notions of fun and excitement. The addictive, adrenaline-driven world of catching killers stole any possibility she might have of returning to the pleasantly ignorant days of her youth. She was a cop junkie with little chance for rehabilitation.

Robbie rubbed her hands together. Not that she was cold; it was the best way to release the pent-up energy without revealing her position in the bushes. The nearly full moon illuminated the canal bank just enough to form phantoms out of shadows and give substance to the low, clinging fog crawling out of the water onto the shore. Hiding among the dense foliage along the bank of the now infamous Tillman Canal, Robbie's dark camouflage jacket covered her Florida Department of Law Enforcement bulletproof raid vest and her gun belt, which pinched against her hip if she moved just right.

She checked her watch: 3:34 a.m. Another slow, possibly wasted night. They'd set up their surveillance every night for nearly three weeks with nothing resembling a lead. She needed to be patient, no matter what it took. The killer would return.

The muggy Florida air and occasional sounds of fish breaking the water's surface added a little ambiance to her secluded, all-night venture. She tucked an errant tendril of her black hair back into the elastic band and tightened her ponytail. She was a city girl, not some rustic chick. Just because she was on a stakeout didn't mean she had to look uncivilized.

Squeaking brakes called from the darkness. A shadowy silhouette of a car, lights off, crept toward her down the pitted, bumpy service road along the canal bank. Maybe one of the other agents was changing position? The car stopped, but no brake lights came on.

"I've got some movement here," Robbie whispered into her radio mic as she stepped behind a palm tree and aimed her night-vision scope toward the car. "Is anybody moving out there?"

"Everybody's still in position." John Russell was a half mile west of her location. "If something's moving, it's not one of us."

Robbie adjusted the volume on her radio and tightened her earpiece. FDLE agents from the Melbourne field office were stationed at intervals along the six-mile-long canal bank. The Tillman had many entry points—some from neighborhoods, some from wooded trails. Florida Power & Light used it to check their power poles, and ATV and motorcycle riders enjoyed the road during the day. Boaters and fishermen trolled along the canal itself, but it was the nighttime activity that concerned Robbie.

In the last four months, three homicide victims surfaced at different points along the canal—one was found underneath a private dock, another in a patch of reeds. And just over a month earlier, the last victim was discovered floating facedown in the middle of the channel. By Robbie's estimate and profile, the killer worked on a thirty-day cycle.

He was past due to strike again.

His victims were prostitutes working the Melbourne and Palm Bay area: women of the night who could disappear and not be missed for days, weeks, months—and sometimes never. As if murdering the women wasn't bad enough, the ghoul had tortured them first.

It was an impossible task to try to keep watch on the all-too-numerous potential victims strolling up and down the U.S. 1 corridor. Another consistent factor of his MO was the dumpsite. This place meant something to him. Maybe he grew up around here. Maybe he lived within a block or two or possibly right along the canal. Robbie didn't know what it was, but something attracted him here—and he'd surely return.

The car stopped about two hundred feet away. No one came out here this time of night just to sit in a car by himself. Robbie zoomed in on him with the night-vision scope. The driver fumbled with something in the front seat. Even if he wasn't their suspect, this guy was up to no good. The man opened his door and used the roof to hoist himself out of the vehicle.

He checked up and down the desolate roadway. The green hues of the night vision made a positive identification impossible, but he was a white male, maybe midthirties, medium build, wearing blue jeans and work boots. Definitely not one of her team. He paced to the front of the car, then quickly to the rear doing "the felony look-around." Whatever he was up to, it should be a treat.

Robbie's pulse quickened as he jammed his key in the trunk's lock and whipped it open.

"All units, move up." Robbie hugged the shadows of the tree line as she inched closer and whispered into the mic. "He's opened the trunk. We have to block him in."

The man bent over and pulled a log-sized lump half out of the trunk, resting it on the edge. Squatting down, he lugged the object out onto his shoulders. Hunched over and staggering like a drunk trying to dance, he two-stepped his way to balance, the limp load draped over his shoulders like a thick, malleable yoke. Lumbering down the canal bank, he picked up speed, and with a primitive grunt, he launched the object into the waiting waters of the Tillman. The loud splash told Robbie what she needed to know—they'd just found their suspect.

"It's him! It's him!" Robbie silently sprinted from the darkness and drew her 9 mm, crouching down as she ran to intercept him. "All units, move in. Repeat, all units, move in."

"Wait for backup!" Special Agent in Charge Alan Cohen commanded. "We'll be there in just one minute."

The suspect marched up the steep bank toward his car. He glanced back at the disturbed waters lapping at the shore, and he rubbed his hands along his jeans. He was nearly in the car. She didn't have a minute.

It's easier to beg for forgiveness than to ask permission.

She skulked along the road about twenty yards from the vehicle without acknowledging Alan over the radio. She had the element of surprise and couldn't wait for backup. The suspect would be gone by then, maybe forever. She had to move now. She lit him up with the flashlight. "Police! Get on the ground. Now!"

He twirled around, his arm splayed out like he was preparing for a tackle. His eyes narrowed and focused in on her. This guy wasn't going down without a fight.

Robbie marched toward him, gun and flashlight freezing him in place. He stole a furtive glance at the open car door. Could she cut him off before he made it to the car?

"I know what you're thinking." Robbie quickened her pace. "Don't do it. On the ground now!"

Raising his hands high, he glanced behind him, then back at Robbie. She was alone, and he had to know that by now. With a smirk and two quick bounds, he hopped into the driver's seat,

slamming the car in gear before his rear hit the seat. The spinning tires sprayed a rooster tail of dirt as the vehicle swerved,
front door still open, and barreled toward Robbie, who back-
pedaled but would never make it out of his path.

"Stop!" She trained her flashlight and 9 mm on the driver's
head. His hateful, sadistic eyes bore down on her, and he
gunned the engine. She had no choice.

Crack. Crack. Two rounds spiderwebbed the windshield
just as the driver ducked down, jerking the car to the right at
the last second.

Robbie dove and rolled down the canal bank, splashing
into the murky soup of the Tillman. He missed her by mere
inches, and his car rocketed along the clumpy canal bank like
a skier taking moguls.

As Robbie struggled for footing, her hand brushed against an
object bobbing in the water. Cold and smooth. She didn't have to
see it to know she'd just touched another victim. She pulled up
her flashlight, hoping it still worked, and shone it on the water.

The milky white figure floated facedown in a way no live
human could.

Robbie grabbed the woman's wrist, heaved her up onto the
shore, and made a quick search for vitals. They were long gone.
Another victim. One more woman forced to pay for this suspect's sick, deluded fantasies.

He was going to be stopped—tonight.

Robbie crawled up the canal bank, weighed down by her
saturated vest and gear.

Another car raced down the dirt road toward her, the dash-mounted red and blues flashing, then skidded to a stop. "Are you okay?" The dust that John's car kicked up overtook them.

"I'm fine." Robbie lit up the victim's body on the shore as she struggled to catch her breath. "But he's killed another one. We've got to get him, John. We can't let him escape again."

"Hop in!" He revved the engine and white-knuckled the steering wheel, his ink black hair slicked back.

The suspect's vehicle was back on the dirt road and nearly a quarter mile away. Robbie sprinted around the car and shook her pistol, hoping the water wouldn't damage it. She might need it again soon.

"He's getting ready to turn onto Fallon Boulevard," John called on the radio as he pulled away before Robbie could shut the door.

"I've got him." Agent Tim Porter's voice brimmed with excitement. "He's turning west. A blue Honda. Florida tag FDC4439. I'm in pursuit. Get the sheriff's helicopter here."

"Catch up, John." Robbie holstered her pistol and then pounded a damp fist on the dash. "I fired at him twice, but I don't think I hit him." She'd been on this guy for too long now to let him slip away like this. But Porter was a good cop. He wouldn't let the suspect escape.

Robbie snatched John's microphone off the dashboard. "We have a confirmed victim, and he tried to run me down. We have at least one more count of murder plus attempted murder on me. Do what you have to do to stop this guy. He's not getting away tonight."

As the dirt road turned into pavement, John's car smacked a dip, scraping the bottom and jostling Robbie. The Buick screamed as they raced toward Tim, who was keeping up with the killer, turn by turn.

"He's heading north on Babcock Street." Tim's voice was a pitch higher than normal, the adrenaline amping up on everyone.

The Brevard County Sheriff's Department helicopter thundered overhead, its powerful spotlight tracking the suspect's car as if it were daytime. He was just ahead of them. John floored it. Alan Cohen's car fell in behind them.

All the agents converged on the suspect as he zigzagged and barreled down the four-lane road, desperate to elude their pursuit. At least the late hour gave them some insulation from killing an innocent civilian in a car crash. The streets were empty save the cops and the killer.

"I'm gonna ram him," Tim's voice crackled over the radio.

"Wait and follow him a little longer. We've got the copter here. Let's be smart."

"Forget smart, Alan. He tried to run over Robbie. I'm taking him out." Tim accelerated alongside the suspect, who swerved into Tim's lane, not letting him get next to him.

"Watch it!" Alan called out. "This guy's desperate. He knows he's going down. Be careful."

Veering out of his way, Tim eased closer and lined up his front bumper just off the suspect's left rear tire. Tim swerved, nailing the suspect's car just behind the tire, sparks flying like two sabers clashing in battle. The suspect spun out of control and crashed into a tree.

Tim's car careened off Babcock Street in the opposite direction, taking flight as he struck the curb and splashing down into a retention pond nose first.

John skidded to a stop just behind the suspect's crumpled heap. Robbie leaped out and raced toward the car, her pistol trained on the man. Smoke billowed from the crushed car, and the suspect's head wobbled back and forth as he fought to open the crinkled door.

"Get your hands up!" Robbie tickled the side of his head with her pistol. Blood trailed down his battered, defeated face, his hands trembling as they extended out of the smoldering wreck.

John seized one arm, Alan the other, and they wrenched him from the car via the smashed-out driver's window. Planting him facedown on the asphalt, they cuffed him. The sirens from the backup units wailed into the night, announcing the end of this killer's reign of mayhem and murder.

Robbie pulled his wallet out of his jeans pocket. *Gerald Williamson.* No one she'd ever heard of. But they would become very familiar soon. She rolled him onto his side. "Mr. Williamson, I'm Agent Roberta Sanchez with the Florida Department of Law Enforcement. You're under arrest for the murder of the young woman you just dumped in the Tillman Canal, and we're going to talk about all the others as well."

Gerald's head dropped to the concrete, echoing like a hollow coconut.

"Hey, is anyone gonna help me?" Tim asked as John passed off Williamson to the Palm Bay police officers for transport. "I need some help over here."

"I almost forgot about Tim." Robbie holstered her pistol. Then she, Alan, and John jogged across Babcock Street's four lanes to where Tim tanked his car.

Tim's Buick, his pride and joy fresh off the line, lurched in the water in a manner reminiscent of the last moments of the *Titanic*. Tim perched on the trunk with his legs dangling off. His back window appeared to have been kicked out.

"Did you get him?" Tim pulled his knees to his chest as the car sunk a little more in the water. Water droplets glistened on his short-cropped afro like a crown, and his thick frame struggled for balance atop his Buick bobber.

"He's bagged and tagged." Robbie slipped off her camo jacket and then her FDLE raid vest and dropped them to the grass. "But it looks like you're gonna have to swim in to see him."

"That ain't right." Tim shook his head. "This is my first new car since I don't know when."

Alan massaged his gray beard as he gawked at Tim's predicament. "Porter, you're not gonna see the inside of a new car as long as I'm here, which, luckily for you, happens to be only six weeks."

"Boss, what else was I supposed to do?" Tim shrugged. "He's a killer who tried to run Robbie down. I couldn't let him get away. Give me a break."

Alan slapped his hands on his hips, his mostly bald head shining under the streetlights. "That's what you said when you smashed the car into the convenience store, and when you wrecked the retirement home, and when you—"

"I get it, I get it." Tim crossed his arms. "But for now, can you just get me outta here?"

Tim's car floated in the middle of the retention pond, a good fifteen feet from shore. Robbie flashed her light all around the shoreline. "Well, big guy, I think you're gonna have to wait for a wrecker or swim your way out."

"Man, I don't want to wait out here an hour for some wrecker." Tim rose, balancing on the bumper like he was riding a wave on a surfboard. "I think I can make the jump."

"No way." Robbie laughed. Tim was so stubborn and just about crazy enough to try. "Just wait and someone will pull you out."

"I *can* make this jump." Tim rubbed his brown hands together. He was in good shape for a man in his late forties, but he had a bit too much bulk for that kind of leap.

Robbie shook her head. "It's not going to happen. Better wait for the tow truck."

"Russell, can I make this jump or what?"

"My friend, if you try it you'll be very wet and very angry." John ripped the Velcro and shed his raid vest, letting it slide to the ground. He stretched out his lean, sinewy frame. "It's not worth the attempt."

"Bah to both of you." Tim pointed to the murky chasm that separated them. "I was a fine athlete in my day, and I can do this."

"I've got ten bucks that says you'll splash down before you touch down." Robbie held up her wallet. For all they'd been through, this would be money well spent.

John leaned toward her and whispered, "Don't do that. It'll only encourage him."

"I know." Robbie smirked. Pushing Tim's buttons was so easy. "Do you have your camera here?"

"You're a really bad girl." John crossed his arms. "It's in the car. Want me to get it?"

"Hey, we've been working this case day and night for four months. It's time we had some fun. Go get it."

John hustled across the street to his car.

Tim pulled his wallet out and waved a ten at Robbie. "Show me the money, lady."

Robbie retrieved a ten of her own and grinned as the currency flapped in the early morning breeze. "Okay, Kermit, let's see if you can make that jump."

Alan walked to the pond's edge. "Please tell me he's not going to do what I think he's going to do." He lifted his vest over his head and dropped it on the ground. His sweat-soaked

T-shirt clung to his broad chest. Sporting a good build for a man in his early fifties, Alan often told Robbie that his daily workouts were the only thing that kept him sane.

John jogged back to Robbie and handed her his digital camera.

"Oh yeah." Robbie raised the camera and focused in on Tim. "And Porter's going to be paying for breakfast too."

Tim alternated his gaze from the bumper to the shoreline. He swayed and worked his arms back and forth. Eyeing the shore, he leaped with all his might.

Robbie snapped the photo.

2

Benjamin removed his glasses as he stood in front of his laboratory door, and the red laser scanned his retina. "Good morning, Dr. Silverstein," the feminine computer-generated voice said. He pinched the bridge of his nose and blinked several times to refocus his vision.

"Good morning." He always felt silly answering a computer, but it felt rude to say nothing. Security wasn't his strong suit, but he certainly understood the need.

After the perfunctory metallic buzz of unlocking doors, he hurried into his lab, late as usual, or right on time, depending on how one looked at it. This morning he'd spent an extraordinary amount of time searching for his BlackBerry; he could never keep track of the infernal thing. More of a nuisance really, but he had to be reachable at all times.

How had human beings survived in the past without all of these gadgets? Einstein got along perfectly fine without a BlackBerry or a cell phone. There was something to be said for a little less rushing and a little more reflection.

The small hallway opened up into a cavernous room with a ceiling two stories high. Computer equipment and monitors lined the walls, and twenty-one amniotic chambers divided into three rows of seven dominated the center of the lab. Most of the lab's light emanated from inside the chambers themselves.

"Dr. Silverstein, we were worried you weren't going to make it." Dr. Neal Meyer stood in front of the first chamber.

A bright young man, Neal made a fine research assistant and partner in this venture. Without his dedication, Benjamin would not have been able to get this far. Neal's brown hair had retreated from the front of his head, and his thin frame and gaunt face revealed a man who was too focused on work and didn't eat well.

"You must be joking, Neal." Benjamin buttoned up his lab coat. "This could be the greatest day of our lives. I'd have sooner missed my own birth."

"Maybe today we'll actually experience success." Warren Finstead emerged from between the rows of chambers, surveying their most important project to date. Steve Glick hung back behind him, off to his left, silent as usual. "That would be a pleasant change."

"I think this will be a most historic day, Warren." Benjamin extended his hand. Warren seized it and squeezed extra tight, locking eyes with an intensity that only Warren could muster.

Benjamin had developed an immunity to Warren's barbs long ago and didn't take them personally. He was used to working with demanding, intense men. The reality was, without Warren Finstead, the Genesis Project would have been the pipe dream of an eccentric professor from MIT. "You won't be disappointed, my friend."

"I hope not." Warren gazed down at the Yorkshire terrier scampering from behind the chamber.

Benjamin lifted the terrier and stroked his head. The small dog's heart purred with the precision of a fine automobile engine, maybe the finest ever engineered. "This fella's been an enormous help to us. Isn't that right, Sammy?" He rubbed noses with his pet.

"I think, Doctor, that you've become a little too attached to that mutt." Warren rolled his eyes. "After all, he is just an experiment."

"This *mutt* should have been the most famous animal in the world, but we all know better than to tout our victories too early. Some before us have replicated sheep and other animals, so even Sammy wouldn't be the first. But he is certainly the most magnificent, a flawless specimen. Sammy's success has taught us much of where we went wrong, and he's the key to getting it right."

"I hope so. For all of our sakes." Warren eyed Steve behind him. "We don't need any more…problems."

Steve nodded with a crease on his face that could be mistaken for a smile.

"We might not have been the first to clone animals, but no one will beat us to him." Benjamin rested his hand on the chamber that contained a man suspended in amniotic fluid, arms floating at his side. His remarkably well-developed physique balanced in his liquid womb, eyes open with a blank stare.

Black swim trunks and a chest harness were his only clothing, and a mask covered his face with a respirator running to the chamber's top. Strands of black hair waved above him, and his sharp, chiseled muscles would be the envy of any bodybuilder. His limbs twitched as the current from the electrodes pulsed in cadence to prepare his muscles for use. The chamber prevented bed sores and permitted the experiments to grow unencumbered in the fluid, a combination of nutrients and enzymes for the skin and eyes. Nothing could be left to chance.

"Are you sure he's ready to survive outside the chamber?" Warren brushed lint off his sleeve. "I'm not in the mood for more drama."

"He's ready. I know it." Benjamin lowered Sammy to the floor. He trotted between Warren and Neal and disappeared around the corner.

Warren's apprehension was understandable, but this time was different. They'd made adjustments and learned so much from each step. Then, as if an angel whispered it in his ear, he'd had an idea to incubate an entire line of experiments, not just one at a time. Neal then tweaked the genetic components to strengthen their subjects. Twenty-one new and improved men now stood ready to make history.

"We've accelerated his growth process to meet your goals." Benjamin slipped on a pair of rubber gloves as he talked. "He's a pure specimen of humanity if there ever was one. He'll have the strength of three men combined. He's not just the first successful human clone; he's a genetically altered—perfect—human being. We are gazing at the future of humankind."

"If what you're predicting proves true, Doctor, then we all stand to be very rich men. And the medical advances Lifetex will be able to accomplish from this point forward are almost incalculable." Warren stepped back with Steve. "There is no limit to where this technology will take us."

"I'm not one to discount monetary gain, but the Genesis Project is so much more than that." Benjamin pulled a surgical mask over his face. "Imagine a world with no disease, with all the genetic flaws engineered out of the human population. Think of all the progress that can be made in science with specimens such as these. Perfect organs harvested to save the lives of others, research to end all suffering. A new day is dawning, Warren. And we are all a part of it. This has been worth the wait."

"It's a shame the press isn't aware of what we're doing here." Neal manned the control panel at the side of the chamber. "A new future begins today, and no one is here to appreciate it except us."

"There will be plenty of time for that," Benjamin said. "We can't take the risk of another problem while the press is here. We'll be filming the entire process for posterity. Nothing will be lost. But we must be wise in how we present our findings to the world. First things first: our friend here is celebrating his birthday today. We really shouldn't keep him waiting."

"Have you come up with a name for him?" Warren folded his arms.

"Why, Adam, of course." Benjamin chuckled. "It seems fitting."

"I think you're right, Doctor. It's most appropriate." Warren glanced at his watch. "Are we ready to get started? We're already a little behind schedule."

Benjamin approached the table directly in front of Adam's chamber. Two nurses stood by, waiting for their signal. Angela and Lois were quite loyal and well compensated for their work—and their discretion.

"Doctor," they said in unison. Both were decked out in blue surgical caps, scrubs, masks, and rubber gloves.

"Ladies." Benjamin bowed. "I think it's time for delivery. Dr. Meyer, would you do us the privilege of birthing Adam?"

Neal typed in a series of commands on the control panel. The hoist above the chamber hummed. With the harness around his chest pulling taut, Adam rose above the chamber, amniotic fluid pouring off his muscular body. Neal worked the control stick as Adam's limp body ascended over the top of the chamber. As Adam descended onto the table set out for him,

Benjamin, Angela, and Lois took hold of his legs and laid him gently on his back. They dried his legs, torso, and arms with towels.

The respirator was still attached to his mask. Adam's brawny chest rose and fell with mechanical precision.

"Okay, remove the mask." Benjamin unsnapped one side while Lois attended to the other. They eased it away from his face, breaking the seal, and Lois and Angela removed the long dual-intubation tube that had been supplying oxygen and nourishment.

Adam drew his first breath of unpumped air—the breath of life. His head flopped to one side, almost staring at Benjamin, if that were possible. Adam's eyes carried no signs of life, just vacant black disks with no more expression than a doll's.

The nurses continued their preparation, and Angela covered him with a sheet while Lois toweled off his hair.

"His vitals seem good and strong. His heart rate is perfect. His brain waves are functioning well. But something doesn't seem right." Benjamin wiped Adam's forehead with a cloth. "I guess I expected a little more movement or something from him."

The group circled around Adam's gurney, the beeping EKG reverberating throughout the lab.

"Maybe there's some sort of brain damage?" Neal shone a penlight into one of Adam's eyes and then the other; both contracted normally. "There must be something that we haven't accounted for."

"We've considered everything. He should be responding." Benjamin shook his head. "This is just like the others. I don't understand. Sammy nearly jumped off the table as soon as he was out. Why is there no responsiveness at all?"

Adam's body convulsed and seized-up, his arms flailing. His heart rate spiked on the EKG.

"Not again! Restrain him." Benjamin grabbed an arm as Neal and the nurses held Adam to the table, his body jumping and thrashing about. Benjamin struggled to keep ahold of him. Adam was even stronger than he expected.

"Give me a readout!"

"His vitals are going wild, Dr. Silverstein." Angela glanced at the monitors, then back to Benjamin. "I don't know what's happening. He's in some type of arrest. Do you want me to medicate him?"

"Not yet." He felt Adam's muscles loosen and relax. "Let's observe him for a moment. I think he's calming down."

Adam's tremors slowed to light twitching, his legs sliding around on the table. The EKG monitor eased back to normal. Adam blinked several times and moved his head from side to side.

Benjamin released his grip. Adam raised his hand and gazed at it, rotating it and opening and closing his fist. He looked around the lab, his eyes now alert and processing the new world around him. He shifted his attention to Benjamin.

"Eureka! Adam lives!" Benjamin thrust his arms in the air like a referee signaling a touchdown. He didn't need that kind of scare at his age. He turned to Neal. "Finally, Adam is here. Thank goodness. I think he's going to be okay. We've done the impossible."

"Congratulations, Doctor, everyone." Warren clapped. Angela, Lois, and Neal chimed in as the applause echoed throughout the lab. "This is what I wanted to see—success. Great teamwork. I know I've pushed you all very hard, but it's paid off now…big time."

"Thank you, Warren, for this magnificent day." Benjamin leaned over Adam. "Can you hear me?"

Adam gazed back at Benjamin and then at those around him. He grinned.

3

Robbie jiggled her front-door key as the sun crested the top of the complex, illuminating the hallway of her second-story apartment. She could barely focus. Being up all night with a demented killer sapped anything resembling energy. She'd hoped that after finally catching Williamson, he would confess his crimes. No such luck. But that didn't surprise her either. Her profile had predicted that he'd invoke his rights and refuse to talk.

She also predicted that her killer was quite intelligent and methodical. The victims had all been dumped in the water to destroy any evidence. Gerald Williamson was an engineer by trade, and he lived two blocks from the Tillman Canal.

Robbie pegged him perfectly in her profile, but it offered her little comfort now. Four women were dead because of his sick, twisted fantasies. She only wished her profile could have provided a name and address before that scum killed anyone, some sort of all-knowing, flawless method of stopping these madmen before they ever murdered at all. But that wasn't reality. She had to work with what her training and experience gave her. Now she had nailed him flat out for one murder, and she believed they could link him to the others. At least he'd be locked away, never able to hurt anyone again.

She fumbled with her keys again while balancing her briefcase and files, the haze in her brain still not lifted. The doorknob rattled and then opened.

"I thought I heard you out here." Kathy Henderson held open the door. Her short brunette hair danced around her shoulders. She stepped back and opened the door wider so Robbie could enter.

"It's been a long night." Robbie shrugged as she steadied her load. "How's Mima?"

"She's up but not dressed yet. She seems to be having a pretty good morning, all things considered."

Robbie hurried past Kathy and placed her briefcase and file folders next to the small dining-room table. Robbie slipped a CD with Ibrahim Ferrer's "Bruca Manigua" into the CD player. The soft Latin tune reverberated throughout the two-bedroom apartment that served Robbie and her mother so well, although not what could be called luxurious by any means.

The couch in the middle of the living room still had a blanket on it where Kathy had slept the night before. Robbie was fortunate to find a woman like her to help out. Young, single, and earning money for college, Kathy cared for Robbie's mother during the day while Robbie worked, and would stay over nights when necessary.

Robbie opened her checkbook and scribbled out a week's payment for her, plus a little extra for the double duty Kathy had been pulling lately. She tore the check out and handed it to her.

"Thanks again for all your help and for staying over. I don't know what I'd do without you. I certainly couldn't earn a living."

"It's my pleasure, Robbie. Your mother is a wonderful lady and a joy to spend time with. But what does *cochinito* mean?"

Robbie covered her mouth and chuckled. "It means 'little piggy.' Why?"

"She was complaining last night about something. I really have to brush up on my Spanish, but she used that word often. Isabel hardly ever speaks in English anymore."

Robbie nodded.

Her mother emerged from her room, draped in a faded blue robe. She looked at Robbie and smiled, not the exuberant greeting of a woman whose daughter just returned home from work. It was a courteous, formal smile she reserved for strangers, something Robbie was fast becoming in her mother's mind. Her mother ambled into the room and glanced at Kathy, then back to Robbie.

"*Buenos días,* Mima." Robbie stepped forward and gave her

a peck on the cheek. She welcomed Robbie with a vacant stare but said nothing. *"¿Cómo dormistes?* Did you sleep well?"

Her mother shrugged. *"Más o menos."* She strolled over to the couch and sat facing the television.

How odd that as the disease progressed, her ability to speak English diminished as well. The cruelty of the malady was only now becoming fully evident, ever so slightly washing away any vestiges of life as she knew it, like the unstoppable torrent of high tide rolling over and over a beautiful sandcastle on the beach until its very memory is erased from the shoreline forever.

"Well, I've got to get going." Kathy grabbed her purse and headed for the door. "I'll see you tomorrow, Isabel." Kathy waved, and Mima returned it reflexively.

Robbie hurried to the kitchen and started her preloaded espresso machine, which appeared as beaten and weathered as she felt. The ancient apparatus rumbled, hissed, and sputtered to life. The aroma of the café con leche enveloped the small apartment, spiking Robbie's heart rate by the mere smell. Moments later she poured a fresh, steaming cup of the potent Cuban coffee, grabbed a package of saltine crackers, and carried them out to Mima.

Every morning of her mother's life included the Cuban coffee and crackers; these little routines were becoming increasingly important to keep her at peace. Mima took the cup and passed the brew underneath her nose and smiled. She nibbled on a cracker and eased back into the couch.

The other detectives made fun of Robbie for drinking her coffee black, but after being weaned on strong Cuban espresso, anything less was like drinking water. Her father often said that he required his espresso strong enough to chip a tooth on.

Mima took another bite of her cracker and a long, savoring sip of her coffee. Her long silver hair suffered the abuse that only a night of fitful sleep can offer.

"Lean back, Mima." Robbie pulled a brush from her purse. "Let me fix your hair."

Her mother placed the coffee cup on the table beside her and wrapped the robe around her legs. Her movements were as elegant and graceful as always.

Robbie gathered Mima's hair and stroked the brush through, dislodging some light tangles, her gossamer locks shimmering under the light. Once a polished black, her hair still remained long and full and striking. Isabel Sanchez was without a doubt the most beautiful woman Robbie had ever known.

She wasn't the only one with that opinion. When Robbie was young, she would walk with her mother to the corner store in Little Havana in Miami. The men drove by, honked, whistled, and called out to her. Mima would glance down at Robbie and just continue walking with her wry smile, not giving them a moment of her time. The constant attention from other men didn't impress her in the least. Her heart belonged to just one man—Jorge Sanchez.

Robbie wondered what a love like that would feel like, a man and a woman utterly committed to each other. Her parents' love and affection was an anomaly in this world, and she doubted that a love that strong and enduring would ever find its way to her. Men didn't treat her as they did her mother. Robbie wished she had inherited some of her mother's beauty and poise rather than having a tomboy nature.

She rested her hand on top of her mother's head and continued to work the brush through the brilliant strands. Robbie glanced at the bookshelf with the wedding picture of Jorge and Isabel Sanchez. Her father was a strong, vibrant man with a sharp, penetrating laugh and round, joyous face. Her parents had fled the tyranny of Castro's regime for a chance at a better life. They'd found that chance in America. Her papi was a die-hard patriot, loving Cuba and the United States with equal passion.

Feeling a sense of debt to his new country, Papi enlisted in the army and did a stint as a Ranger in Vietnam and then twenty-two years as a Metro-Dade police officer. Jorge Sanchez commanded respect when he entered a room. It was that same respect that had drawn four thousand police officers to his funeral. He was labeled a hero for foiling a bank robbery that went terribly bad and taking two crazed gunmen with him to the grave. But Papi was fighting three gunmen that day, and it was the third who shot him in the back.

Robbie passed the brush a bit more easily through her mima's hair as she sought to wipe the memory from her mind. She was too tired to go through it again. After all these years, the sting of the murder was still fresh. She gazed back at her father's picture. Robbie yearned to hold him one more time and tell him how much she loved him. Now, with her mother's illness, Robbie felt as if she'd already lost both of her parents.

Her mother reached up and patted Robbie's hand. "Roberta?" She beamed, a sparkle of recognition in her eyes as her hand stroked Robbie's.

"*Sí,* Mima." She savored these moments, becoming fewer by the day. Joy chased the fog of exhaustion from Robbie's mind. It had the makings of a great day.

Robbie typed away on her keyboard at work, the last several days blurring into a jumbled narrative on her screen. There would be time to edit later. She'd caught another killer, a man driven by his perverted lust and evil desires. Like most she'd dealt with before, Gerald Williamson made mistakes—big ones. He did have the good sense to leave the driver's licenses of his victims underneath the computer monitor in his house, which the police gathered while executing the search warrant.

She knew that he'd have trophies, small portable trinkets from each victim to help him relive the crimes again and again. She'd pegged him well. Conviction was pretty much a slam dunk at this point. It was only a matter of cleaning up the mess and preparing all of her evidence for a court presentation sometime in the future.

The back door opened, and someone was walking toward

the agents' desks, which were cubicles positioned in a square with an open space between them. Robbie flashed a look at John, who was in his desk chair. He nodded at her and smiled. Alan rushed into the area and hurried into the chair next to John. The plan was in place. Robbie stifled her smile and pasted on her serious work face.

"He's coming," Alan said as Tim entered the workspace.

"Good morning, all." Tim plopped down into his chair and switched on his computer. "No need to thank me for catching your guy, Robbie." Tim held up his hand. "I'm sure if you were in my position, you'd have risked your life to solve someone else's case. I have no doubt of that."

Tim spun in his chair, his back to his computer as his login sequence booted up. He folded his hands across his stomach and glanced at Robbie. "I assume that you *are* gonna carefully document in your report how I, nearly single-handedly, apprehended your suspect with a precision PITT maneuver."

Tim held his hands in front of him as if they were on a steering wheel. He treated them to several renditions of this takedown technique, with mad jerking motions and a bizarre sound that she assumed was supposed to be a car engine.

"Oh, I'm going to mention your contribution, something like that…sort of."

"I don't like the sound of 'sort of.' If I'm gonna risk my life, the least I could expect is a kind word or two in your report, since some people in this office don't appreciate aggressive law enforcement anymore." Tim eyed Alan, who was still mumbling with John. "It doesn't matter, though, because I'm going to file a detailed supplement for this case myself."

Robbie glanced past Tim to his computer. The background on his screen switched on, and the photo from the night of the arrest sprang to life. Robbie covered her mouth to suppress a giggle, but she lost it when Tim's full form—splashing into the retention pond—filled the screen. The picture was Pulitzer quality. Tim's arms shot straight out and his legs kicked up, just as his bottom entered the water. The look of horror on his face was clear in every detail. A masterpiece.

Tim scowled at Robbie and then turned to see her handiwork. He leaped to his feet and pointed at the screen. "That's just wrong. Wrong, I tell you! Which one of you is responsible?"

Robbie, John, and Alan roared with laughter, Alan slapping his knee.

Robbie raised her hand. "Guilty as charged."

"Oooh, Sanchez, when the time is right, you're gonna get yours. You can bet on that." Tim jammed his hands in his pockets and pivoted in a circle.

"Don't fret, big guy." She rose and walked over to him. "I can delete it off your screen."

"You all know I would have made that jump if I hadn't slipped on that wet bumper."

Robbie rolled her eyes. Porter would never admit defeat. "I'll take it off your background." She sat in Tim's chair and clicked into his settings. "But I don't think I can delete it from the department newsletter that comes out tomorrow. I heard you made the front page."

"Sanchez," Tim wagged an angry finger at her, "when you least expect it—expect it."

"Well, I have some news that might lift your spirits." Alan stood, still grinning. "I was able to get you a car from impound. I think you'll find that it fits your personality quite nicely."

"At least that's something. I spent all of yesterday drying out my equipment, my guns, my wallet—everything was soaked." Tim shook his head. "Smelled like swamp water too. Nasty."

"Let's go out and see your new ride." Alan dangled the keys for Tim to grab.

Alan led the rest of the team down the corridor and out the back door to the parking lot. "There she is." He held his hand out to the car parked in Tim's normal spot. "She's ready to set sail when you are."

"You *can't* be serious." Tim stared in disbelief at the abomination before him.

John laughed as they beheld the hideous vehicle. A 1968 yellow Volkswagen Beetle, decorated with several peace signs on the hood and the trunk. The headlights had black paint on them that made it look like eyes with mascara. It was seized from a hippie who ran pounds of marijuana from one end of the state to the other.

"Alan, what are you doing to me?" Tim grabbed the sides of his head. "I can't enforce the law in this thing."

"You're a great cop, Porter, but you can't drive to save your life—or anyone else's." Alan slapped his hands on his hips. "Maybe the peace signs will calm your demeanor a tad."

Tim opened the door, stepped away from the car, and fanned his nose. "It's a stick shift, and it reeks in here. Smells like a reefer factory. And it has an eight-track-tape player. How in the world am I gonna listen to any music? I can't use this."

"Well then, you can walk to all of your cases." Alan crossed his arms. "Because this is your ride until I leave here."

"Boss, this could be considered cruel and unusual punishment." Robbie rested a hand on Tim's thick shoulder.

"He's earned it."

"Russell, are you gonna help me or what?" Tim's sad expression almost made Robbie feel sorry for him. Almost.

"You can ride with me." John was a softy, always feeling sorry for whoever had a problem.

"Thanks, Russell, you're a good egg."

"I don't know how good of an egg I am. I just know that I wouldn't get in that monstrosity if it was the last car in the fleet."

4

"Y ou trying to get us both killed, rookie?" Willie Farmer asked as he waved at Brad Worthington, who just turned into the alley and flashed the squirrelly informant with his headlights. "Turn those things off."

Brad flicked off his lights and stepped from his unmarked police car, adjusting his cross tie tack, keeping it straight. The humid night air mugged him at once, sweat beading across his forehead. His long-sleeved shirt and tie didn't help, but they were a part of the job, just as his uniform had been before he was promoted to detective. Another unbearably hot summer encroached on the horizon. He tugged twice at his collar, loosening the noose some.

Willie raised the Miami Dolphins cap off his head and ran his fingers through his stringy brownish gray hair in his usual overly dramatic fashion. He scanned up and down the alleyway.

As challenging as informants could be, all the work paid off for Brad when one gold nugget of information was mined from his contacts. Many were drug addicted or working off criminal charges, so their information needed to be vetted in the highest order.

Willie required little supervision and was generally reliable, as informants went. He breezed in and out of Brad's professional life with the capriciousness of the El Niño winds, offering up intriguing flurries of information, only to disappear again with no fixed date of return. Several months had passed since his last call, until tonight.

Willie's bike rested against the white block wall of the rear of the convenience store where he had asked to meet. A bedroll and all the accoutrements of his life were tied, hung, and balanced on a set of baskets over the rear tire. Faded blue jeans and a green army field jacket adorned a man perpetually down on his luck. He'd walked the streets of Palm Bay since before Brad started as a police officer eight years ago and would probably be there long after he left, a near-permanent fixture on these city streets.

"How are things going, Willie?" Brad extended his hand. Even though he wasn't an exceptionally large man at five-foot-ten, he towered over Willie, who might stretch out to five-five on a good day.

"Been a bit crazy." The wiry man in his fifties firmly squeezed Brad's hand. "Didn't the police teach you how to be a little stealthier? A stint in the Special Forces woulda done you

some good. Woulda made you sneaky…like me." He pointed
to the army patch on his well-worn jacket.

"We can all use a little more sneakiness in our lives." Brad
rested his elbow on the pistol's handle at his hip and crossed his
arms. He'd listen to what Willie had to say, touch base with
him, and then hurry home. "What do you have for me
tonight?"

"How much you know about that new Life-something-or-
nother place down by the community college?"

"Lifetex?" Brad shrugged. "It's some sort of medical research firm. Why?"

"They've got weird things goin' on there." Willie shook his
shaggy head. "Weird things."

"Don't make me play twenty guesses tonight, Willie. I'm
worn out." Brad checked his watch—already after ten. The
kids would be in bed, but Julie should still be awake. If he hustled, he'd make it home in time for at least a few minutes with
his wife. "Just tell me what's up."

"Dead bodies. That's what's up. They're carting dead folks
out the back of that place."

Brad cupped his hands over his face and let out a fatigued
sigh. So much for his plan to hurry home. It just crumbled
with the mere mention of dead bodies. "Are you going off the
deep end? What are you talking about?"

"I'm telling ya, they're up to no good." Willie aimed a bony
finger in the direction of Lifetex. "A couple months ago, I set
up my hooch in the woods behind there. It's quiet, and I don't

like having my bivouac near any of the other homeless camps. I need to be off by myself. Anyway, I had a real sweet spot that no one knew about, and I had a good recon position of the back of that place too."

"What did you see?"

"One night I wasn't sleeping so well, so I stepped out of my tent and heard a noise. It was early in the morning, maybe two or three, something like that. As I scooted up to their fence, I see a couple of fellas coming outta the back loading dock, carrying a body."

"What did the victim look like? Male? Female?"

"I couldn't see what the person looked like. I could just tell they were carrying a body in a body bag."

"How do you know it was a body bag?"

Willie planted his hands on his hips, glaring at Brad. "I filled more than my fair share in Vietnam. I know exactly what a body bag looks like, and I know what two men look like when they're carrying one, all hunched over and such."

Willie bent over and took a couple of steps to demonstrate. "Not only did they have a body, but they tossed it into a van like they was throwing away some trash. I heard the thump from all the way back where I was. And they sped outta there like nobody's business."

"Willie, how much did you have to drink that night? Could you have tipped a few too many *cervezas*?"

"I know what I saw, Detective Brad. I wouldn't waste your time with nonsense. I was sober as could be."

"What happened after that?"

"I don't know. I broke down my bivouac and got outta there in a real hurry. I'm not hanging around a place like that. No tellin' what they're up to."

"Why didn't you tell me this sooner?"

"Aaah." Willie flicked a dismissive hand toward him. "There were warrants out on me for shoplifting and disorderly conduct, so I was laying low. I was afraid that if I called you, you'd have to pick me up on the charges. I finally got busted by the sheriff's department, and the warrants are all squared away. I'm free and clear now."

Brad rubbed his chin. Willie was a bit loopy, but everything he'd ever told Brad had proven true, even some solid leads on a homicide case. But bodies whisked away in the middle of the night was a bit much. Willie probably just saw what he thought was a body in a body bag. The night can play funny tricks on the eyes and mind.

He'd give the information its due attention, though, and would check it out, if for no other reason than as a courtesy to Willie. Brad pulled out his wallet and dug into his informant funds.

"No booze with this, Willie." Brad let the twenty flap in the breeze for a second before handing it to him. "Just food and water and necessities."

Willie snatched the bill and squinted as he held it close to his face. "Now you gonna give me the God-and-country speech?"

"Yeah, I think it's about time for that." Brad slipped his wallet back into his pocket and cleared his throat. He and Willie had a ritual, and he didn't want to disappoint. "You know I can help you get off the street if you need it. I have lots of contacts. I'll help you get on your feet."

"Ah, I'm doin' all right." Willie smirked. "I take care of myself just fine."

"You know God loves you and wants His best for you." Brad bent down to look him in the eye. Willie wasn't a bad guy, albeit entangled in a depressed, beaten-down life. Like many people, he just didn't know the Truth. From what he knew of Willie, after his Vietnam experiences the man never adjusted back into society. Brad would love nothing more than to help him build some sort of life for himself and know the Lord— and finally find some peace. Willie would have to take the first step; Brad couldn't do that for him. He would keep better tabs on him, though.

"I knew you were gonna say that. You always do, rookie."

"Well, I mean it. If you need something, just let me know. I'm praying for you."

"You're all right...for a cop." Willie winked at Brad and crumpled up the twenty and stuffed it in his pocket. He grabbed the handlebars of his bike and pulled it away from the wall. "I'll call you if I hear something else." Willie pushed his bike around the corner and through the alley toward the front of the store.

Brad hurried back into his car and glanced at the picture

of his wife and two children taped on the dashboard—a constant reminder to be smart and safe. God blessed him with Julie and the kids, and he vowed to do whatever it took to come home to them every night. But it wasn't only the bad guys that Brad feared. The violent, grubby world of police work tainted and seared some of his co-workers, destroying many officers and their families. The very same specters haunted the outskirts of his personal world as well, only kept at bay by his relationship with the Lord and the solid grounding of his wife and children. One of his many prayers was that God would strengthen him enough to deal with the horrors he encountered daily but keep him tender to the needs of those around him, like Willie. The balance was often tough but absolutely necessary.

He checked his watch again. As much as he yearned to just head home and forget all about Willie, the nagging cop instinct teased and tugged at his curiosity. He didn't know much about Lifetex, and as implausible as Willie's story sounded, it did merit at least a drive-by and a respectable look around.

Flipping open his cell phone, he used his thumb to speed dial his partner. He got the message service. "Hey, Eric, this is Brad. I've got some weird info I'm working. I guess I'll share it with you tomorrow. See you then, bud."

Brad snapped his phone shut. Eric was his prayer partner as well as his cop partner. He wouldn't mind having his good friend with him if he went rooting around a little tonight. Maybe he'd try to page him and see if he wanted to join him.

He shook off the thought. No need to get Eric out this

time of the night for what might just be some kooky information. He'd check it out himself first and talk with Eric in the morning.

Now to Lifetex.

"Interesting place."

Brad stepped off the roadway at the edge of the Lifetex complex. The full moon cast its jaundiced eye on the woods next to him as a stray cloud crawled overhead. He never used to believe the malarkey about full moons making people crazy—until he worked as a police officer. Now he was a true believer. Those nights tended to be wild and unpredictable.

Having parked his car about a quarter mile away in the Rolsen Corporation parking lot, Brad walked up the road to Lifetex. He wanted to see the back of the complex as Willie had seen it, at night and preferably undetected. Maybe he was picking up a little of Willie's sneakiness.

The three-story complex covered two city blocks with a few more acres of undeveloped land surrounding it, probably for future expansion. He hadn't seen a car pass by since he'd arrived. Other than the community college off to the north and Rolsen to the south, much of the area was undeveloped. With the city growing like it was, Brad wondered how long that would last.

Lifetex blazed on the side of the building in giant red let-

ters with the company logo behind it—a Leonardesque Vitru-
vian man formed the *t* in *Lifetex*. Mounted cameras hung on
the corners of the building, focused on the front parking lot.
The back employee parking area had a security gate with a keypad entry, not a bad idea in today's world. Lifetex looked like
any other large corporation—it screamed of big money.

A chain-link fence surrounded the rear of the complex,
where Willie had camped. The parking lot lights and brilliant
moon chased complete darkness away and offered the possibility of getting into position without using a flashlight. Several
cars were in the lot, probably some midnight-shift workers.

He followed the fence line toward the rear but stayed in the
shadows as much as possible. The night dew had already settled on the ankle-length grass. His feet felt each wet step; his
shoes were soaked. Now he felt foolish for being out here.
Willie must have been seeing things. At the back of the complex, Interstate 95 was maybe two hundred yards behind him.
The constant rumble of cars in the distance provided a surreal
hum in his ears.

The back of Lifetex didn't appear outstanding in any way.
The loading dock was visible. A male exited the back door and
entered a white company van. Brad slipped his digital camera
from his pocket and focused on the license plate. He snapped
a photo, then another, as the van pulled up to the gate, which
rolled open. The van disappeared into the night.

Brad snapped more photos.

A Dumpster sat in the corner of the lot a couple of feet away from the fence. Brad walked over and used it as conceal-ment as he clicked off another round of pictures. A clump of papers lay scattered on the ground behind the Dumpster. It wouldn't hurt to get a heads-up on the company's goings-on. Once something was left in the trash, it was free pickings as far as he was concerned. Dumpster diving was one of the more unpleasant aspects of the job.

The threefold row of barbed wire at the top of the fence precluded him from hopping over and taking a closer look, not that he was inclined to try that anyway. He tried to slip his hand through the fence. No good. He searched the ground around him and picked up a three-foot-long stick. He worked it through the fence and stabbed it on top of the papers. He scraped them along the concrete until they were next to the fence. The scratching sound was a little louder than he'd hoped.

As he pulled the fence back to get his hand underneath, the thump of another car door closing stopped him cold. Peering around the Dumpster, he saw two men enter another Lifetex van. They backed up and drove ahead to the security gate. It rolled open, and they pulled onto the street. *Busy place at night.*

"This is just plain creepy." Brad reached under the fence and grabbed a handful of papers. "Time to go."

He retraced his steps and hurried back to his car. As he was almost to the street, palmettos rustled, maybe a hundred feet or so behind him. He picked up his pace. No telling what kind of vermin was traipsing around back here. And Willie wanted to live in these woods? No, thank you.

Arriving at the Rolsen parking lot, he stepped up his pace until he reached his car. He sat in the driver's seat, flicked on the dome light, and thumbed through the papers. He'd check out the photos and meet with Eric in the morning.

A shadow breezed across the parking lot in front of his car. Brad looked up but couldn't see anything moving. He clicked on his headlights. Nothing but empty parking lot. The full moon was making him as crazy as Willie. Definitely time to move on.

He inserted his key in the ignition and started the engine. Something darted on his left. He turned. The driver's door whipped open, and a giant hand snatched him by the throat, squeezing tight.

"Aaaggh." Brad grabbed the radio mic on the dashboard to call for help. He keyed up but couldn't speak.

The man jerked him out of the car, flinging him through the air and bouncing him onto the pavement. The attacker straddled him and squeezed even harder.

Brad couldn't tear the hand off his throat. *Who is this maniac?* Brad brought his knee up, nailing the loon in the ribs and knocking him on his back.

Brad rolled up, sucking air, and drew his pistol. The shadowy assailant bounded toward him and snatched his wrist, forcing the pistol down.

Crack! The first shot ricocheted into the parking lot, sending chunks of asphalt flying.

"ID 230," the dispatcher's voice crackled over the radio. "Where are you calling from? ID 230?" He had to get to the radio.

The thug rammed his shoulder into Brad's gut and drove his back into the car, knocking the wind out of him. Brad punched him twice in his rock-hard stomach. He didn't budge.

I can't do anything with this guy. Brad kicked his ankle to sweep him to the ground; it was like kicking a telephone pole.

The attacker used his body to pin Brad against the car. The pistol slipped from his hand. Brad felt his arm snap.

"God, help me."

The goon grabbed the gun and smacked Brad with the butt. His legs gave way, and he slid to the ground.

Brad stared down the barrel of his own gun as the towering menace hovered over him. The moonlight gave Brad nothing more than a giant silhouette of his attacker. Brad's ribs screamed with pain; several had to be broken. He held his arm close to his chest and fought to stay conscious. "Lord, watch over Julie, Kaylee, and Brad Jr."

His assailant's low growl transformed into laughter.

5

Palm Bay police detective Eric Casey turned the corner onto Nesbitt Street, a route he was all too familiar with, although he never dreamed he'd be making this trip. It was the darkest night he'd ever seen, even with the full moon. The morning sun was still a long way off.

He checked his rearview mirror, and Chief Patrick Gailey followed his turn with Wilson Perry, Brad and Eric's pastor, riding with him. Two more unmarked cars snaked around the corner behind them, carrying the upper echelon of the department.

Eric stopped in front of the home he'd grown to love as his own. The robin's-egg blue house sported white trim and a wooden swing set in the side yard, the one he helped build. The house was still, quieted by an ignorant slumber not yet disturbed by the news. How he wished it would stay that way forever.

Every experience in his eight years of law enforcement all rolled together couldn't begin to match the pain and angst he felt at this moment. He and Brad went through the academy together. Brad led him to Christ and discipled him. Eric had spent so much time with Brad and Julie that they were more family than friends.

"Lord, how could You let this happen? It's not fair, and I don't understand. It should have been someone else—me, but not Brad." Eric chewed on his lower lip as he heard the chief's car door slam.

It was time.

Pastor Perry embraced Eric at the end of the driveway. "God is in control. No matter what."

Eric's arms barely reached around Wilson's meaty frame. "I'm having a hard time with that right now." Eric fought back the tears filling his eyes. "And I don't know if I can keep it together."

Wilson left an arm on his shoulder. "He'll be here for us. He promised, and I believe Him, Eric. God will get us through this."

Eric hoped that was true; he needed all the help he could get.

Chief Gailey adjusted his gun belt and squared up with Eric. "I'll make notification."

"No, Chief." Eric raised his hand. "Julie should hear it from me."

The chief nodded, and he, Pastor Perry, and Eric walked to the front door with a line of officers behind them. Squeaking brakes and headlights announced the arrival of more friends at the home. He imagined the officers would continue to pour in.

Lord, help me. Give me the words. If it's even possible to have the right words. What can I say to her?

Eric knocked on the door and then rang the doorbell. A light flickered on inside. Julie Worthington passed across the living room window as she wrapped a white robe around her.

"Who is it?" she called from behind the door.

"It's Eric, Julie. It's important. Please open the door."

The door unlocked and swung open.

"Eric, what's…" Her smile melted as she scanned the crowd of solemn officers whose faces told the story more than any words could express. She staggered back with her hand covering her mouth. "No. Nooooo! Oh, Lord, please no."

"I'm so sorry." Eric's voice quivered as he stepped into the house, taking her hand. "Brad's gone home."

The dual nuisance of her pager and phone going off simultaneously disturbed Robbie's slumber. Sitting straight up in bed, she stared at the wall for a moment as the pulsating beep competed with the ringing phone for her attention. Passing her hand over her face, she shook off the stupor and fought to keep her eyes open. She glanced at the digital clock: 2:05 a.m.

"Hello," she said tentatively, not really wanting to hear a voice on the other end. Early morning phone calls and pages were never good news.

"Robbie." Alan's ominous tone carried through the receiver long before he spoke his next words. "We have an officer down."

"What?" The paralyzing thought surged down her spine. She was awake now as the possibilities whirled and collided in her head. "Is it Tim? John? What happened?"

"No. It's a Palm Bay detective."

"What's his prognosis? Is he gonna make it?"

"Robbie...he's been murdered. We've been asked to step in and take over the investigation. The Palm Bay chief doesn't want his guys going vigilante, and they need an independent agency to work this case. This is gonna be real high profile. I need you to come in, and I want you to be lead."

"Have you called the team?"

"John and Tim are on their way. I'm getting dressed now, and I'll meet you at the scene."

"I have to make a couple of calls first, but I'll be there soon."

"One more thing, Robbie."

"What?"

"From what they're telling me, this is going to be a bad scene. Vicious. I just want you to be prepared."

Alan hung up before Robbie could say anything more. He wasn't much for civilities to begin with, and he needed to make plenty more calls. She kicked the sheet off and headed into the bathroom.

Splashing some water on her face, Robbie worked to kick-start some life into her.

A cop killer.

Why did she have to get this case? Alan couldn't have known about her father or he probably wouldn't have assigned her to be lead. It wasn't his fault; she'd never told him. Maybe she should have. But it always provoked the kinds of questions she just didn't like dealing with: *"So, how did he die again?"* *"How many times was he shot?"* Or her personal favorite, *"How does it feel to lose your father so young?"*

"Well," she always yearned to say, *"it's like having your heart ripped from your chest, leaving a gaping, excruciating hole forever. Thanks for asking!"* But she never responded like that. She'd deflect silly inquiries and often found it best to never mention it in the first place.

She took in her reflection in the mirror and shook her head. "This is going to be a tough case, in more ways than one." She tied her black hair back into a ponytail, where it would stay at least until she cleared the scene. Less to mess with.

She'd arrested every type of pervert, lowlife, and murderer, with the exception of a cop killer. This was new ground. The detectives from Metro-Dade who had investigated her father's murder were first rate. They had the suspect in jail in less than twenty-four hours. A tough standard to meet, but she'd aim for it.

Kathy was at her door in less than fifteen minutes to watch her mother. That girl was getting a huge Christmas bonus for this.

Robbie's apartment was about ten miles from the scene. As she rocketed toward the site, she scrolled through her mental checklist for examining the crime scene and debriefing witnesses. She needed to be ready when she arrived.

While she was still a good mile away, the kaleidoscope of pulsating lights seized her attention. Two police helicopters thundered above, circling the scene, their searchlights crossing like two giant swords dueling in the night. Two more Palm Bay police cars zoomed past her, rattling her small Buick. She parked on the outskirts of the Rolsen property, which was surrounded by dense wooded lots on either side, perfect escape routes for any suspect on foot.

The police cars fashioned a semicircle around the property, and crime-scene tape stretched for three hundred yards in either direction, completely encircling the building and parking lot. Temporary lighting stands fully illuminated the area.

Robbie grabbed her legal pad and digital audio recorder. She clipped the power microphone to her shirt to pick up her verbal notes. Checking her look once more in the rearview mirror, she tightened her ponytail, then gazed out the windshield. With all the emergency lights, passing patrol cars, and roaring helicopters, the scene had all the tranquillity and order of a three-ring circus.

John, Tim, and Alan huddled with several other detectives, probably Palm Bay PD, at the edge of the parking lot, just outside the crime-scene tape.

She stepped out of the car and slid her badge onto her belt next to her pistol. Her blue jeans and FDLE T-shirt were not exactly office apparel but appropriate and comfortable for crime-scene work. She hurried toward the group of detectives.

"Robbie." Alan moved back to let her into the circle. "This is Detective Eric Casey with Palm Bay PD. He was Detective Worthington's partner. Eric will be shadowing us on the case as a liaison. He'll be able to guide us through any trouble spots."

"I'm sorry for your loss." Robbie extended her hand.

With eyes as red as his hair, Detective Casey just nodded and worked his jaw back and forth. His body was bladed toward Robbie like a boxer's stance. He was definitely a veteran cop. She'd seen him in passing at a couple of south-county detective meetings. He was handsome, though somewhat reserved, especially for a cop. A dusting of freckles covered his chiseled cheekbones. His powerful, athletic build rose with each purposed breath and seethed with every exhale. The man was having a tough time keeping it together. Clearly this wasn't just another case with him—it was personal.

"We all are." Eric set his hands on his hips. "Now let's get to work and find Brad's killer."

"Tell me what happened." Robbie raised her notepad.

"Brad called me earlier tonight." Detective Casey pulled

his cell phone from its case. "I was out jogging and left my phone at home. He said he came across some 'weird' information. That he'd check it out and get with me in the morning. When I got home I tried to call him back, but there was no answer, so I called Dispatch to see if he was still working. The dispatcher told me that Brad had keyed up on his radio but wasn't answering. We have GPS in all the radios, so they sent an officer out here to check on him. That's when they found Brad."

"Did he say anything over the radio, any suspect info or license plates?" Robbie jotted down in her own shorthand what Eric said.

"Nothing. He just keyed the mic but for some reason didn't transmit." Eric's voice cracked, and he stepped back. "I'm guessing he was already fighting with the suspects. If I'd just been home or had my phone with me...maybe—"

"This isn't your fault, Eric." Alan pointed his flashlight at him. "Don't go owning something that doesn't belong to you. We'll find the person or people responsible. But you can't start this investigation by blaming yourself. I've been a cop for thirty years. I know what I'm talking about."

Eric nodded and sucked in a deep breath.

"What else do we have?" Robbie lowered her pad.

"Every Palm Bay cop is out here looking now, as well as some from the Brevard County Sheriff's Department and Melbourne PD." Eric waved a finger at the hovering helicopter.

"There are probably three hundred officers searching the area. We don't know if the suspects left on foot or in a car. We aren't taking any chances, though. We're checking everywhere."

"Robbie, we don't have good suspect info right now, but we do have a bit to go on." Alan scratched his beard. "I was hoping you could put together a profile on the killer. You'll know what I'm talking about after you view the scene."

Alan turned to John and Tim. "I want you two to interview some of the officers here. Run a background on Detective Worthington and find out if anyone had a beef with him. We're going to start shaking some trees and see what nuts fall out."

Robbie's soul twinged. She loved the process of hunting a killer and the satisfaction of taking a violent felon off the street. But having just come off another high-profile case, she didn't know if she had the energy to carry it through. And with a cop killer, how much more of a toll would this case take on her?

A photo from her father's crime scene flashed in her mind, one of him lying on his stomach, his pistol at his side. She wished she'd never looked at those stupid pictures. She shook them from her memory.

Get focused, Robbie. Stay focused.

She surveyed the hundreds of officers around the scene and Detective Casey, who was about to burst. She wasn't the only person having issues with this case. More people than she could count were hurting. She'd toughen up, as usual, and find a way to work through it and catch this maniac.

"I've got it, Alan." She pulled her notepad to her chest. "I won't let you down."

"I never thought any different."

"We've got your back on this one, Sanchez." Tim's fists were clenched. His anger-management training didn't appear to be working.

As much as she jabbed and prodded Tim, she respected him. He'd spent a good number of years as a uniformed officer before becoming a homicide detective with Orlando PD, and then finally with FDLE.

"We're on this until it's solved." John slipped his hands in his pockets. One of the best criminal interviewers she'd ever known, John would be an asset here. "Let me know what you need."

"I want to get a look at the scene." Robbie noted the time. "Then we can plan our next move. Seems like we have enough officers searching the area."

Robbie passed the line of police cars and stood next to the crime-scene tape. It looked like the responding officers took great care to leave the scene as they found it. That would be helpful. Many crime scenes she went to were destroyed by first responders trying to administer first aid or secure the scene. She silently commended the Palm Bay guys for preserving evidence while in such an emotional state.

She nodded to the officer keeping the crime-scene log and lifted her badge so he could document her ID number and the time she entered the scene. A silly detail, but one that, if not followed to the nth degree, could give a defense attorney something to sink his teeth into. She wouldn't give him the pleasure of such an easy morsel.

Detective Casey followed her. His feet landed heavy on the pavement, and she felt his rage with each purposed step. It was an added distraction she didn't need, although she did understand. She'd be a mess if Tim, John, or Alan were the victims of a horrendous crime like this. She was impressed that Eric could function at all.

Alan trailed behind Eric. They would enter the scene at the same point and follow a narrow path to the car and Detective Worthington's body. One way in, one way out. The less trampling of any potential evidence, the better.

She cleared her throat and clicked on her digital recorder. "I can see the victim down about one hundred feet from the roadway. His car is running, and the headlights are still on. I wonder why. Did he stop the suspect, or did the suspect come to him?"

She oriented her legal pad and sketched a hasty diagram showing the positions of the building, Detective Worthington's car, and the body.

Robbie approached carefully, using her flashlight to scan the parking lot for any evidence as she walked. Eric and Alan hovered behind her. They stopped just about ten feet away from him.

"The victim's—"

"Brad." Eric stepped closer to her. "His name is—was—Brad."

"I'm sorry." Robbie lowered the pad to her side. "I didn't mean anything by it. It's just easier for me to refer to him that way for my notes."

"Well, it means something to me. His name is Detective Brad Worthington, badge number 230, and I would appreciate it if you would show him—and us—that respect. He's not a piece of meat or some junkie dumped in a vacant lot somewhere. He was my best friend."

Eric trembled as a tear hung on his cheek. He was on the verge of a meltdown, and Robbie didn't want to push it with him or any of the other officers around this scene. This would be even more difficult than she first thought.

"Detective Casey." Alan slid between him and Robbie. "Robbie's the best criminal profiler in the agency. She will find the person who did this, but you'll need to back off a bit. Maybe you're too close to this investigation to be working it. We're gonna need your help with a lot of things, but if you can't keep your emotions in check, I'll have you yanked off this case. Nothing is going to stand in the way of us solving this—friend or no friend."

Eric's glare didn't fade, but he took two steps back and raised his hands. "Look, I chose to be here right now, working this scene instead of staying with Brad's wife. I want a piece of whoever did this, so I'll do whatever I have to do to stay on this investigation."

Robbie nodded. It was best to let his comment die a dignified death. She understood the sting of loss and wouldn't want to relive it for anything in the world. She drew a deep breath and concentrated on her scene. She never should have answered the phone this morning.

"Detective Brad Worthington is lying on his back next to the driver's door with his arms splayed out. Small plastic cones mark the numerous shell casings scattered around his body. My goodness—maybe two dozen rounds fired."

"Twenty-six, by our count anyway." Eric stood off to Robbie's right. At least he was trying not to get in her way. That was all she could ask for. "All 9 mm from Brad's gun."

"Thank you. Whoever did this is an angry, angry person."

"All murderers are angry, Detective Sanchez. Especially someone who'd kill a cop."

"True. But this person had a special beef."

Eric frowned. "Why do you say that?"

"To fire twenty-six rounds, the suspect would have had to reload. If he were simply trying to get away, he would have shot Brad several times and then fled the scene. Who's going to take the time to reload in an open parking lot and empty another magazine into a police officer who is already dead?"

Eric nodded. Calmer and composed, he had his cop's face on now.

"Only someone mentally unbalanced would do something like that."

"Maybe that profiling stuff does have some value." Eric attempted a smile as if to say he was sorry, which was probably as close as she would get to an apology in the cop world.

"Those are just my off-the-cuff observations. As we document the scene, I hope to put together a little better profile." She stepped closer to Brad and leaned over. Most of the rounds had hit his face, head, and neck. She had no idea what he must have looked like before the attack. Her stomach churned. Figuring out motives and seeking keys to personalities was one thing, but standing over dead bodies had never been the part of the job she looked forward to. But it had to be done.

"What's this?" Robbie pointed to a metallic clump next to Brad.

"Looks like his camera," Eric said. "They issue digital cameras to all the detectives. I'm guessing that's one of ours. It's a little hard to tell."

"Digital camera is on the ground next to Brad," Robbie plotted it on her diagram. "It appears to have been smashed. Did it happen during the attack, or was it smashed on purpose?"

Eric eased alongside her. "Hey, where's his cross?"

"What cross?"

Eric shone his light around Brad's body and then the car. "His cross tie tack. It was a present from his daughter, Kaylee. He wore it every day. Now it's gone."

Eric pointed to a slight tear on Brad's navy blue tie. Robbie initially thought it was another bullet hole, but now, as she inspected it closer, it was certainly a tear. The suspect had ripped the cross off the tie.

"Why would someone do that?" Eric massaged his forehead. "I understand someone snatching the badge, but a little cross? This whole nightmare is crazy. This can't be happening."

"Suspect removed a cross tie tack from the—from Brad's tie," she whispered into her recorder while making a note on her legal pad.

Robbie scooted around to the open car door. She peered in, careful to keep her hands from touching anything. A picture of a beautiful young woman with two small children—a boy and a girl—was taped to the dashboard. They were on the beach with waves rolling in behind them.

Robbie was going to be sick. She stepped back and drew in a deep breath. Why did she have to answer the stupid phone?

"Don't just leave him lying there! Cover him, take him outta there! Do something!" a uniformed officer screamed from the outskirts of the crime scene as Tim, John, and two other officers held him back from sprinting toward them. "It's not right." He sobbed uncontrollably as the two officers embraced him on the spot.

Eric turned to Robbie. "Agent Sanchez, everyone loved and respected Brad. He was the best cop and best friend anyone could ask for. All I've got to tell you is that if the FDLE doesn't catch the person who did this—we will. And may God have mercy on his soul…because we will not."

6

He seems to be responding surprisingly well." Neal rested his chin on his hand as he peered through the window of the speech-therapy room. The resident therapist, Joyce Sherwin, worked with Adam in the sterile, white room.

"A, B, C." Joyce pointed to each letter in succession.

"A, B, C." Adam mirrored her movements and voice without error.

"He has exceeded all of our expectations." Dr. Silverstein's eyes never left Adam as he drew closer to the window, captivated by the work of his creation. "He'll astound the world."

Seeing Dr. Silverstein so happy warmed Neal's heart. A jovial man to begin with, Benjamin was nearly euphoric with Adam out of the chamber. A scant eight days and Adam was already forming words, walking on the treadmill, and working with weights. Maybe even the great Dr. Silverstein underestimated his creation.

Considerably shorter than Neal and with a bulbous middle, Dr. Silverstein could have been mistaken for a storefront Santa Claus minus the beard. His white hair encircled a bald patch on the top of his head, and a bushy mustache hid under his nose like an out-of-control caterpillar. But behind those grandfatherly eyes churned the mind of one of the most brilliant men Neal had ever encountered.

The therapist showed Adam an object, named it, and ask him to do the same. He flawlessly followed her direction.

Neal was honored to be part of the Genesis Project. His specialties in the area of genetic alterations and the repair of damaged or mutated genes were enough to impress Dr. Silverstein. Not that it was all that difficult. Many others had laid the groundwork upon which their discoveries were built. But now was the time to take the collective knowledge of those before him—Crick and Watson. The prestige and honor of working with Dr. Silverstein would have been quite enough for Neal. But when Mr. Finstead revealed what his salary would be, he was on the first flight to Florida.

The Genesis Project would propel them to the top of the scientific community, not that Dr. Silverstein wasn't already there. But the chance to accomplish something that future generations would look back on and thank them for was unfathomable.

Working at the Lifetex labs was not without its problems though. All the secrecy associated with the assignment had troubled him at first. He was not some sort of covert agent dealing with national security issues. But the research had to be protected. Industrial espionage was everywhere. If they were to make the most out of their discoveries, seclusion and privacy only made sense.

After the first several weeks, however, it became quite routine, even comforting. Only a small team of researchers and medical personnel were involved. Limited distractions. No financial considerations—at all. The only concerns came from the sensitive legal and ethical issues that could be raised.

Lifting humankind to a whole new level of life was well worth their small dance in the gray area of scientific ethics. As far as potential legal problems went, Mr. Finstead assured them that he had skilled lawyers already prepared for that fight. Lifetex was a scientist's dream come true. Neal eased next to Dr. Silverstein.

"He's going to be ready soon," Dr. Silverstein beamed. "Who knows? At this pace, he just might be calculating algebraic formulas and learning Greek in a month."

Adam stood with the therapist and mimicked her writing on a whiteboard. He followed her movements with precision and skill as they wrote the alphabet. His penmanship was already quite extraordinary.

"It could be a little…dicey for a while. Some people might not respond favorably to Adam." Neal tapped his foot. The thought of the numerous and possibly hostile inquiries didn't sit well with him. He wasn't the confrontational type and didn't relish the thought of being dragged before committees and questioned.

Dr. Silverstein waved off the comment. "We'll be fine. Warren has everything accounted for. Besides, if they imprison us for repairing, perfecting, and replicating the sacred codes of the human body, so be it. Once our research is revealed, tested, and verified, and diseases like diabetes, Alzheimer's, and cancer fall off the chart of human experience, we won't remain imprisoned. I have more faith in my fellow man than that. Our work will be recognized, respected, and revered; you can count on that."

"Well, Doctor, I wish I shared your faith." Neal slipped his hands in his lab coat. "You know, Adam's personality is what astonishes me the most. I quite expected him to be more temperamental or confused, like an infant or a small child instead of his adultlike mentality. But he seems at ease in these surroundings and has an eagerness to learn. He just seems a little too well adjusted for having just been born, pardon the expression, into this world."

"True. But that can only enhance our case for not only cloning but for accelerating the growth rates as well. The time it takes to train them in any endeavor will be greatly reduced."

Dr. Silverstein rested a hand on Neal's shoulder. "Feel free to see the cup as half full, my friend. At least if you're going to work yourself to death, revel in the victories for a moment anyway."

"You do have a point, Doctor."

"When are you ever going to stop calling me 'doctor'? I

have a name, you know. It's Benjamin, but my friends call me Ben." Dr. Silverstein extended his hand as if it were the first time they'd met.

Neal would have sooner called his own father by his first name. To call the finest mind in the world *Ben* seemed so... irreverent. He sighed and extended his hand. "Okay, Ben. This is all very fantastic, but Adam's behavior does seem to go against our expectations."

"That's not a bad thing. So we miscalculated a few behaviors—to our advantage, I might add. You worry far too much. When all this is finished, we're going to make sure you go out and have some fun. You've been cooped up in the laboratory for too long. You need to find a nice young woman and go dancing or get out in the sun. You look anemic. These silly fluorescent lights aren't good for anyone."

Neal shook his head. The doctor was always trying to get him to live a bit more. Sure. It was so easy for him. Just show up and be brilliant. Neal had to work hard for his success. Maybe he should lighten up a little, but only after the work was finished.

Dr. Silverstein glanced at his watch. "Well, let's go in and see what our Adam has to tell us."

Neal and Dr. Silverstein walked around the glass partition to the doorway and entered the classroom. The fluorescent light radiated around the all-white room, forcing Neal to squint for a moment.

Adam and his teacher turned toward them.

"Please, don't let us interrupt you." Dr. Silverstein beamed and held up his hand. "You both were doing so well."

"Thank you, Doctor." The therapist turned back to Adam.

Dressed in blue scrubs and sandals, Adam sat at the table with the whiteboard next to him and a laptop computer on the desk with a language program open.

"Adam," Joyce enunciated with clear precision. "Can you say hello to Dr. Silverstein and Dr. Meyer?"

Adam turned to them and grinned. "Hello, Dr. Silverstein."

Adam's voice, much deeper than expected, rumbled like the growl of a prowling lion and echoed in the small laboratory and down Neal's spine.

Dr. Silverstein clapped twice and held his hands to his mouth. "This is wonderful. Just wonderful, I tell you. I cannot believe what you've done."

Joyce shrugged. "I haven't done much. Adam is an amazing student. It's as if he's known the English language his whole life... Well, you know what I mean. He really is incredible."

"You've digitally recorded all his training, haven't you?" Neal asked.

"Yes, Dr. Meyer. I've also finished the outline on his progress that you asked for."

"Neal, Neal, everything is being done just as we've planned. Stop your incessant worrying. The Genesis Project will be preserved for generations to come. Students a hundred years from now will be learning about what we've accomplished here. Rest easy, my friend. The hardest work is behind us."

Neal glanced down at Adam's feet and tilted his head. Was he seeing things? That was unusual. "Has Adam been able to go outside for a walk yet?" Neal rubbed his chin.

"Of course not." Dr. Silverstein walked to Adam and laid a hand on his mountainous shoulder. "That would be quite foolish. He's exercising with his physical therapist in the gym and walking around the lab. Why do you ask?"

Neal shook his head. "No reason. Just curious about if he's had some fresh air."

"There will be plenty of time for that. I'm so glad you're concerned for Adam's well-being. If you could only show the same concern for your own, you'd be a much happier man."

Neal rolled his eyes, but then glanced back down at Adam's feet. He wasn't seeing things. A spot of dirt was underneath Adam's toenail. There was no soil anywhere inside the facility.

Adam scooted his body around and checked Neal from head to toe. The corners of his mouth curled up, and his eyes pierced through him.

"Hello, Neal."

7

Florida Department of Law Enforcement, Melbourne

Robbie perused Detective Worthington's personnel folder as John, Tim, and Alan filed into the war room before their meeting. Brad had received numerous citations, commendations, and letters of appreciation—and the lifesaving medal for pulling a mother and her newborn from their vehicle after it careened into a lake. A citation for Officer of the Year. He was nothing short of a stellar cop.

Robbie held up his picture ID. Handsome. Smart, dedicated father of two. Respected and loved by his fellow officers. And gunned down by some slimy, no-good, filthy lowlife, probably on a drug high. She taped Brad's picture up on the whiteboard and rubbed the back of her neck.

Her emotions were frayed like a cheap sweater. Her father's face, the memories of his funeral, and crime-scene pictures melded together in an amalgam of loss and pain. *Concentrate, Robbie. Keep the past in the past so you can make it through this case.*

"Robbie, how's your mom holding up?" Tim asked as he slipped past her.

"Seems like more bad days than good anymore." Robbie shrugged. "Thanks for asking."

"John and I prayed for you in our Bible study last night." Tim plopped down in his chair. "I know it's got to be tough."

"With everything you have going on, just let us know if you need some help." John took his chair. "We'll keep you on the prayer list."

"Thanks. We're making it." Okay, so she lied a little. She was barely making it, buried with her mother's care and case after case piling on. It was sweet that they kept praying for her. Since Tim became a Christian, Robbie noticed subtle but substantial changes in him. Even though he was the same difficult man at times, he was at peace and had a renewed purpose for his life.

What must that be like? Peace and purpose? She couldn't even keep her schedule together, much less the thought of a life that meant more than day-to-day survival. The closest thing to peace Robbie felt was as a little girl at St. Mary's. But that was a long time ago.

"I guess we should get started." Alan dropped his notebook on the table. "Besides, all this prayer talk is giving me a headache."

"I'll pray about that too." Tim and John snickered.

They scooted their chairs up to the oblong table in the middle of the room. On the table, empty coffee cups intermingled with police narratives and photos, a hodgepodge of a chaotic night's work. Shirts were pulled out and ties were long removed as each slumped in his chair. The early morning call-out didn't allow for a lot of sleep. They worked the scene straight through the morning, took a half hour to clean up, then reported back to the office.

"I wanted to wait for Detective Casey to arrive, but I think we should get started." Robbie belted down a long swig of her room-temperature, bitter coffee, which drew a reflexive grimace. Good thing she wasn't drinking it for the taste. "I'll brief him when he gets here."

The disheveled team nodded, no one offering objections.

"All we have right now is what we learned at the scene. Detective Worthington keyed up his radio at 12:02 a.m. in the Rolsen parking lot." On the whiteboard, Robbie stuck an aerial photo of the crime scene that the sheriff's department's aviation unit just e-mailed to her. All of the local agencies were stepping up to help. "The crime scene, as well as the surrounding area around the Rolsen building, are mostly wooded commercial lots waiting to be sold." The photo provided context for their investigation.

Palm Bay was one of the fastest-growing cities in the nation. Soon all the vacant land would be gobbled up by developers, but for now the only other business in the area was

Lifetex, the parking lot just visible on the top left of the photo. Interstate 95 marked the top right with the community college at the bottom.

"What was our suspect doing in the Rolsen parking lot?" Robbie circled the area with her laser pointer. "Where was he coming from, and where was he going?"

"Maybe our suspect just came off of 95." Tim stood and stretched his arms above his head. "Maybe he's from out of state."

"Well, let's start with what we know; then we'll move to the maybes." Robbie rested back against the wall. "There are an awful lot of maybes and possiblys."

"I've called the media, and we have a major news conference in an hour at Palm Bay PD." Alan rocked back in his chair, rubbing his gray beard as he spoke. "I'll take care of that so you all can keep the investigation moving. We'll put out the info we have and see what happens."

Holding a briefing with pros refreshed Robbie and made her job as lead a lot easier.

"John, Tim, can you two check out Lifetex and see if they have any security cameras that could have picked up anything?" Robbie circled it with her pointer. "You never know. If they have some cameras pointed toward the street, we might get a picture of our guy coming or going. We can hit the community college after that."

"We're on it," Tim said while he and John collected their

legal pads. "If we stay here much longer, it'll be nappy time for us all."

"Sorry I'm late." Eric strode into the room with a smile on his face for the first time since Robbie met him. "But I think I have something that will make the wait worth it."

"The floor's yours." Robbie stepped aside. "What do you have? Anything at this point would be good."

"Him!" Eric slapped a picture on the whiteboard with enough force that Robbie thought it would crack—a booking photo of a guy with a grimace on his pasty, pockmarked face. His stringy hair resembled a mop dipped in ink.

"Elvin Jacob Marasco." Eric's voice thundered with verve and purpose. "Not only does he have a criminal history that would be the envy of every felon in the cellblock, but he's also six foot three and 220 pounds. That's a pretty large doper. Large enough to attack and kill a cop."

"Sounds like a lowlife. But there are a lot of lowlifes." Alan rose and edged closer to the photo. "What's Marasco's connection to this case?"

"Brad arrested him two weeks ago for possession of methamphetamine and burglary. Sweet Elvin here then threatened Brad, saying if it was the last thing he did, he would kill Brad and his whole family."

"That's our first good piece of information so far." Robbie examined Elvin's photo closer. If being ugly was a crime, he'd be on death row. He looked every bit the drug-addicted felon.

"Oh, it gets better." Eric punched his fist into his hand. "I just got off the phone with our narcotics unit, and they have probable cause for a search warrant for Elvin's house. They're walking the warrant to a judge as we speak."

"We do need to meet with Mr. Marasco." Tim bounced on his tiptoes and grinned. "I think it's high time for a visit."

"I took the liberty of assembling our SWAT team. For your use, of course." Eric's eyes sparkled and his cop nature beamed. He was ready for war. The look suited him. "The SWAT commander was more than happy to put together a plan on short notice. I hope you don't mind."

Robbie's gut swirled with excitement. Having a search warrant ready to go was more than she could have asked for. Maybe they'd find Brad's gun or his cross tie tack or something that would link Elvin to the case. If nothing else, it would give them a great opportunity to talk with this guy after SWAT softened him up.

She smiled. "Mind? This is the best news I've heard all day. Mr. Marasco needs a cop visit in a bad kind of way."

Neal hated this part of the job more than he could articulate. He just hoped he wouldn't have to articulate anything today. Lifetex's lobby echoed with media murmurings and rehearsals of their monologues as ninety journalists elbowed and pushed their way to the podium, vying for the closest positions to the stage. Warren Finstead knew his business well and could get worldwide press to a frog-eating contest.

Warren strolled out to a salvo of camera flashes from the waiting press corps. He posed for several seconds, giving everyone plenty of time to capture a grand picture of him for various front pages around the world.

"Thank you for coming today. Our staff at Lifetex and I are so pleased that you could attend our open house." Mr. Finstead's clear, baritone voice carried well in the lobby and hushed the waiting mass. "First, we'd like to take you to our medical wing, where we will highlight some of the work that Dr. Silverstein and his team have overseen. I believe that each and every one of you will be pleasantly surprised by our research and development and the many cutting-edge medical innovations."

Dr. Silverstein remained to the left and rear of Warren; Neal hovered behind Dr. Silverstein as much as he could. Mr. Finstead's natural acumen for handling the press and publicity astounded Neal, who possessed none of those talents and desired to have them even less.

The crowd applauded as Mr. Finstead stepped back and nodded. He passed his hand down his red power tie and then engaged them again. He was as smooth as he was smart.

Dr. Silverstein leaned toward Neal. "Can you imagine the press conference we'll have when we introduce Adam to the world? It will make this look like a Cub Scout meeting."

"That will be an interesting day." While he was as excited as Dr. Silverstein about releasing their research, Neal still felt uneasy about Adam. All the tests and research validated the Genesis Project as a phenomenal success. So why couldn't he shake the notion that something was wrong? Neal couldn't put his finger on it, but there was something in Adam's demeanor, the way he carried himself so confidently…almost cocky. And his eyes. They pierced through Neal like those of someone who hated him.

"If everyone could please line up, I'd like to direct you to our medical wing." Mr. Finstead hopped down from the podium and hurried to the front of the line of reporters, escorting them through the huge double doors and into the medical section.

A secretary stood as they entered the waiting room. An attractive blond woman, she wore a short dress and had a headset on.

"Good morning, Mr. Finstead." She pressed the security button, and the piercing metallic buzz vibrated down the hallway.

"Follow me, please." Warren led the group through the door into an expansive foyer of the Lifetex Children's Care Unit, "Where the Science of Miracles Happens Every Day."

The walls were covered with painted bears and toys and action figures—Dr. Silverstein's idea. He dreamed of a place where terminally ill children could come and be treated with the latest innovations. But he never wanted them, or anyone else, to forget they were still children in need of an emotionally fertile place to heal and grow whole again.

Two girls, both about twelve, were playing a video game against the wall.

"This is Emma and Christy. Both of these pretty young ladies are here being treated for Ewing's sarcoma, a devastating form of cancer." Warren crouched down and looked on as they played, seemingly oblivious to the throng of reporters.

"Hey, Mr. Finstead." The red-headed Emma smiled at him. "Do you want to play with me when we're done?" The reporters' cameras lit up the room at their interchange.

"Maybe later when I'm finished with these fine people." He patted her on the head and faced the reporters again.

"Just a short time ago, the prognosis for these girls would have been very poor. But now, with the innovative research conducted at Lifetex, these young ladies—and many more children like them—are offered real hope of a cure."

Another round of photos flashed around the room.

An African American reporter raised her hand. "Mr. Finstead, to what do you attribute the success of Lifetex's revolutionary medical breakthroughs?"

"It's simple really. I've assembled a fantastic team of the greatest minds in the genetic research field and provided them with the funds and materials necessary to empower them to do what they do best. Everyone has their part here at Lifetex. And as you know, Dr. Benjamin Silverstein has been the lead on this research." Mr. Finstead waved to him to come forward. "Doctor, would you like to explain what's happening on the developmental end?"

"I'd be honored to." Dr. Silverstein stepped in front of Mr. Finstead.

A male reporter with a microphone in his hand eased closer to the doctor. "Dr. Silverstein, while there have been some amazing medical breakthroughs here, there have also been rumors of some secret testing, possibly even research into human cloning. Do you have any comment?"

Neal swallowed hard and held his breath. He gazed over at Mr. Finstead, whose smile never abated. He was good. Neal feared he would have crumbled with that question alone.

Dr. Silverstein chuckled and shook his head. "If it were a secret, I wouldn't be very smart to tell you, now would I?" He winked at the reporter and grinned with his bushy white mustache. "It's true that I have more than a passing interest in human cloning and have written several papers on the viability of human cloning in today's world. And much of our work at the Children's Care Unit is in the area of genetics and genetic manipulation, so I'm sure more than one science fiction writer has put two and two together and come up with nine."

Several reporters chuckled with Dr. Silverstein. "But as for your rumors, they are just that—rumors. We have many things in development, and a certain level of security is required, so people can speculate all they like. Nothing but work that is benefiting all of humankind is going on here at Lifetex, I can assure you, and I'm honored to be a part of this team. But the real genius of this project is Dr. Neal Meyer. I'm sure he'll answer any of your questions."

Neal's stomach flipped, and water beaded on his forehead like a glass of ice water on a hot, humid day. Dr. Silverstein snickered as he passed Neal. The crazy old man was always doing things like this to him.

"Dr. Meyer, how have you been so successful in cancer research?"

"Ah, well, ah, it was easy really. We…we worked off of a lot of previous research in this area." Neal rocked back and forth on his heels. "We synthesized a small molecule called a chimera. It has the capability to find and fasten itself to a certain part of a gene and create a genetic vehicle designed to trigger a cell's normal DNA repair system into action. The repair mechanism scans the DNA, looking for any mismatches or two strands of DNA that don't seem in sync. When it finds a mismatch, it replaces one of the chemical bases with one that fits better."

Neal feigned a grin. His legs wobbled, and he was about to throw up. "We've also enhanced the speed with which a cell multiplies and grows, so once a damaged series of cells are repaired and enhanced, they are injected back into the cancerous area and the healthy, faster-multiplying cells overtake the cancerous cells…with amazing speed, I might add."

"Can you translate that into English?" a reporter asked. The room erupted in laughter.

Neal smiled but didn't understand what was so funny.

"We've prepared a press packet that explains much of what Dr. Meyer just said." Dr. Silverstein rested his hand on Neal's shoulder, the torture apparently now over for him. "You should find it most helpful."

"We need to be moving on." Warren led the crowd back toward the lobby. "There are many marvelous things to see here at Lifetex."

8

Dude, you just need some sleep." Zeke plopped onto the couch, launching a dust cloud around him. "You're schitzing out, man, and making me crazy too."

"Who can sleep?" Elvin trod a path on his living room rug, his face prickly and alive. He raked his nails up and down his cheeks, his bloody fingernails ripping another sore open. He'd take care of it later, as well as the scrapes on his forearms. He couldn't help it if bugs were crawling all over him. Maddening! His heart throbbed; he must be having a heart attack. What was taking Josh so long? Something was wrong; he could feel it. The punk was ripping him off.

"Just sit down and relax." Zeke waved his wimpy hand at him. "You're making me nervous."

"I'll give you nervous." Elvin pulled the Colt .45 from his

waistband and zeroed in on Zeke's head. "Josh better be here soon, or we're gonna have a real problem."

Zeke's eyes widened, and he squeezed the arm of the couch so hard his fingers looked like ivory. "Elvin, you need to chill and point that thing somewhere else. He'll be here. Trust me."

"I'll chill when Josh gets back—with my meth. He's got five hundred dollars of mine and my stash." Elvin slipped the pistol back into his waistband and patted the handle. Not that he couldn't pound Zeke by himself, but the dude was such a coward, he might have a gun of his own.

Elvin wasn't about to be jacked by him or anyone else. Zeke was out of his mind if he thought Elvin would just stand by and let them rip him off. But Zeke did have the connection that would keep Elvin surfing this high as well as get him enough meth to cut and trade for more money. For that reason alone, he wouldn't shoot him yet.

But he still didn't trust the weasel. Zeke was always looking at Elvin like he was getting ready to pounce or something. Josh and Zeke would probably try to jump him as soon as he turned his back. After seeing his .45, Zeke wouldn't be stupid enough to try anything—for now. Elvin would watch them both.

"You look like crap." Zeke peeked out the window above the couch. "How long has it been since you slept?"

"Two…three days maybe. I don't know. What does it matter? I want my stuff—now!"

"Okay, okay." Zeke held up his hands. "Just settle down,

and Josh'll be here with your stuff. We've done business before. You know the drill."

Coward. Elvin hurried to the window, hiding behind the drapes as he peered out at the street. He couldn't be too careful. He was sure he'd been followed earlier today. Someone had been following him for several days. He'd doubled back two or three times in his car just to make sure.

Someone was always wanting to take what was his or to take him out. Maybe Josh and Zeke were setting him up. Maybe some other jitterbug was waiting in the wings to punch his ticket. Then there was the cops. There was always the cops. Someone was out there. He could just sense these things.

Easing the drapes back into place, he drew a deep breath. He'd heard whispers in his head all day, small voices with unintelligible words. The meth monster was on his back bad now. Was he losing it? His head was foggy and pounded like a jackhammer digging into his brain. Just one more hit would set him right, and then he could get some rest. He wiped his face with both hands just as he heard a creak on the front porch.

"What was that?" Elvin drew his pistol from his waistband and slipped next to the front door.

"What was what?" Zeke didn't even budge at his warning.

"I heard something out on the porch."

"You're losing it, man. Nothing's out there."

The doorknob jiggled. Elvin stepped back and aimed the pistol at the door.

Zeke leaped from the couch. "Someone *is* out there."

A knock came at the door. Zeke posted alongside the door-frame, Elvin on the other side.

"Who's there?" Elvin called out.

"Josh, who do you think? Open up. I've got the stuff."

"How do I know it's you?"

"Don't be an idiot. Open the door."

The pistol rattled in Elvin's hand as tremors racked his body. Every inch of him screamed for another meth hit. He nodded to Zeke and then slipped the pistol back into his waistband. He opened the door a sliver.

Josh stood on the step with his hands in his jeans pockets, rocking back and forth on his heels. His blue ball cap was pulled down low on his forehead.

Elvin opened the door all the way. As Josh ambled in, a trail of shadows scurried behind him up onto the porch. Elvin blinked and shook his head to clear the hallucination.

One of the figures tossed a small cylindrical object over Josh's shoulder and onto the floor.

Boom! A brilliant flash and huge explosion rocked the house.

Josh screamed and his body lurched forward as one of the specters nailed him from behind, knocking him past Elvin and slamming the door open against the couch.

Another silhouette bounded through the door like a gorilla, straight toward Elvin, who reached for his pistol as he back-pedaled away from the beast.

"Aaah!" All the air rushed from his lungs as the monster lowered his shoulder and rammed him in the gut, bashing him to the ground. The fiend jumped on top of him as Elvin struggled to get the .45 out of his waistband.

Elvin made out the bright words printed on the gorilla's chest: POLICE. The beast's fist raised, then crashed down onto his chin.

Everything went black.

"Police! Search warrant!" The frenzied commands of the SWAT team rang in the air as they poured through the front door of Elvin Marasco's home. "Everyone on the ground!"

Eric trailed the entry team and aimed his Glock at the floor, because everywhere he looked was a cop's back, a chaotic scene ripe for an unintentional shooting. Robbie and the other FDLE agents brought up the rear. A good twenty cops hit this house with some fifteen others on the perimeter. Nobody wanted to miss this show. Brad's killer could very well be in here.

Three suspects were on the ground in various stages of being handcuffed and secured. The acidic fumes of the stun grenades mixed with the noxious stench of the soiled drug house. Eric felt grimy just standing here. This should be fun.

A column of SWAT cops surged down the hallway to clear the back bedrooms. Another stun grenade exploded; team members rushed into a room with the rest of the squad speeding up to the next room, precision moves practiced time and time again until it was the real thing—like now.

Eric rallied in the living room with Robbie, Tim, and John as the last room in the back was cleared. Fast-food wrappers and beer bottles decorated the floor, and the house had all the order and hygiene of a landfill.

One by one, the SWAT members exited the back rooms and huddled with Eric and the rest of the officers. Robbie holstered her pistol and fanned the haze from in front of her face. A cool criminal profiler, Robbie Sanchez carried herself like a salty crime-scene veteran. She'd caught Eric's attention with some sharp observations and how she'd handled the investigation so far. It didn't hurt that she looked a little like J.Lo either.

But on the personal side, Robbie didn't radiate the same kind of confidence. With a smooth olive complexion and a fit build, she was an attractive woman but acted like she either didn't know it or didn't believe it. Even though she, John, and Tim seemed close, Eric sensed that Robbie kept everyone at a distance. She was a difficult one to figure out.

"Thanks, guys. I think we have it from here." Eric holstered up and surveyed the messy scene. "Which one of you morons is Elvin Marasco?"

A suspect sitting on the floor with his hands cuffed behind him pointed with his chin to the corner of the room, where a young man with a black T-shirt, dirty blue jeans, and greasy black hair lay crumpled in a heap. His pacified hands were cuffed as well. One of the SWAT team members stood guard over him.

"Hey, Eric, is this the guy we're looking for? Is he the one who killed Brad?" The hefty officer reached his large mitt down and snatched the felon by the scruff of the neck. "Get up. We got somethin' to talk about."

Elvin's limp body didn't respond, his head dangling toward the floor like a rag doll.

"He's unconscious." Robbie pulled a miniflashlight from her belt and shone it on his face. "We'll need to get him some medical attention before we talk with him."

"Medical attention?" The cop sneered. "This guy should be takin' a dirt nap for what he did to Brad. And he was reaching for this when I grabbed him." The angry officer held up a Colt .45 semiautomatic pistol.

"We don't know if he's the guy yet or not." Eric stepped forward and took the cop by the arm. "And if he is, we're certainly not going to let his lawyer get him off because we didn't do things right. Now back off and let us do what we need to do."

The cop dropped Elvin to the floor and snarled.

"John, I really want you to interrogate this guy."

Robbie stared at the monitor that led into the interview room, which was wired so agents could watch a particular interrogation from different points in the office, even from their desks. The more eyes and ears in on an interrogation, the better. It was easy for one agent to get caught up in the moment and miss vital information or body-language cues. Through the monitor, Eric, Tim, John, and Alan observed Elvin, who held a cold pack underneath his jaw.

Robbie decided to conduct the interrogation at the FDLE office instead of Palm Bay PD. Fewer distractions and hassles. She imagined that the one hundred and fifty or so Palm Bay cops would have been vying for position to watch Elvin spill his guts. She didn't want to push her luck.

Elvin resembled so many junkies she'd seen before. His oily black hair hadn't been under a shower in some time, and his pasty, pitted face sported the texture of stucco with several open sores around his chin and mouth. Crystal meth addicts itched constantly, ripping and tearing at their skin. Wicked stuff, that meth.

In the eighties, when she was going to school in Miami, the crack craze seized the town. Turf wars erupted, and she lost several friends to a new party drug. They were never the same. Her father warned her incessantly about drugs as a child, which she appreciated. But even if he hadn't done that, she still didn't understand the attraction. Young women would throw their lives away and sell themselves and their souls just to get high. Men would beat, stab, and murder for it. If the brand name "Evil" could ever be attached to something, it would be drugs.

And it looked as if Elvin Marasco could be the poster boy for "Just Say No" to drugs.

"You sure you don't want to take a shot at him?" John rubbed his chin and smirked.

Like Pavlov's dog, Agent John Russell salivated at the chance to interrogate this felon. He was showing due respect because it was her case, but he wanted to slowly strip away the layers of Elvin's psyche until he crumpled into a heap of emotion and confessed to killing Detective Brad Worthington.

Robbie would love to interrogate Marasco in a more clinical setting, to plumb the recesses of his tortured mind. But when John Russell was under the stress of a police investigation, he outpaced every detective she knew. Tim was tactical, streetwise, and fantastic at finding any felon who didn't want to be found. But John was the best at retrieving those gold nuggets of truth in confessions. Tim often teased John, calling him "Father John" because he'd heard so many confessions. She couldn't let ego get in the way. She needed John to interview Elvin.

"If you don't want to take a shot"—Eric rose to his tiptoes—"I'll certainly be glad to."

"I don't think that would be a good idea." Robbie shook her head.

Eric smirked. "Me neither, but I thought I'd ask."

Eric had restrained himself well during the search at Elvin's house. She could see him struggling between knowing what had to be done and what he wanted to do—personal vengeance.

She couldn't imagine how she'd react if a guy like Elvin had killed John or Tim. Would she be able to keep her composure? Would she conduct herself like a professional? She hoped she'd never have to find out.

Eric gazed at the monitor and forced a tense exhale. He was a good man, but human all the same. Robbie would be a happy girl when they finally locked someone up for Brad's murder.

"I think he's ready." John closed his case file and pointed to the monitor. He outlined Elvin's body position in the chair—slumped, shoulders down, head hung low. The sure signs of a defeated, ragged-out suspect. "He's been on ice for about two hours since his arrest. He's peaked and should be crashing now. It's a good time to approach him."

Tim rested his hand on John's shoulder. "You can take him, Russell."

"Thanks, partner." John nodded at the crew and rounded the corner, entering the interview room.

Elvin scooted up in the chair as if startled. John dropped the thick folder on the small table in a dramatic motion, the *slap* echoing through the audio of the monitors.

The tiny room was designed to steal any comfort from the person being questioned and to amp up the stress level. Gray carpet covered the walls and floor to moderate acoustics and dampen the mood. Elvin's chair was metal with hard plastic yellow pads for the seat and back. John's chair was large and soft. Sometimes an agent could be in the room for hours; a good chair was a must. The key was to make the suspect feel isolated and vulnerable in that room. Police work was ugly business, and Robbie felt no shame in using tried-and-true techniques to help solve crimes.

"Elvin Jacob Marasco. Date of birth: October 2, 1979. Is that correct?" John eased into his chair, his eyes never leaving Elvin.

Marasco wiped his hands along his jeans and fidgeted in the chair. "That's me."

"Do you know what all this is about?"

Still not making eye contact, Elvin nodded. "You all have been dogging me for a while, following me around. I know about that kinda stuff."

"Seems like you're a smart guy. That should make our talk a little easier."

"I know what you want. I'll do what I gotta do to get outta this. I'll tell you what you wanna know."

Robbie turned to Tim and Eric; both were smiling. How great would it be to wrap up everything and give the Palm Bay guys a bit of peace? They were burying Brad tomorrow. At least there could be some closure.

John carefully read him his Miranda rights, ensuring that Elvin wouldn't have his confession overturned in an appeal.

Robbie held her breath as Elvin signed the consent form to talk to the police without a lawyer present.

"Elvin, tell me what happened." John bent forward and rested his hands on the table that separated them.

"You all seem to know everything anyway." Elvin picked at a sore on his chin. "That rat Josh set this whole thing up."

"Josh Miller?" John canted his head. "The one in your house with you when we hit it?"

Robbie flipped through her file to the driver's license photo of Josh. Twenty-three years old. A couple of arrests for drugs and traffic stuff. Nothing violent, especially anything that would point to a cop killer, but it wouldn't be the first time she'd been surprised by a suspect.

"Why would Josh set up such a thing?" John's easy voice carried as if they were talking about the weather. "What beef did he have with Detective Worthington?"

"Detective Worthington? What are you talking about? Josh set me up to buy five grams of meth to cut and resell. I thought he was working with you guys. What's this Worthington stuff?"

John opened a file and spun Brad's photo across the table to Elvin.

"I know who he is. He's the pig who arrested me a couple of weeks ago."

"Pig!" Eric stepped around Robbie and Tim and marched toward the interview room.

Just as Eric's hand reached for the door, Robbie sprinted in front of him, cutting him off, and braced her hands on his rock-hard chest. His heart pounded.

"Don't do it, Eric." She kept her voice low. If he was truly intent on entering the room, she didn't know if she could hold him back. She stared deep into his tear-filled eyes and saw the same hurt she'd felt when she lost her father. Robbie understood his pain and wished she could take it from him, but she knew better. She could, though, keep him from doing something monumentally stupid.

"We have to do this right. We can't let Elvin or anyone else skate on this. Brad would want it that way. Just keep it together. John will break Marasco."

Eric growled, his face nearly the color of his red hair. He stepped back and raised his hands. "You're right. I know you're right. This is just tough."

"I know how hard it is, believe me." Robbie led him back to the office cubicle to watch the interview again. This time she positioned herself between him and the door.

"When Detective Worthington arrested you, you threatened to kill him and his family, didn't you?" John scooted his chair closer to Elvin, nearly on top of him. "And tonight you tried to pull a gun on the SWAT team. Seems like you have a real problem with cops."

"Look, I was angry and high when I said that. I didn't mean anything by it. I was just talking trash. So I said something stupid. I'm sorry. I keep that gun on me to protect myself. It's a crazy world, and you never know what people are gonna do."

"It's more than just what you said, Elvin." John tossed another photo to him. "It's what you did. You are a man who keeps his word."

Elvin picked up the crime-scene photo of Brad lying murdered next to his patrol car. Marasco grimaced and recoiled, laying the photo facedown on the table. "What's this? What are you all trying to pull on me?"

"Just showing you a little of your handiwork. Maybe Josh put you up to this. Maybe it was all your idea, getting a little retribution against a cop who arrested you."

"You're out of your mind, cop! I don't even know what happened to this guy." Elvin held up his hands and shook his head.

"What, you don't watch the news? Detective Brad Worthington was murdered two nights ago, and you're the only one with a motive for wanting him dead."

"This is insane. I never did nothing to that cop or any other cop. I thought we were in here talking about the dope, and you're trying to set me up." Elvin brushed the photo to the floor and faced the wall.

"So you're telling me that two nights ago you didn't shoot and kill Detective Brad Worthington? Because from where I sit, you're the guy and we don't need to look any further."

Elvin opened his mouth and stopped, sitting back against the chair and gazing at the floor. "Two nights ago?"

"Yes, Monday evening, about midnight. Is your memory improving?"

A completely stupefied look covered Elvin's face. He glanced back up and grinned. "I was in the Orange County jail Monday evening. I got locked up by Orlando PD for driving on a suspended license. You can call and check. I wasn't even in this county when it happened. I'll talk with you about the drugs. I'll even help you bust my source, but I didn't have anything to do with no murder. And that's a fact."

John backed off and glanced into the camera. Tim was already on the phone with the Orange County sheriff's office. After a few moments, Tim regarded Robbie and nodded.

For once in his pathetic life, Elvin Marasco was telling the truth. Their best suspect just evaporated with an airtight alibi.

Robbie gazed at Eric, whose head dropped. He had probably hoped that this part of the nightmare would be over. Robbie laid her hand on his shoulder.

"We're going to find the person who did this, Eric. I give you my word."

9

Lifetex

D r. Silverstein. Thank you for coming so quickly." Warren hurried around his mahogany desk and extended his hand. The doctor wore his usual gleaming white lab coat that matched his mustache and the remaining hair on his head.

"Never a problem, Warren. I'm always available for friends. How can I help you?" He took Warren's hand with both of his and then with a smile greeted Steve Glick, who stood next to the window. Steve returned the smile with as much enthusiasm as was possible for him.

Warren walked around his desk and eased onto his new chair. He loved the smell of fresh leather and the feel of a fine chair. He made sure he purchased a new one every three months or so. It reminded him of what was possible with Lifetex. Rejuvenation, a total human makeover, and the promise of a greater, longer life…among other things. Now it was time to move beyond names and mission statements into the potentially limitless and lucrative world they had just unlocked.

"Ben, how's Adam's progress? Is he on track?"

"Astounding. I couldn't be more impressed."

"That's very good." Warren steepled his fingers and rotated toward the window. The radiance of the midmorning sun in the cloudless sky brightened Warren's office. There was no disputing that it was a new day. "When do you think we will be able to unveil him?"

"I know you're excited, Warren, as we all are, but we need a little more time. Adam will set the scientific community on its ear, as well as whatever legal busybodies will rear their heads. I expect some consternation, to say the least, from the religious groups too. They might be a bit fanatical about such things, so we need to be prepared to defend our actions. We must introduce Adam and all the enormous benefits to the world that this research has led to in as flawless a package as possible. Success and the greater good served will be our vindication."

Warren tapped his fingertips together as he swiveled in a semicircle. Dr. Silverstein's methodical, cautious approach frustrated Warren. He had friends, globally and within the Defense Department, with a financial stake in these decisions. These men didn't care one iota about public opinion or any legal and ethical considerations. They wanted a product, one that would enrich their power, their portfolios, and their positions.

Should Warren not deliver a product or prototype very

soon, his "friends" would certainly look to one of Lifetex's competitors—and they were not far behind, so his sources informed him. If that were to happen, the investors he'd assembled would flee as well, leaving Lifetex in the lurch—with billions of dollars lost. They'd missed three deadlines so far. There couldn't be a fourth.

"Ben, I'm sure you understand that all of the amenities you see here are not cheap, by any means. There are many factors that I've worked hard to protect you from so you can focus solely on your vital research."

"I appreciate your contribution. More than you can imagine." Dr. Silverstein lifted his chin. "So what's troubling you? We've been friends long enough for me to know when you're concerned about something."

Warren nodded and shifted his gaze to Steve, then back to the doctor. "I had hoped we'd be further along with our project. The most difficult portion of the project—cloning and producing a genetically perfect human being—is finished. We need to unveil Adam now and let the press and the scientific community watch you run him through the paces." Warren made a jogging motion with his arms. "I'm just concerned that if we wait too long, someone will beat us to this."

"Warren, you needn't worry so. I just like to have answers. Yes, Adam seems perfectly healthy now, but what if we miscalculated? What if there's a glitch, a mistake in his DNA coding? We can only find this out by testing and observing. Time gives us that luxury. If something surfaces later that we should have discovered, we stand not only to look like a cadre of fools, but a criminal cadre of fools. Believe me, I would like nothing more than to stand alongside Adam as he is introduced to the world. But we must have *all* the answers first. If we move too early, we'll only be setting ourselves up for a potential disaster."

Warren pursed his lips. It was highly unlikely that Dr. Silverstein would reverse his opinion. His obsession with scientific methods and verification had created his reputation and success. Normally Warren could simply order what he wanted done, and it would be done. Silverstein was different, and Warren needed his loyalty—for now.

"How long do you need?" Warren placed his elbows on the desk and folded his hands. "What's your time frame for going public?"

Ben shrugged. "I have Neal working on the final reports, collating the files and research together. Two and a half, three weeks, I suppose."

"I think we can accommodate that time frame." Warren wanted tomorrow, but Dr. Silverstein's estimate was at least workable, barely. He'd press him again toward the end of the week to shave off a few more days. "One more thing, Doctor. When we do introduce Adam, I'd rather not disclose the number of other experiments we have."

Dr. Silverstein paused for a moment. "We can do that, but what would be the point of holding back after Adam is unveiled?"

"I'm asking you to trust me on this one, Ben. I know what I'm doing."

"Very well."

"Wonderful things are in store for all of us, Doctor. Wonderful things."

"For the entire world," Dr. Silverstein added. "I believe Adam, much like his namesake, will usher in a beautiful, new Utopian era."

"Me too, Doctor. Me too. Thank you for your time."

"Always a pleasure, Warren." Dr. Silverstein glanced at his watch and hurried for the door. Steve beat him there and opened it for him.

Warren waited for Ben to leave the office, then regarded Steve. "As soon as we're done here, get General McNally on the phone. Explain the situation to him. The general will get his test run very soon."

"Will do, sir." Steve unhooked his BlackBerry and held it at his side.

"Steve, when you were in the marines, what would you have given for a platoon of Adams?" Warren wiggled the mouse of his computer to wake it from sleep mode. "What about a battalion? a division? Can you imagine what soldiers like that could accomplish? Countries would be willing to pay a fortune for an army like that. It boggles the mind."

"Soldiers like Adam could change the face of warfare, bring it to a whole new level." Steve brushed back his jacket and planted his hands on his hips, his Smith & Wesson .40-caliber pistol in full view. "And I can't wait to see it happen."

"Dr. Silverstein has been more than useful, but I worry that he lacks our vision for this project. He only sees half the equation with Adam. The medical advances and spin-offs will play out nicely for us, but equally as profitable is the defense industry. I don't think Dr. Silverstein would ever go for that."

"How do you think he'll react when he discovers your plans?" Steve raised his eyebrows.

"Let me worry about Silverstein." Warren tapped his fingernail on the table. "I'll deal with him when the time comes. You just need to stay focused and do what you always do—make sure that nothing, and I mean nothing, keeps this project from moving forward."

Robbie stepped from her unmarked car as Tim got out of the passenger's seat and John from the back. Alan drove separately and would meet them inside. Robbie slipped on her coat, adjusting it around her pistol and badge—with a black band around it. She'd attended enough police funerals to know the protocol.

Clusters of police from every law enforcement agency in the state, and some from out of state, lined New Life Fellowship's parking lot because there was no more room in the church, which was able to seat three thousand people on a good Sunday. Each agency huddled together, one alongside the other. The various uniforms came together like a patchwork quilt, stitched together in tragedy and pain. Patrol cars and unmarked vehicles stretched for blocks around the church, along side streets, and down Malabar Road.

The clamor of jostling gun belts and the shuffling of boots reverberated throughout the parking lot. The officers moved into formation, as they would soon be called to attention. Wearing suits and sober expressions, detectives remained behind the rows of uniformed officers. Robbie trailed Tim and John as they walked toward the church door.

The front of the broad semicircular sanctuary contained a raised pulpit backed by a ten-foot-high lighted cross. In spite of the circumstance, Robbie felt a brief moment of peace. Raised Catholic, she was no stranger to church. Even though this was a bit different than she was used to, a breath of familiarity welcomed her, much as it had when she was young. Her father had made sure the family was in church every Sunday, and he would often go by himself before his police shift.

Although he rarely spoke about his faith, Papi's actions had demonstrated much to Robbie. A twinge of guilt assaulted her, bringing her back to the moment. She hadn't been to church other than for funerals and weddings since before college. She did still pray occasionally, when she needed to. But in truth, she drifted away from God a long time ago. Between apathy and activities, she just didn't have the time or desire to make church a priority.

Detective Worthington's coffin lay just behind the pulpit. The casket was closed, as Robbie figured it would be. A picture of Brad in uniform was displayed on an easel next to it. In full-dress uniform, he appeared handsome and professional. Even though Robbie had never met him before, his photo exuded the countenance of a kind, caring person.

As they approached the front of the sanctuary, Eric rose from his seat next to Julie Worthington and met them in the aisle. Without a word, he pointed to the pew behind them. While Eric shook John's hand and then Tim's, Robbie slipped into the pew. John and Tim followed her.

Julie's three-year-old daughter wiggled in her mother's arms as she glanced back at them. Robbie saw the loss and confusion on Kaylee's face. She didn't know where her daddy was or what had happened. By the time Kaylee was old enough to understand, any memories of her father would have slipped away. Though her mind might not remember, Robbie was sure the little girl's soul would forever feel her father's absence. Robbie's did.

Hardly a day went by that she didn't feel the sting of loss. She hadn't even been able to visit her father's grave since his funeral. She just couldn't bring herself to it. She'd spent all those years pursuing what she thought her father wanted her to do, to follow in his footsteps and become a cop, to push herself more and more. But now it all felt so ridiculous. She'd achieved every goal she ever set for herself and…nothing. Emptiness and longing was the reward for her toil.

Robbie gazed into Kaylee's confused eyes. She simply wanted her daddy. Robbie knew that feeling well.

Their son, Brad Jr., maybe six, turned around to look at them as well. He bore his father's features. Robbie forced a smile at him, then felt foolish. But what else could she do? Eric told her he would save a spot for them in the sanctuary. Robbie was sure that Eric wanted them to sit behind Julie and her children so their emotion would keep the team moving forward to find Brad's murderer. It worked. Robbie drew a purposed breath, alternating between sorrow and rage. Brad Worthington went to work to protect others and provide for his family, and some lowlife came along and took his life simply because he was a cop.

Robbie checked her watch. She couldn't wait to get through the service. She had business to attend to.

Eric eased down next to Julie and adjusted his coat so he could rest his muscular arm behind her on the back of the pew, as if erecting a protective shield. He glanced back and locked eyes with Robbie, then nodded. His red hair was perfectly combed. He looked exhausted. He wasn't just investigating the homicide; he was comforting and caring for Julie and her children as well. Eric had a lot on the ball to be able to juggle everything. Robbie was concerned that when he did crash—and he would certainly crash—it would be painful.

Pastor Wilson Perry negotiated the three steps into the pulpit and set his notes on the podium. Dressed in a dark suit and tie, the pastor was a large man with a heavy face and thick brown hair. At first Robbie thought he was a church worker or someone else. She was used to a priest in robes, not like this casual atmosphere. It felt strange.

"Tragedy!" The pastor's voice boomed throughout the sanctuary and carried into the parking lot. Speakers had been set up outside the church, so the officers there could hear as well.

"Tragedy!" he thundered again. "The life of Detective Brad Worthington was snatched from this earth in what could only be called a tragedy of immeasurable proportions."

Pastor Perry paused, letting his words resound from the speakers. "Brad leaves behind a loving wife, two wonderful children, and a legacy of faith that can scarcely be rivaled. And in the midst of this unexplainable heartbreak, I'm here to tell you that three days ago, Brad Worthington experienced his greatest triumph as well."

Robbie snapped to attention. Maybe this pastor was deluded, because she was at the crime scene and triumph was certainly not there, only the horror and violence of Brad's last moments of life. She closed her eyes to close off the memory.

"Three nights ago, Brad heard his Lord and Savior say to him, 'Well done, good and faithful servant. Your mission here on this earth is finished. You've finished the race. Enter My rest.'"

Robbie wanted to believe that. It sounded good, but any faith she had suffered from more holes than a target at a pistol range. She didn't know what she believed now. She only knew that Brad Worthington was dead and a killer remained free.

"But as we meet here today to grieve our loss, we are also here to celebrate Brad's life and where he ultimately has gone. We either believe that he's where the Bible says he is, or we choose to disregard what God has clearly revealed to us in Scripture. Brad Worthington placed his faith in Jesus Christ as his Savior. He walks with God today."

Pastor Perry covered his notes and bowed his head as a photo montage played on a wide screen behind the pulpit. Pictures of Brad in uniform, with his family, as a boy playing football cycled across the screen to the music of Mark Schultz's "Remember Me."

Julie wiped the tears from her cheeks as snippets of their life together scrolled by. She covered her mouth and laughed out loud when a picture of Brad wearing a gaudy, pink woman's hat, which must have been taken at a party, flashed on the screen.

Although she didn't know either of them, Robbie admired the life the two of them had built, even if it was cut short. They looked so happy and were blessed with two lovely children. At least they had the memories and the feelings of a life lived together, shared with the person they loved.

Robbie would trade places with Julie in a second, even knowing the love of her life was gone forever, just to have those memories of eight years with a true soul mate. Robbie yearned for a love like Julie and Brad's and Mima and Papi's.

Robbie's love life, or lack thereof, consisted of a lot of first dates, very few seconds, next to no thirds. She'd always get to the part of the relationship where she was supposed to open up and reveal a bit of her true self—and she just couldn't. She hadn't found a person she felt comfortable enough with to let down her defenses and allow him to get close to her.

The slide show ended, and Pastor Perry continued with his sermon. Robbie heard little else he had to say. Consumed by the memories of her own father's funeral, watching the suffering of the Worthington family, and mourning the loneliness of her own life, Robbie moved as if in a trance through the rest of the ceremony.

Later she drove John and Tim in the funeral procession, which was several miles long, to the grave site. John and Tim made small talk; Robbie said nothing. She quietly took her position at the grave site and stood at attention when commanded. John and Tim flanked her on either side.

A Palm Bay police officer from the honor guard stepped out of formation and raised a trumpet to play "Taps." Cops were supposed to be tough. They weren't supposed to feel emotion or succumb to the fears and pains of this life. Cops were supposed to be superhuman, maybe even inhuman. Robbie couldn't stand it anymore. Her facade cracked, and the tears poured down her cheeks.

It wasn't right. Why did things like this happen? How could God allow a good man like Brad to be murdered by some monster? How could He allow her father to be murdered too? Did only the good die young while evil men seemed to live forever?

Her shoulders quivered, and she battled not to crumple into a heap on the grass. John slipped his arm around her shoulder. He was crying too, the big softy. Tim closed in on her other side. She didn't feel as alone now. She did have good friends who would help her find the person responsible for this. But it wouldn't be easy.

Crack! Robbie jumped as the first volley fractured the air. The honor guard raised their rifles again. Another series of seven shots rang out. Twenty-one times the rounds fired.

An officer wearing a kilt and sporting a set of bagpipes pushed through "Amazing Grace."

Robbie had nothing left. The bagpipes always finished her.

10

Neal Meyer strolled down the aisle between the tubes that contained twenty more physical triumphs like Adam. Nearly ten thirty at night, the lights in this part of the lab were dimmed to acclimate the experiments to the same schedule as everyone else.

Neal chose evening duty. He savored his time alone, with only his work to keep him company. Silence and solitude were friendships he took great pleasure in cultivating, much to the chagrin of Dr. Silverstein.

While he had immeasurable respect for the doctor, Neal couldn't make the man understand that his work *was* his entertainment and his fulfillment. He told him so in one conversation only to be greeted with a back slap and an admonishment to go dancing with some fun young women. For all the passion they shared for the project, they didn't communicate well on any other level.

Neal stopped in front of Beta. At least that was his name until they could come up with a better one. Dr. Silverstein didn't think it wise to use laboratory references for the projects once they were unveiled to the world. He felt it dehumanized them and could cause the press and other scientists to treat them with less respect.

With the physique of a fifteen-year-old boy, Beta was curled in the fetal position, suspended within his watery cocoon somewhere between life and nonlife. It couldn't be "death" because there had to have been life for death to occur.

Neal surveyed the control panel on the side of Beta's home. Tubes extended from the top, providing oxygen and all the elements Beta needed to thrive. He was being cared for and monitored even better than if he were in a womb.

Beta's foot twisted, and his leg extended, then curled again. Good. The pulse therapy seemed to be working fine, just as it had for Adam. Beta's physical therapy hadn't started yet, so the movement must have been independent. Neal jotted down notes on his clipboard.

The careful labeling of the chambers proved to be a better idea than he had first thought. From Adam to Beta to Gamma, only their apparent ages gave distinguishable differences. That would change soon as the accelerated growth of the rest caught up with Adam.

Dr. Silverstein didn't like surprises. He wanted to chart their progress and have one genetically ideal prototype to present to the world. After a couple of weeks, the twenty others would burst forth, and a never-ending stream of flawless humanity would follow. Additional staff was already prepped and on standby.

Neal marveled at how Beta mirrored Adam in every way, even his early physical responses, even though this had been planned. Produced from the same genetic combination, their movements, and ultimately their thoughts and actions, should follow the predetermined pattern. After all, since they shared the same exact DNA sequence—the essence of all life—every part of themselves would be exactly the same. That's why so much focus was placed on Adam. Once his tendencies and capabilities were charted and measured, all the others would follow that precise outline.

So much had been accomplished here. Neal never imagined being involved in something of this magnitude. Science simply fascinated him from an early age, and he excelled at it. Sports, music, and girls were things he never quite understood or related to.

His mother had encouraged him at every turn. "God's given you a brilliant mind, Neal. You need to use it for His glory." Mom was special, always believing in him, but she never seemed to get his passion for science.

His mind wasn't a gift from a god or higher being. It was the product of having a brilliant father, a CPA who read four to five books in a weekend, and a college-educated mother, who had a fancy for trivia. Pure genetics. A product of a giant sifting process, sluicing genes this way and that, washing out the weak, recessive genes in favor of the stronger, dominant ones. Not nearly as romantic a tale as his mother's, but much more grounded in reality. But like an athlete born to run, without proper training and discipline he would have never reached the genetic potential fate had given him.

If his father had married a nice but slightly dull woman, would Neal have taken after his father or mother? What if both had lacked any intellectual capacity? Would he be a mere simpleton, scurrying about aimlessly, clueless about the world's complexities? Difficult to imagine.

Neal inspected the control panel next to the chamber. Everything was working just as it should. The low hum of the life-care machines reverberated throughout the lab, supplying a harmonious backdrop as soothing to Neal as a symphony orchestra. Bending down, he checked the oxygen pressure gauge at the bottom of the chamber. A foot stepped out in his way.

"Ah!" Neal hopped backward and dropped his clipboard.

Adam crept from behind the tube and grinned at Neal.

"Adam." Neal slapped his hand on his chest, his heart pounding. "You scared the life out of me."

Adam continued to grin as he turned to face Beta's chamber. Adam's blue hospital scrubs stretched to their limit over his tall, muscled frame. Eventually, they would have to get him some "real" clothes. He was such an impressive sight.

"You're supposed to be in bed. You need your sleep." Neal picked up his clipboard. How did Adam get out of his room anyway? That part of the lab was locked down at night. They couldn't have their experiments walking around and doing goodness knows what in the lab.

"I'll help you back to your room." Neal took Adam by the arm, but he didn't budge. It was like grabbing a granite pillar and expecting it to move.

Adam glared at Neal, his eyes piercing him, then shifted his gaze back to Beta's chamber. Neal stepped aside. Adam's demeanor was considerably different than it was when the therapist and others were around. Neal's curiosity overrode his desire to get Adam back to his quarters. What was he up to?

Adam stared at Beta, reached out, and touched the glass. Beta twitched and convulsed, stirring the fluid in his chamber as much as he would during his morning therapy. His heart-rate monitor spiked, beeping faster and faster. Beta opened his eyes. Adam's smile morphed from benign to sinister. The two locked eyes for several moments, and then Adam removed his hand.

Neal's stomach flipped, and tremors racked his hands.

Beta closed his eyes and curled back up into fetal position, his heart rate dropping to normal.

Adam faced Neal and trained his eyes on him like machine guns; a totally different countenance emanated from him. Something wasn't right. Adam stepped closer to Neal, lording his physical prowess over him.

Neal trembled. Adam could snap his neck like a dry twig, and no one was around to stop it. Neal lowered his head.

Adam pointed to the chamber. "When?"

"Wh-what did you say?"

"When will he be complete?"

Adam had a good grasp of the English language and could speak in small sentences, but how did he understand what was going on with Beta? He didn't have the context to recognize that Beta was yet being formed. His education was rudimentary at this point—basic language, manners, physical training. He'd never watched television or experienced what other adults his physical age had.

"Soon." Neal swallowed hard. "A couple of weeks, maybe."

"Good."

"We need to get you back to your room." Neal reached for his arm again but stopped short.

Adam turned and strode confidently toward his room at the rear of the lab. Neal followed at a distance.

He needed to talk with Dr. Silverstein, immediately.

"Man, what an impressive place." John slid on his jacket, which snagged on his pistol handle. He brushed it aside. The Lifetex facility bustled with activity, cars cruising through the parking lot and a steady stream of people hurrying in and out of the building.

"Yeah, some pretty nice digs." Tim examined the wall of concrete and mirrored glass before them.

John had wanted to check out Lifetex before they got jerked around by Elvin and his crew, an aggravating dead end and waste of time. The hottest leads always got the most attention. Then they would move on to other investigative concerns, like canvassing the neighborhood. Now, with much of the early chaos in the case out of the way, they could return to a little more methodical approach to the investigation.

John turned to the south and could see the Rolsen building and parking lot about a quarter of a mile away. Maybe the cameras captured Detective Worthington's murder or the suspect coming or going from the scene. He'd take what he could get.

"I appreciate your giving me a ride here and not forcing me to drive that…thing."

"No problem, partner." John chuckled. "Friends don't let friends drive VWs. It's a little life philosophy I've developed over the years."

"You're a good egg, Russell."

"Yeah, but don't tell Alan. He still wants to punish you."

"I know, I know. It'll be our little secret."

John and Tim entered through the double doors and met the receptionist, a young woman with long brown hair. A cool air-conditioned breeze washed over them. Another steamy Florida summer lay just ahead.

"Can I help you, gentlemen?" She stood to face them.

"We're agents with the Florida Department of Law

Enforcement." John pulled back his jacket, exposing his badge and pistol. "We have an appointment with Warren Finstead."

The girl whispered into her headset, "Alice, two police officers are here to see Mr. Finstead. Okay. Thank you." She gave her attention back to John. "His secretary will be right with you."

John checked out the lobby, which was split into two sections with stairs heading up the middle of the room. Posters with children's faces on them—all children being treated at the Lifetex Children's Care Unit—decorated the walls. A collection of metal sculptures of Greek forms held prominent places in the lobby. Lifetex appeared to have it all together.

"Detectives." A large blond woman, maybe in her late forties, stood at the bottom of the stairs. "Mr. Finstead will see you now."

She hurried up the stairs before John and Tim reached her. They both jogged to catch up and hurried down a corridor to a single desk with a lone office door behind it. "Warren Finstead, CEO of Lifetex, Inc." was emblazoned on it. Pictures, presumably of Mr. Finstead, dotted the secretary's office wall: him shaking hands with two former U.S. presidents, an NFL quarterback, a golf pro, and numerous others that John probably should have known but didn't. Warren Finstead exuded confidence, good looks, and power. Should be interesting to meet with the real thing.

Alice opened the door and with an extended hand ushered

them into the office. Warren reclined in his chair, phone in one hand as he held up one finger on the other.

A muscular, well-dressed man stood in the corner and covered the distance between them with a smooth, balanced gait for a person of his size.

"Steve Glick." He extended his hand, engulfing John's. "Mr. Finstead's assistant."

Glick's knuckles were gnarled and calloused; he'd punched many a hard object with those fists. On the right side of his thick neck, a tattoo of Japanese writing peeked out from his shirt collar. This guy was a martial artist for sure. The pistol-shaped bulge on his hip underneath his suit coat confirmed that in Glick's lexicon, *assistant* meant "bodyguard."

John introduced himself and Tim. Glick returned to his position, like a well-trained attack dog. His demeanor at least attempted to be warm and inviting; his eyes betrayed the civilities, though. He didn't like law enforcement one bit.

The office was somewhat modest for a man of Warren's stature. A mahogany work desk held a picture of himself with his arm around an attractive blonde, who was a good ten years younger than he was. It appeared to have been taken on a boat somewhere. The bookshelf behind him was stocked with mostly motivational books and autobiographies. Nothing ornate or showy, but Warren did have more pictures of himself with celebrities and corporate leaders.

Whenever John went into someone's home or office, he

compulsively assessed the bookshelves. Books provided many clues about a person. Warren Finstead was a powerbroker and jet-setter.

After a solid two minutes of chatting in French with someone, presumably overseas, Warren finally hung up the phone. "Gentlemen, sorry to keep you waiting." He folded his hands on top of his desk. "Can we get you any coffee?"

"No, thank you." John eased into a chair in front of Warren's desk. Tim followed suit.

"Well, I assume that you came to talk about the tragedy that happened down the street."

"You're the CEO for a reason." John crossed his legs and opened the case file.

"Nasty business," Warren said. "We sent some flowers to the Palm Bay Police Department for the funeral. We've had a very good working relationship with the department ever since we moved here. They keep a good eye on the place. It just makes us sick that someone would shoot an officer like that, especially so close to our facility. I tell you, they don't pay you law-enforcement officers enough for what you do."

"Well, we appreciate that." John slipped his pen out of his pocket. Finstead should be in politics; his smooth tongue could cajole whatever crowd he was working with. "I don't want to take much of your time, but maybe there are some things you can do to assist our investigation, if you don't mind."

"Anything." Warren spread his arms open wide. "Like I said, we feel the loss to the community deeply here at Lifetex."

"I noticed coming in that you have a pretty elaborate security system. Is there any way we can get copies of your security footage from the other night?"

"Our cameras focus on the complex itself, so I don't know what you hope to find. I'm not sure they'll be of any value."

"You never know. Maybe they picked up a car driving by or someone walking. The suspect might have cut through your property to make his escape. We just want to check to see if there's anything on them. I've been surprised more than once at what security tapes can pick up."

"Steve, please do as these detectives have asked." Warren regarded Glick, who raised his eyebrows. "Pull the DVDs and get them to me as soon as possible."

John smiled. "Excellent. Also, could we get a list of all of your employees, especially those working the other night? We'd like to interview them."

Warren crossed his arms and leaned back in his chair. His confident Hollywood smile disappeared. John scribbled down a note.

Tim glanced at John and then asked, "Is there a problem with that?"

"No problem." Warren's voice carried a hint of consternation. "We just have a lot of employees. I don't know if you're aware, but we have a thirty-bed children's hospital as well as a research facility. Many doctors come and go. Some are on the Lifetex payroll, and others are contractors and independent researchers, so the request might not be as easy to comply with as it seems."

"Mr. Finstead." Tim pointed to a picture of Warren with President George Herbert Walker Bush. "You strike me as a get-it-done kind of guy. I'm sure that type of request won't be too difficult if you want it to happen. I get the feeling that around here, when you say jump the only question is, how high?"

"I am a get-it-done type of man. But I don't get caught up in Lifetex's day-to-day operations. I'm responsible for a number of other entities as well. So I'm sure you can appreciate that this request will take some time. It's not a matter of just making a phone call. I'll have a meeting later today with the Lifetex staff, and we'll make arrangements to get you the information you need. We have nothing to hide."

"Thank you, Mr. Finstead." Tim rose from his chair. "You've been more than helpful."

"Well, then." Warren stood. "I think we're finished here, gentlemen."

John and Tim shook hands with Finstead and then Glick.

Making a hasty retreat from the office, John picked up his pace as they walked down the hallway.

"What's stuck in your craw, Russell?" Tim nearly jogged to keep up with him. "You've got that look on your face."

"Something Finstead said is bugging me."

"What's that?"

"We weren't there asking about Lifetex. We simply wanted the security footage and to speak with potential witnesses."

John stopped and turned to Tim. "It's an odd statement and just enough to have me concerned."

"What do you think it means?"

"Maybe there *is* something to hide at Lifetex."

11

D r. Silverstein." Neal rubbed the sleep from his eyes as he made it to the lab earlier than normal. "We need to talk."

"We'll talk when you finally get around to calling me by my name." Dr. Silverstein continued typing on his computer, undaunted by Neal's insistence. The doctor's office hardly fit a man of his stature and prestige. Uneven mounds of paper covered his desk, some on the floor as well. The cramped bookshelf bulged with manuscripts ranging from quantum physics and genetic splicing to cookbooks and the latest on Pilates.

"Okay." Neal sighed. The eerie feeling in the pit of his stomach had not left him. In fact, it had only increased during a fitful night of attempted sleep. "Ben. I really think we need to go back through the research. I'm not comfortable with some of the things I'm seeing now."

Dr. Silverstein stopped typing and peered over his glasses at Neal. "What has you so concerned?"

"Well, I think something's wrong with Adam. He's just not acting right." Maybe they had miscalculated, possibly a glitch they hadn't accounted for. Neal had pondered the possibilities well into the night. He was stumped.

"What do you mean? I've watched all of his training tapes and monitored many of his sessions. He's nothing short of a miracle."

"Sure, when he's studying and around others, he appears to be well ahead of schedule. But when he's not around everyone else, I mean, when I've been alone with him, it's like there's something...sinister about him."

Dr. Silverstein smirked. "Neal, we're both men of science. Feelings aren't measurable and can easily fool us. You'll have to be more concrete. Give me an example of what you think is wrong."

Was Neal just being paranoid? By all measurable indicators Adam was perfect. How did he explain a look or Adam's behavior in a way that another scientist would understand? Neal reviewed Adam's mannerisms and what he observed. He wasn't just crazy or paranoid; Adam *wasn't* what he seemed to be.

"Last night I was in the lab. Adam snuck up on me and scared the daylights out of me. Then he went over and placed his hand on Beta's chamber. Beta wiggled and thrashed around. As soon as Adam lifted his hand, Beta went back to normal. It was like the two were communicating in some unseen way."

"Don't be ridiculous. You must have been imagining things. I've told you that you need to have a life outside of this place." Dr. Silverstein pointed at his head and swirled his index finger around. "Being in here all day and night will make you batty."

Neal massaged his forehead. "The way Adam looks at me, it's more like he's looking through me, smirking, like he's mocking me. It's truly eerie."

"Adam is the most magnificent human to ever walk the face of this earth. He doesn't have the genetic disposition that leads to crime and malevolent behavior. He's been cleansed of all the problems that plague us backward humans. These thoughts of 'sinister' and 'eerie' are simply not possible. They're the ruminations of a tired, burned-out mind late at night in the laboratory when he should be out in the company of a young woman or friends."

"Ben, we need to keep a closer watch on Adam's progress. Just keep an open mind on this. That's all I'm asking."

"Your observations are duly noted. And, of course, I respect your scientific mind, my friend. We're documenting Adam's behaviors, and I promise that if I observe something wrong, we will discuss it. So put your mind at ease."

There would be no convincing Dr. Silverstein. Neal wasn't even sure himself what he'd seen. Was it mere feelings, or was something else at play? Being a scientist precluded him from reacting on feelings alone, but should he ignore them completely? That didn't make sense either. Neal couldn't shake the tremors that racked his body when he was alone with Adam.

And what about Beta? It wouldn't be long before he'd be ready to be released from the chamber. They were about to go public with their findings too. So much was happening. Maybe he was just letting the stress get to him.

"Have you seen Sammy?" Dr. Silverstein shifted the computer mouse on the pad.

"Not since sometime yesterday."

"That little rascal is quite the mischief maker. I'll find him."

"The lab is huge, and who knows if he got out and is in the back area. Really, Ben, we should keep that experiment locked up. He could escape, or someone could steal him. Then the most valuable ball of fur on the planet would be gone."

"*Tsk, tsk,* Neal. Sammy's much more than an experiment or a ball of fur. He's my best comrade, and I don't relish the thought of losing him. I should have a location on him in just a second."

"What are you doing?" Neal gazed over Dr. Silverstein's shoulder.

"Look. I should see him here in a second." Ben clicked the mouse and brought up a new screen: Pet-Be-Found.com. He typed in his password and brought up a map of Palm Bay with a small light flashing on the screen in the area of the facility. He clicked the mouse again and zoomed in for a closer view of the facility itself, a single light blinking just behind the life chambers near the back wall, by Neal's estimate.

"I've grown so fond of Sammy that I subscribed him to this service. It's really quite handy, and my heart would break if I lost him."

"And you say that *I've* been in the lab too long."

"Put your concerns to rest now." Dr. Silverstein pushed his glasses up on his nose. "You see, Neal, technology and scientific advances work to benefit humankind. You have nothing to fear from them."

The FDLE office was quiet for the first time in several days. John and Tim had gone to follow up leads. Alan was meeting with the Palm Bay chief of police to update him on the investigation. Eric and the Palm Bay detectives were shaking up their informants for anything they could dig up. Maybe, with a little peace and quiet, Robbie could start fitting the pieces together.

The adrenaline from running the first few days of the homicide was all used up. Now it was time to sit back and reflect on the information they'd gathered. She'd seen it in cases before. Once the investigators get a chance to settle down and examine the evidence, the answer pops out, having been there the entire time undetected. She hoped and prayed that would happen this time.

Robbie slipped Brad's crime-scene picture onto the white-board next to the department photo of him smiling. Had she not been told who he was, she wouldn't have been able to identify him at the scene.

The crime-scene photos were hard to view. The scene itself could be the key to an entire case. What could they reveal about the killer? Every killer left some kind of evidence at a crime scene, be it fingerprints, latent fibers or hairs, maybe even DNA. There was no such thing as a pristine scene. It was just a matter of digging in and finding it.

Robbie had witnessed death in every manner possible, but the memory of Brad lying there provoked a pain beyond what she thought she could bear. Images of her father's murder ran inescapably through her mind.

When Robbie was preparing to leave for college, she'd met with the detective who worked her father's homicide. She needed to know what happened to him that dark day in Miami, beyond what they'd been told. She wanted to know everything—or so she thought.

The detective begged her not to look at the photos, to remember her father as he was in life, not death, but she wouldn't listen. She demanded to see them. He then said something that stuck with her all these years. "Once you see these images, you can never get them out of your mind. You can't just wipe it away like it never happened." He was right. The images of her father's crime scene had never left her mind—or her heart. That day she knew she would be a cop. She'd stop people who did these savage things and hold them accountable. Maybe she couldn't save the world, but she could make a difference.

"Hey, you okay?" a voice came from behind her.

Robbie started and spun around.

Eric hopped back. "A little jumpy today, aren't we?"

"How'd you get in?"

"The door was unlocked. You FDLE types should really work on your security here. You all are starting to slip."

Robbie controlled her breathing and felt her pulse come down. He'd gotten her good. Eric looked better than he had in the last few days. He might have actually gotten some sleep last night. His light blue shirt was tucked in, accentuating his athletic build. "Tim said you played college football at UCF. Says you were a pretty good defensive back."

Eric shrugged. "Football paid my way through school. I doubt I'd have been able to go otherwise. I had a lot of fun, but it seems like forever ago now. What about you? I heard you played softball in college."

"How'd you hear that?" Robbie placed her hands on her hips and feigned an angry look. He'd been checking up on her. Not a bad thing. Most men Robbie met, cops especially, would have gladly bragged all day about being a football star. Eric played it down and seemed quite comfortable with himself. She liked that.

"You ever heard of Google?" He smirked. "I am a detective, you know. Some habits are hard to break."

"You shouldn't Google people you work with." She faked a pout. "It's not polite."

"I'll try to remember that." Eric chuckled and turned his attention to the whiteboard. "Have we found out anything new?"

"Nothing yet." Robbie folded her arms. Back to business. "I'm trying to put together my profile. It's hard being the lead detective and working on a profile at the same time, but I do have some ideas."

"What does your gut tell you?"

"Well, it appears the killer didn't necessarily plan this. The suspect didn't bring a weapon with him but instead disarmed Brad." Robbie glanced at Eric to make sure he was pleased with her use of Brad's name rather than *victim* or any other faux pas. Eric seemed to appreciate it.

"From the autopsy report, Brad had a broken arm and several broken ribs, and since the suspect was able to disarm Brad—an experienced cop and former wrestler—I think we're looking for someone who's large and strong and probably a trained fighter. Possibly a prior military type or more than one assailant. It's really hard to tell right now. I'm hoping there is more than one suspect."

Eric cocked his head back. "Why's that?"

"Because the more suspects, the better chance of someone getting chatty about the crime. Suspects always get drunk or high and shoot off at the mouth."

"I never thought of it that way." Eric put his hands into his pockets. "I'm learning quite a bit hanging out with a professional profiler. What about the cross?"

"I don't know what to make of that yet." Robbie shook her head. "It's unusual that someone would rip the cross off of Brad's tie. We used metal detectors all around the parking lot and the wooded area. Nothing. It certainly appears that whoever did this wanted to make a statement."

"Certainly looks that way."

Robbie wasn't sure what it would mean to her investigation. As much as she liked delving into the psychological aspect of the profile, she also knew its limitations. It wasn't like she could pull a suspect out of a hat or come across some miracle explanation. As best she could tell now, he was a cop-hater who not only killed a cop, but did it in a vicious manner. A very angry person was responsible for this crime.

"So we've got a cop-hating killer in the Rolsen parking lot at 12:02 a.m." Eric tapped his finger on the long-range shot of the scene. "What was he doing there that late, and why did he think he had to kill Brad? Was Brad looking to arrest him? Did Brad know him? Did he know Brad?"

"And why did he reload with Brad's extra magazines? The killer had to know Brad was already dead. Why the overkill, so to speak? I've never run into anything like this before." Robbie was flummoxed. How she wanted answers right now. Solve this thing and give some peace to the family.

When the detectives told her and her mother that they caught her father's killer, they were initially filled with joy and celebrated. But the years passed by—birthdays, Christmases, graduations, all missed. Time eroded the once-vivid memory of her father, leaving scattered recollections she struggled to hold on to. It was all she had left. There was only so much healing Robbie could bring to the Worthington family, of course, but she'd do her best.

Eric's jaw worked back and forth, and he glanced out of the corner of his eye at Robbie. Something was on his mind. She didn't have to know him real well to see that.

"You know, Robbie, my whole behavior since this started has been horrible. I've been so focused on revenge and catching the person that I've let it cloud who I really am."

Robbie folded her arms. Not quite what she expected. "Who are you, Detective Eric Casey?"

"Well, first, I'm a follower of Jesus Christ, and I know my actions thus far haven't shown much of that. I've been an angry, vengeful buffoon, and that's not what Brad would want. I became a Christian because of his witness to me. I owe him and God a whole lot better than that. I'm an extremely flawed vessel and a work in progress, so I hope you can forgive me."

This guy was a mystery, an intriguing one at that. Even with his bouts of anger and frustration, she saw a man who was committed to finding his friend's killer. Nothing out of the norm in law enforcement, but his attitude must have truly bothered him to bring it up. Not many cops she knew apologized for anything.

"I'm also sorry about jumping on your case at the scene. I

was pretty hard on you and your team. It's been bugging me since the other night. I can see that you all are good cops—the best—and you're busting your tails to find Brad's killer. I—we appreciate that. I just wanted you to know."

"Thank you." Robbie touched Eric's firm arm. "We're going to find the person responsible. I give you my word."

"I don't doubt that, Ms. Roberta Sanchez. I don't doubt that at all."

12

In his home office, Pastor Wilson Perry scribbled the last of his notes for the morning's sermon. He was scheduled to finish his series on the bride of Christ, but with Brad's murder and his congregation hurting and searching for answers, he changed his teaching to "The Refiner's Fire."

Wilson leaned back to the all-too-familiar creak of his chair. The subdued glow from the desk lamp offered only partial illumination of the stacks of paper, his open Bible, and a Greek dictionary scattered about the desk. He couldn't even see his phone. The fan on his laptop fired up, humming like it was ready to take off and fly away.

Wilson rested the tips of his forefingers on his lips and turned around in a slow half circle. He was preaching on God's sovereignty in all situations, even and especially this one, but he would be lying to himself and to his congregation—and worst of all, to the Lord—if he didn't admit he had no idea why God would strike down a young man in his prime like Brad Worthington. It made no sense to him whatsoever.

Wilson had married Brad and Julie not seven years before. It was a beautiful ceremony. Now he'd buried Brad, neither by disease nor accident but by the hand of another human being. If that person could have listened to Brad for five minutes, it was entirely possible this senseless tragedy would have never occurred.

Wilson yearned for more men like Brad in his church. He simply loved God and followed His commands, loved his family without limits, and loved others as himself. Although certainly not perfect, Brad was the benchmark by which other Christians in their church could be measured. Wilson lost track of all the church members that Brad was responsible for either leading to the Lord or just bringing to church to learn more. How could a servant like him be heartlessly butchered in a deserted parking lot? Wilson could scarcely understand what God was doing in this.

He tipped his head back and prayed that he would capture God's will in communicating to his devastated flock. He would trust and lean on the Lord. What choice did he have, and where else could he go? God was still God regardless of tragedy or triumph, pain or pleasure. But it was still tough. He wouldn't and couldn't lie about that.

Wilson checked the clock on the table: 11:44 p.m. He needed to get to bed. Sunday mornings came early, and he'd need to be at his best. Brad's friends and family and the rest of the congregation deserved that.

As he stood up to join his wife in bed, the doorbell rang. *Awfully late for visitors.* Being the pastor of a three-thousand-person church, it wasn't unusual to get late-night visits, but this was pushing it.

He hurried from his office, not wanting the doorbell to ring again and wake Joan. He glanced up the stairway as he walked to the door. Too late. Joan arrived at the top of the stairs, tying her bathrobe, her hair tossed about.

"It's all right, hon." Wilson waved to her. "Go back to bed. I'll be up soon after I take care of this. Love ya."

She nodded, then plodded back down the darkened hallway out of view.

Wilson flipped on the porch light and checked the peephole. A stranger hovered directly in front of the doorway. Wearing a trench coat, he had coal black hair and rugged features. Wilson was sure he'd never seen this man before; he would have remembered.

Wilson unlocked the door and cracked it open, leaving the screen door closed and locked. "Can I help you?"

"Pastor Wilson, can we speak? It's urgent."

"Have we met before?"

"Yes, but it was a long time ago." The man looked up the street and then back at him. "I really need to speak with you."

"It's kind of late. Can we talk at the church tomorrow? I

have to be up early to get ready for my sermon. I could make some time before services."

"It's imperative that we talk tonight."

Wilson couldn't imagine Jesus turning anyone away regardless of the hour. He'd promised himself years ago that he'd never turn away anyone in need; he wasn't about to start tonight. Besides, the man appeared to have nowhere else to go. Wilson opened the front door and unlocked the screen.

"I'm sorry. Please come in." He held the door open as the hulking visitor slipped past him. "We can talk in my study."

Wilson led the man past the staircase, through the kitchen, and into his cluttered office. He lifted a jumbled stack of papers off the chair in front of his desk and pushed it back so his visitor could sit down. He was a bit embarrassed by the messiness, but there was only so much he could do.

Joan badgered him to straighten up so he could find things, but that would destroy his system. Maybe tomorrow afternoon he would organize everything, so as not to put off any visitors.

"I'm sorry. I didn't even get your name." Wilson extended his hand to the visitor, who squeezed so hard it felt as if his hand would be crushed.

"Call me Morek."

"Pleased to meet you...Morek." *Strange fellow.* He wasn't the first odd person to seek Wilson's counsel. He'd have to be patient, but he was tired.

Morek didn't respond but brushed his coattail behind him and settled into the chair, smiling at Wilson. His broad shoulders spread wide like a billboard, and his athletic frame sat tall in the chair. Although he had handsome features, his penetrating blue eyes held an icy stare that caught Wilson's attention.

"So, how can I help you tonight?"

"I've come to talk about Brad and everything that is going on at New Life Fellowship."

Now it made some sense. This guy was probably a cop struggling for answers to his friend's senseless death. Wilson felt ridiculous for being anxious. He relaxed and sighed.

"Believe me, we're all taken aback by this. Right before you came I was wrestling with many of the same questions you probably have. I wish I had easy answers for you. I don't. But I know and trust that the Lord is in control, and He knows best. We have to lean on that during difficult, painful times."

"So you say." Morek picked at his fingernails and then regarded him. "More and more people seem to be coming to *your* church. It has been quite a little revival, as you might call it."

"It's not my church." Wilson pointed up. "It's His. And we've been blessed as of late. Brad was a large part of that blessing. He'll be missed. But the Lord will still be moving at New Life Fellowship regardless of our loss."

"We'll see about that. It has been my experience that when humans lose people they love and their shepherds are struck, the sheep scatter...and lose faith. Humans are remarkably weak and cowardly and don't respond well to adversity. Wouldn't you say so, Pastor Perry?"

"Sometimes." Wilson folded his hands on the desk. "But often the worst experiences drive people to their knees, then to faith in Christ."

Morek cringed and his smile faded as he drew a purposed breath and stood, looming over the desk. He gripped the edge and hissed, "Do you really believe that?"

Wilson gulped and rolled his chair back. He was accustomed to having others challenge his faith and hoped he could give this man some comfort, but he hadn't mentally prepared. He needed help.

As he stood before him, Morek was considerably larger than Wilson first thought. *Lord, give me the wisdom to help this man. I'm wiped out here.*

A flood of comfort and peace filled him. The Spirit was here with him in a way he hadn't felt in years. "'The message of the cross is foolishness to those who are perishing,'" he said.

Wilson rocked back. *Where in the world did that come from?* That wasn't at all what he wanted to say. "'God did not spare angels when they sinned, but sent them to hell....' 'Then he will say to those on his left, "Depart from me, you who are cursed, into the eternal fire prepared for the devil and his angels."'" Wilson no longer controlled his own tongue. He couldn't believe what he just said. What was happening?

Morek growled and stepped back, tipping over his chair.

As the veil lifted from Morek, a dark, sinister aura encircled him, casting a malevolent shadow over the entire room. This was no mere man standing before him. Why didn't he see it at the door? Wilson had made a terrible mistake—evil just entered his home.

"This is the true *offense*." Morek tossed a small round object at Wilson, who caught it with both hands. He tried to examine it while keeping a cautious eye on this Morek. He rolled it around in his hand. A metal cross bent at the sides and the top, almost into a ball.

"This was Brad's offense." Morek snickered. "And now it's yours as well."

Wilson trembled and swallowed hard as he glanced at the telephone on his desk. Could he call 911 before something happened? Or would this dark visitor smash him like an ant for trying? Would it matter now?

"It won't do you any good." Morek shook his head. "You should know that Brad's last act as he begged and cried out for his life was to deny the *Offensive One* once and for all."

Wilson lowered his shaking hands, and he was sure Morek could see the sweat beading on his forehead.

Lord, help me.

Despite his fear and the presence of evil in his midst, Pastor Wilson Perry's spirit quieted and was quelled. Another Presence was right next to him, unseen but felt. He grinned back at Morek.

"I know who and what you are, and I know that your father is the father of lies. Brad no more turned his back on the Christ than you could ever turn to Him. You are a liar!"

Morek drew a black pistol from his jacket pocket, and Wilson gazed into the barrel trained at his head. "Renounce *Him*, or your fate will be as Brad's."

Wilson stood up and bent forward as close to Morek as he could get, nearly touching the barrel of the gun with his forehead. "No matter what happens here tonight, no matter what you do, no amount of bullets can stop the kingdom of God. But you already know that. You're doomed. Jesus Christ is and always will be Lord—"

Crack.

Joan Perry sat bolt upright in bed. "What was that?" She'd heard something, she was sure. Several loud pops. An ache tore across her heart with a dread she couldn't imagine. *Wilson?* She grabbed her bathrobe and wrapped it around her as she sprinted out of the bedroom to the stairs.

A large man loomed at the bottom, leering up at her. "Good night, Joan. See you soon." He tucked his hands in his pockets and hurried out the front door.

She raced down the stairs and lost her footing, almost falling as she rounded the corner to her husband's office. A strange, pungent odor hung in the air. She didn't see her husband anywhere. "Wilson!" As she walked into the office, she saw his feet sticking out from the side of the desk.

"Wilson!" She hurried around the desk. "No. Oh please, God, no!"

Robbie parked behind Eric's car on the jam-packed street. Crime-scene tape encircled a quaint, wooden two-story home in the Lockmar neighborhood of Palm Bay like a ribbon on a present. Not the kind of present anyone would want, though.

The constant late-night pages and phone calls dogged Robbie, wearing her down. But Eric had told her it was critical to come to the scene. It was related to Brad's murder. His voice quivered; he sounded extremely upset, then hung up. What choice did she have? She had to come.

The Palm Bay PD crime-scene van was parked in front of Eric's car, and several more detective vehicles and marked patrol cars lined the street. A covey of neighbors gathered on a lawn across the street. A uniformed officer stood at the edge of the driveway with a clipboard, probably the place to check in. Robbie grabbed her notepad and digital recorder and hurried to the curb.

"Robbie." Eric marched down the driveway toward her. John and Tim were already standing at the doorway. She was always late. But having to wait for Kathy forced her to be the last one at the scene. The guys understood. Tim had always told her, "Well, there's no reason to hurry. They're not going to get any deader." Porter had a disturbed sense of humor. Still, she didn't like being behind the curve.

She waved and passed her hand over her hair. She hoped she looked all right. What was she doing? She was getting flirty at a homicide scene. How schoolgirlish. Something was really wrong with her life when the closest thing she had to a date was meeting someone at a brutal crime scene. That would have to change.

"Robbie, I'm glad to see you." Eric's eyes were bloodshot again, and his shirt was crumpled and disheveled. He lifted the crime-scene tape and nodded at the officer. "Roberta Sanchez, FDLE."

The officer scribbled down her name and the time.

Robbie ducked under the tape, and Eric took her by the elbow and escorted her toward the front door.

"This is bad." Eric talked as he glared straight ahead. "It's a nightmare."

Robbie stopped in the driveway. "What's going on, Eric? You sounded terrible on the phone."

Eric quaked. "It's Wilson Perry, Brad's pastor. Mine too. He's been murdered. Shot in his own house, practically with his wife watching. I'm betting it's the same person who killed Brad. This is all so insane, Robbie. Is the world going crazy or what? You gotta help me make sense of this."

"I'm so sorry." She touched his forearm. "We'll do everything we can. Just tell me what happened."

"Our Dispatch got a 911 call at about 11:52 p.m. from Wilson's wife." Eric composed himself and continued. "They had a late-night visitor, a really big guy with strong features. Joan said she'd know him again if she saw him. Anyway, Wilson let him in. She went back to bed. Several loud noises woke her up, and she went downstairs to check on her husband. The suspect walked right past her. Even told her good night. Joan found Wilson dead in his office, shot in the head."

Robbie raised her eyebrows. "I'm sorry, Eric. This has got to be difficult for you."

"I've had better weeks." Eric shook his head. "You need to come inside and see the scene."

"Hey, Robbie." John and Tim waited under the porch light. "Another long night."

"Looks that way." Robbie slipped a pair of rubber gloves from her jeans and hurried to get them on. Eric opened the top of the screen door with his knuckle, careful not to disrupt any evidence.

Robbie followed Tim, John, and Eric into the home and passed through the foyer. A woman, presumably Mrs. Perry, perched on the couch to their left. A young female victim's advocate for the state attorney's office sat next to her, holding a blanket around Mrs. Perry's shoulders. Two detectives were questioning her. The catatonic stare and robotic answers told Robbie everything she needed to know about Joan's mental state right now. They would talk with her, but Robbie needed to see the scene first.

Eric led them past a staircase on their right, around a corner with the kitchen on her left, and into a small office area. She'd diagram the house later for her notes. Palm Bay Police Department was the lead agency on this, but if Eric was correct and there was a connection, she would need all of her own info on this scene as well.

Two crime-scene techs in blue jumpsuits snapped photos of the room. Wearing white sneakers with long khaki pants, a man's legs jutted out from behind the desk. Robbie leaned in. It was ugly. She couldn't imagine a wife finding her husband like this.

Robbie tried to visualize the same man she saw in the pulpit at the funeral just a couple of days ago. It was difficult. The window behind the desk was broken, probably from the rounds that penetrated the victim or missed altogether. Two shell casings rested on top of the desk, another on the carpet. There were probably more. A detailed search would reveal them.

"Take a look at this." Eric pulled a small black flashlight from his pocket and shone it on the floor just to the right of the body. A small silver ball lay on the carpet with a red piece of crime-scene tape next to it to mark its location and to give a perspective on its size in the crime-scene photos.

"What is it, part of a round?" Robbie eased as close as she could without touching the body and squatted down to get a better look.

"No. It's a lot more important than just a spent round." Eric glanced at Robbie.

"You gonna let me in on it?" Robbie stood back up.

"It's Brad's cross tie tack." Eric's eyes narrowed. "It has been bent up, crushed, and left here. These cases are definitely related."

Robbie's pulse quickened. This was bad. Really bad. Or good in a cop-world perspective. At least there was a chance for more evidence, something lacking from Brad's case. "How can you tell?"

"I saw that cross every day." Eric clicked the flashlight on and off as he spoke. "I was there when his wife and daughter gave it to him. I know what I'm talking about. And that's not all." Eric shone the light on the shell casings on the desk. "Speer 9 mm casings. The same ammo we carry. I think the killer used Brad's gun. Ballistics will be able to confirm this, but I know I'm right."

"So the killer left the cross here and used Brad's gun to commit the murder?" John scratched his head and sighed. "He's got to be leaving a message. This was deliberate."

"But why?" Robbie jotted more notes on her pad. With the cases blending and blurring in her mind, she needed to keep things straight. "Why would Brad's killer come and murder Pastor Perry like that? What's the connection? Is it possible that Pastor Wilson knew something that even he wasn't aware of that could lead to the identity of the cop killer?"

"Which leads us back to the original motive for Brad's murder," John said. "We know the hows, but we don't know the whys."

"We've got a mess." Eric jammed his flashlight back into his pocket. "And I have no idea what to make of any of this. Do we have a deranged serial killer here, or a methodical cop killer, or both?"

"None of this makes any sense." John stepped back to let the crime-scene tech snap another picture.

Silence weaved through the room for the first time since Robbie arrived, and she sensed everyone else's frustration. Why in the world were two men from the same church murdered?

Tim uncrossed his arms and raised an index finger. "I'm gonna need you all to follow me on this, but what if we're looking at this thing all wrong?" His face was focused as he paused. "Maybe we are turned around and backward on this."

"What do you mean, big guy?" Robbie yearned for help from her team right now. Any ideas were good at this point.

"We're assuming that Brad was murdered because he was a police officer or that he stumbled upon something criminal and the suspect had to kill him."

Everyone nodded.

"But what if Brad's murder had nothing at all to do with him being a cop?"

"We've probed his personal life and every kind of angle that we could," Robbie said. "No extramarital affairs, no financial problems, no gambling, drugs. None of the things that would put him in a high-risk category. He was everything he appeared to be—a good husband, father, and a solid Christian."

"My point exactly." Tim jabbed a finger in the air. "Now what's the common denominator between the two?"

"New Life Fellowship?" Eric raised an eyebrow. "That does make sense. When the shooter left the house, he said, 'Good night, Joan.' The killer knew her name. This wasn't some random robbery. Nothing's missing. It's a flat-out premeditated murder."

"Not just New Life Fellowship." Tim held out both hands. "The killer ripped Brad's cross off his tie and dropped it here. That means something."

"Because they were Christians?" Robbie stepped back. "Seems farfetched, Tim."

"Makes more sense than about anything else we've come up with so far." Tim folded his arms and tapped his foot.

Her profile revealed that ripping the cross from Brad's tie and taking it was significant, but killing them because of their beliefs? Robbie shone her light onto Wilson's legs. "I don't know if that theory holds water right now."

"Do you have a better one?" Tim smirked. "Just think about it. That's all I ask."

"There are millions of Christians all over the United States." Eric scanned the room. "If your theory is true, Porter, why is this guy striking now? What is there about Palm Bay and New Life Fellowship that is significant? And why's he messing with us by leaving Brad's cross here?"

Robbie respected Eric's cop sense. He'd lost his best friend and his pastor in one week but could still think through the tough details of police work. He must be running on adrenaline.

"I wish I could answer that." Tim shrugged. "I'm just posing this as a possibility. It really struck me as odd about that cross, especially bent and twisted up like it is."

"You have a point." Robbie's arms fell to her sides. "That really is a sign of anger and hate, and one we're meant to find. Our suspect doesn't seem to care about being detected."

"Joan said he just walked past her and smiled." Eric rose to his tiptoes, then came back down, and color returned to his face. "This guy doesn't care one whit about getting caught. He's brazen to do these things."

"Brazen, maybe." John rubbed his chin with a gloved hand. "But certainly stupid, because now we at least have a good description of him. We can start working on a composite and get the information out to the press. I don't mean this the way it sounds, but this murder gives us more evidence and a much better chance of catching this guy."

"No offense taken." Eric waved his hand. "I feel the same way. I can't bring back Brad or Wilson, but I'm gonna do everything in my power to catch their killer and stop this insanity."

"We've got your back on this, Eric." Robbie loved working with these guys. Nothing would stand in their way. "We'll get with Alan, link these cases, and make up a task force. Whoever did this is going down—and going down hard."

13

S ir, I have the security DVDs you requested." Steve Glick entered Warren's office.

Steve had proven his loyalty many times over and was the only person Warren allowed to enter without knocking.

Warren finished typing the last portion of his e-mail. His friends at the Defense Department would be pleased to hear the latest. As everything proceeded according to plan, he'd just need to sew up the last of the details to unveil Adam at a press conference a week from Friday. Ten days would be plenty of time for his staff to get the events coordinated. General McNally and his business associates would want to know the date and time so they could be prepared as well. Much of Dr. Silverstein's notes and material had already been sent to them to give them a head start on any competition.

Steve placed the plastic container of DVDs on his desk.

"Thank you. You've done a fine job again." Warren picked up the DVDs. One was labeled Lab. That DVD wouldn't be going anywhere, and he slid it off to the side. Even if he were inclined to produce it, it wouldn't help the police in their investigation. So what would be the point?

The second was marked Exterior/Parking Lot, which he placed on top of his desk. He'd have Alice contact the detectives and get it to them as soon as possible. Keeping good PR with Palm Bay PD was important, especially since one of their own was killed so close to Lifetex. They didn't need any added attention.

"Sir, I don't mean to disturb you, but there's one more thing you should know. When I was copying the DVDs, I noticed a problem with the camera at the rear of the lab. It seems to be going in and out. I'll have the security company take a look at it."

"Those cameras are top quality and practically brand new." Warren grabbed the lab DVD and examined it. "There shouldn't be any problems at all."

"We'll get it taken care of right away, sir." Steve nodded to Warren and hurried out the door.

Tapping his fingers on the DVD case, Warren considered Steve's observation. That was odd. With mountains of work to get through, he didn't have time to dillydally around. E-mails needed to be sent, calls made, arrangements taken care of. But his curiosity wouldn't let him concentrate on any of those tasks.

He opened the DVD drive on his computer and slid the Lab disk in.

As it booted up and played on his monitor, Warren eased back in his chair. Several minutes of uninspired viewing passed. "This is ridiculous. I need to get back to work." As he moved his mouse to click off the program, an image appeared at the top of the screen. "What was that?" He clicked back and watched it again. It couldn't be.

Ejecting that DVD, he inserted the camera view of the grounds. He fast-forwarded to the proper time stamp. Several seconds ticked by. "Oh my."

"Mr. Finstead," Alice called on the intercom. "Should I contact Agents Russell and Porter and tell them their DVDs are ready?"

Warren popped the disk out of the drive and placed it in its case. Lifetex teetered on the threshold of a history-making, life-altering revelation. Billions of dollars and countless lives hung in the balance. The discoveries here would make him the richest, most powerful man on the planet. And the benefit to humanity was incalculable.

"Mr. Finstead?"

"One minute, Alice." Warren bit his lip. He couldn't be sure what all this meant, although he hadn't risen to his position by being a dolt. The police could never see this footage. Nothing would derail the destiny of Lifetex and its magnificent potential, and now he had to deal with the treachery before him.

"Alice." He slapped his hands onto the arms of his chair.

This wasn't going to take him or Lifetex down. This could be dealt with. "Please contact Agents Russell and Porter and tell them that our system had a slight…*glitch* while trying to download."

"I'll let them know."

"Thank you. Tell them we're very sorry for the delay, and we'll get the DVDs to them by the end of the week."

"I'm sure they'll understand, Mr. Finstead. I'll take care of it right now."

That should slow up the detectives until he could get a handle on what was happening. Did the police know more than they let on, and were they way ahead of him?

Warren smacked the plastic DVD case on his forehead. Could his employee really be behind this? Warren felt so stupid for not seeing it before. He'd trusted him only to have this man flip on him like this.

He clicked up Steve on his BlackBerry.

"Yes sir."

His suspicions gnawing at him, Warren paused before he spoke. "Steve, meet me in the lab, pronto."

"I'm on my way."

Warren wouldn't let him get away with this, not while he was still in charge.

Robbie let her files plop on the kitchen table. Who needed a gym membership when she got such a tough workout just carrying her junk from the car to the apartment? With all the craziness in the office, she needed some serious quiet time to get her profile finished. Now that Pastor Perry was another victim, the profile needed considerable tweaking if it was to be of any use at all.

"I'm sorry about being so late, Kathy." Robbie stretched to work the kinks out of her back. It had been a rough couple of days.

"No need to apologize." Kathy stepped into her shoes next to the table and wiggled her feet to get them on. "I brought a change of clothes and can stay as long as necessary. I know you need to find this nutcase. I'll do my part to help."

"Well, thank you. I've got the duty tonight, so you can head home and get some rest yourself."

"Isabel is watching TV in her room." Kathy grabbed her purse and gym bag and hurried to the door. "Just to let you know, she's had a tough day so far. I hope it improves for your sake. I'll see you tomorrow. Call if you need me."

As Kathy closed the front door, Mima sauntered into the kitchen and glared at Robbie. "*¡Ya me quiero llevame pa' casa!*"

"You *are* home, Mima." Robbie removed her badge and laid it on the table. "This is home. There's nowhere else I can take you."

Mima looked away and ambled back into her room, the profanities flying.

"It's the disease, not Mima." Robbie reminded herself daily of that. It still made it difficult to listen to her mother's anger.

The torment of witnessing her mima slide into the abyss of her own mind escalated with each day or new behavior. The profanity was difficult to digest, especially since Robbie had never heard her swear until she got sick.

Robbie straightened the uneven stack of files and papers before her. The description from Mrs. Perry was monumental and could break the case wide open. Robbie would have to watch the eleven o'clock news to see how the coverage would help the case.

She had spent a few minutes with Mrs. Perry before coming home. The woman was crushed by the barbaric attack. "Why would someone do this?" she asked with a probing stare, as if Robbie could actually provide a sufficient answer for such an evil act. Robbie vowed to find one, for Mrs. Perry and for Mrs. Worthington.

What would happen if someday she were to meet the same fate? What if some felon got the drop on her and punched her ticket, snatching her forever from this earth? Who would Alan or John come to tell? Who would take care of her mother? Who would grieve her loss? The thought unsettled her on many levels.

She'd worked and studied hard to build the career she wanted, needed. But now, the longing to share her life with someone, as Brad Worthington or Wilson Perry did, haunted her. Even with their losses, both families built a life and a history and memories, something no demented killer could take away.

They had love and time together. Robbie had responsibilities and a job and a career—nothing more. A deep yearning to fill that void in her life took hold of her as Eric's face intruded on her thoughts. Was something there between them? Or was it just the stress of the case drawing them closer for a time, only to dissipate when all was finished, like the mist from a cool, refreshing summer rain?

She sighed and dropped into a chair, her arms dangling carelessly over the sides. She was hitting overload. The lack of sleep blunted any attempt at rational thought, but she still had so much to do. She needed some rest, a vacation, and a life. But first, Brad and Wilson's killer needed some personal attention. One thing at a time.

Mima passed Robbie again without so much as a glance and ambled into the living room, seemingly enthralled by the newscast on the television. She eased onto the couch with the familiar grace that only her mother possessed. The disease hadn't robbed her of her ballerinalike gait and fluid gestures. She floated as she walked.

At last Mima was settled and Robbie could get some work done. She pulled her shirt out and removed the elastic band from her ponytail, scratching her scalp and shaking her hair into a clumped-up mess—to match how she felt. A little nutty gesture she was glad no one else was there to witness. It felt pretty good. Now she could work.

With a deep sigh, she opened her file folder and started to review her notes. Sifting through the information and organizing it into a coherent package might sharpen her perception of the case and reveal new insights. While no two criminal acts or offenders' personalities were exactly the same, many behaviors offered a tremendous perspective into a killer's personality, education level, and sometimes profession. The tedious process often left her psychologically and emotionally drained. But that didn't matter now; she didn't have anything left anyway.

While she did enjoy plumbing the recesses of the criminal mind, she questioned whether all the time and energy of getting into the Criminal Profiling Program was worth it. Even with her doctorate degree, the program required at least five years' experience investigating violent crimes, an apprenticeship with another profiler who monitored her cases and observations, ninety days' worth of course work at the FBI's Criminal Profiling Unit, classes in blood-splatter analysis and criminal interviewing, and more training in every kind of deviant behavior imaginable.

An epic journey of study and work brought her to this point, but somehow, even though she was considered quite successful by her peers, she felt a cavern of emptiness in her spirit. Was this all there was? Would she be reviewing nasty, violent crime scenes for the rest of her life? There had to be more.

Get on track, girl. Pay attention.

Massaging the back of her neck, Robbie worked the kinks out and focused on getting her work sense back. She logged on to her laptop and created an file for Brad Worthington. She spread out the main crime-scene photos on the table, the ones that gave her the best overall views of the scene. She'd go through the rest of the stack later. Each photo needed to be examined from top to bottom, every image identified and vetted.

She placed a snapshot of Brad on the edge of her computer. It would help her finalize his victimology, a detailed analysis of the victim and every aspect of his life—age, marital status, profession, hobbies, interests. These facts wove into a biography of who the victim really was, providing more insight into potential suspects or motives.

Often a crime centered around some association within the victim's life, even if not immediately recognized. Maybe the victim worked out in the same gym as the suspect. Maybe they crossed paths in a college class. Or the victim had secrets that led directly to the murder. Nothing could be taken for granted and nothing assumed.

Brad Worthington, white male, thirty years of age, married (happily), two children. College educated, former wrestler, weightlifter. Police officer, eight years' experience, by all accounts tactically sound and an astute observer of suspects. No pushover. No extramarital affairs—a huge suspect/victim factor. No outstanding financial debts or problems. No gambling, drinking, drug habits. The guy was Johnny Straightlace. No high-risk factors there.

Delving into Brad's personal life was not a part of profile development she relished, but it was an absolute necessity. A thorough debriefing of all the people associated with Brad revealed nothing but a dedicated husband and father of two living as a devout Christian.

Robbie picked up a closeup of Brad from the scene that focused on the missing tie tack. This troubled her more than almost all of the other evidence. Why, during a violent battle with a police officer, did this suspect take the time to tear off a small trinket? Easily the strangest incident in the cases.

Tim might have pegged this guy right as a cop-hater and a God-hater, but this would be the extreme. He'd fired over two dozen rounds into Brad—an act of hate, anger, or revenge unrivaled by anything she'd ever seen. The cross had gone missing. Then the cross turned up on another case of serious overkill with Brad's pastor.

Although a detailed examination of Wilson's background hadn't been completed yet, she guessed it would be similar to Brad's—strong father, husband, and pastor. Time would tell. Why were both victims from the same church? Is the answer there? Or is it something else entirely?

Hissing an exhausted exhale, she bent back and wiped her eyes. The computer screen and a frantic day were wearing on her vision. Could she get any more meaningful work done today?

The sum of the mound of paperwork and photos before her and her observations just began to weave into a cogent story of Brad's and Wilson's murders. Their murderer had to be one and the same and was not crazy by any stretch. He displayed deliberate, rational thought throughout the process of subduing Brad, using his extra magazines against him, and having enough wherewithal to flee the scene and escape just minutes before the responding officers arrived. This guy was intelligent, strong, and a capable fighter, maybe prior military, an extreme hater of police and…

Robbie struggled with the last portion. What was the significance of the cross? The guy might be a God-hater, but that didn't seem to cover everything. An unknown dangled right in front of her that she couldn't quite grasp.

What was she missing?

14

We have a big problem." Warren burst into Dr. Silverstein's office.

"Warren?" Dr. Silverstein remained seated at his desk as the
mutt snuggled in his lap. "What are you doing working this
late? I thought I was here alone."

Steve Glick entered just behind him. Now Warren could
get to the bottom of everything.

"I'm glad you're both here." Warren closed the office door.
"There are some things we need to get out in the open and
some answers I think you owe me, *Doctor*."

"What are you talking about?" Dr. Silverstein lowered the
dog to the floor and removed his glasses.

"Don't play me for a fool." Warren stepped to the edge of
his desk and jabbed a finger at him. "So, how long have you
been working behind my back to undercut me? I want to know
whose payroll you are on."

"Have you been drinking?" Dr. Silverstein chuckled. "You're not making any sense."

"Explain this, then." Warren held the DVDs in front of Dr. Silverstein.

"What is that?" The doctor scrunched his face.

"The surveillance footage from the night that police officer was murdered." Warren waved the DVD back and forth. "And it's all the evidence I need. You've sold out to someone. You cooked up this little scheme a long time ago and have been using my money to bankroll your plan."

"Warren, you've lost your mind." Dr. Silverstein held out his hands with palms up. "I have no idea what you're talking about."

"Well, let's just pop this in and see if it refreshes that brilliant but twisted mind of yours." Warren brushed Dr. Silverstein aside and dropped the DVD into the doctor's computer.

The system booted up and his options menu filled the screen. He clicked onto the date and approximate time of the murder. The screen divided into fours squares. The picture at the bottom right was black, but the other three seemed to be working fine, all different views of the interior of the lab.

"I fail to see the significance of this, Warren." Dr. Silverstein bent down and squinted at the monitor.

"Be patient, Doctor, like you've always told me." Warren scrolled back until the black screen showed a functioning picture. "Everything will be revealed, and then I want the truth."

He returned the view to normal speed. The night lights

were on, and the camera captured the back doors that led to the rear portion of Lifetex that faced I-95.

The camera provided a good view of the back of the lab, and he could just see the room where Adam slept. The lights were dimmed but working. Adam's room was dark, at least from what he could tell from underneath the door. Holding his clipboard, Neal came into view for just a second as he passed the last chamber, performing his nightly rounds, which would have been his last for that evening.

Shortly after Neal passed, Adam's door opened, and a shadow slipped by. Several seconds later, the camera wobbled and then went black. Warren checked the time stamp on the monitor: 11:47 p.m.

"Right there is where you or your minion Dr. Meyer disabled the camera." Warren tapped the screen with his finger.

"You're mad." Dr. Silverstein crossed his arms, his eyes never leaving the image. "I have no idea what you're talking about."

"Well, let's check the outside cameras now." Warren removed the first DVD and loaded the second, bringing up the menu. "You can see if I'm crazy or not." He selected the side/rear view with the same date and an 11:45 p.m. time stamp.

The outside lights illuminated the area well, except near the interstate, where a line of trees and foliage obstructed a full view of the highway. Headlights of passing cars on I-95 flashed through gaps in the foliage. A human form walked along the edge of the fence line. Two flashes followed. The man then could be seen reaching around the Dumpster, grabbing something. He hurried out of view of the cameras.

"That, good Doctor, was the detective who was murdered down the street."

"What was he doing here taking pictures at the back of our complex? Could he have known about the Genesis Project?"

"I don't know, but you should." Warren glanced at Steve, who still blocked the door. "Keep watching. It gets better."

As the video continued to roll, another shadow emerged from the back door of the lab and raced across the grass to the dark wood line along the interstate. The person scaled the fence, vaulted the barbed wire, and ran south toward where the officer was murdered. The figure moved with incredible speed and agility.

"How do you explain that, Doctor?" Warren stood and faced Dr. Silverstein.

The doctor rubbed his chin and alternated his attention between the computer and Warren. "I'm not sure what we just saw there."

"I am. On the night the officer was murdered, someone from this laboratory left Lifetex and killed that officer in cold blood. And I think I know why."

"You think I had something to do with this?" Dr. Silverstein's head cocked back. "How do I even know that these DVDs are real, Warren? It's like you're playing some kind of bizarre game here. What you're suggesting is not possible. The back door is alarmed. Anyone coming in or leaving would have set it off."

"We need to check out the camera and door." Warren nodded to Steve, who opened the office door. "And when we do, you need to come clean about this whole thing."

Warren, Steve, and Dr. Silverstein walked to the rear of the laboratory, the clicking of Sammy's toenails tapping behind them. Dr. Silverstein's portly frame struggled to keep up with Warren, who refused to slow his pace. How had he let the old man dupe him like this? He'd have an answer soon.

They passed Adam's room on the right side of the lab, then pressed on past the gym and therapy rooms to the viewpoint of screen four.

The camera was mounted in the corner of the room, elevated a good eight feet up, and poised to capture any intruder coming into the lab from the back door. Only no one had broken in.

Warren, Steve, and Dr. Silverstein hustled to the area. Warren looked up at it but couldn't tell if the camera was working or not. Steve walked over toward the chambers, then returned quickly with a folding chair and opened it.

Warren stepped up on it and inspected the camera. The pinpoint red light that showed if it was activated was off, and a thin wire had been pulled out from the rear.

"It's been tampered with." Warren hopped down and regarded Steve and Dr. Silverstein. "Just as I suspected."

Warren picked up the chair and hustled the forty feet to the formidable security door along the back wall. The alarm connector wires on the door appeared intact at first, until he leaned in. They, too, had been cut or pulled out just enough to look as if they were still functional. The door was specifically designed to keep people out, not in, a foolish mistake he'd correct today.

"It's been disabled too." Warren nodded to Steve, who slid his hands to his hips, exposing his pistol. "Now, Doctor, are you going to tell me the truth, or will I have to pull it out of you?"

"I had nothing to do with any of this." Dr. Silverstein's arms fell to his sides, and he rotated around, examining the entire lab. "Why would someone do this thing?"

"Here's what I think." Warren went face to face with Silverstein. "You were planning to auction Adam as some sort of soldier or assassin to the highest bidder, undercutting everything I've dedicated years to put together. You saw that officer out there and unleashed your creation on him as some sort of evaluation run. It's the only thing that makes sense. You've been training him back here in your little dungeon of horrors to do your bidding, all the while acting like the great professor out to save the world. Who got to you? Was it the Iranians? the North Koreans? Or was it General McNally, trying to take out the middleman and go right to the source?"

"What do you mean, undercutting you?" Dr. Silverstein pushed his glasses up and leaned into Warren. "Who is this

General McNally? What machinations did you make for Adam? You've lied and used me the entire time."

"Don't try to change the subject and turn this around on me." Warren adjusted his tie and peered over to Steve, who inched closer to Silverstein. "I only wanted to use this technology in a controlled setting. An environment where the Defense Department could run Adam through the paces, not release him on the community. Your recklessness brought a policeman's murder investigation down on our heads, for goodness' sake. Have you lost your mind?"

"You and I have worked together for a long time." Dr. Silverstein wiped his brow. "The only reason you would accuse me of such a monstrous thing is because that's what's been hidden in your dark heart the entire time of the Genesis Project. But not everyone thinks like you, Warren. The world aches for peace and healing. Adam was never meant for war and violence. He was to achieve the best of the human spirit, all that is great and possible. He was to lift us from our woes, but you've corrupted all of our work with your greed and lusts."

"If that's what you really believe, Doctor, you're brilliant but naive. The world wants perfection and bigger and better toys—and the means to protect what they have. It's human nature, survival of the fittest. And Adam would have provided that, to our great benefit, I must say."

"Is there no end to your depravity?" Dr. Silverstein said. "I had nothing to do with this, and you know it."

Warren scratched his head. "Well, Doctor, if you aren't

responsible for this, then it would have to be Dr. Meyer, because one of you is behind this. You saw the monitor. It was Adam, and there's no way he could pull that off on his own. He's only been alive three weeks. He had to have been trained to do that."

"This whole line of reasoning is preposterous." Dr. Silverstein examined the door alarm again. "I know what the DVD showed, but there has to be some other answer. Neal isn't involved in anything malevolent here either. It makes no sense, Warren. Adam is the perfect man. And although his intellectual capabilities are without peer, he has no knowledge of electronics or security doors, and he doesn't have the social tainting to make him devious or worse. He's just now mastering the language. For what you're proposing to be true, he'd have to have—"

"A knowledge base from somewhere else entirely." Adam's rumbling voice carried throughout the lab like the deep, ominous growl of a prowling lion.

The hair on Warren's neck stood on end.

Robbie prepared for her late-night briefing in front of the war room at the FDLE office. No rest for the weary. Alan stood beside her while Eric, John, and Tim lounged in the chairs in front of the whiteboard. The task force was fully assembled and ready to move on the new information. Pizza boxes and empty Styrofoam coffee cups decorated any exposed surface.

A large picture of Brad with arrows pointing to a fresh picture of Wilson Perry covered the whiteboard. A composite from Joan Perry's description hung between them with notes in red marker and more arrows underneath, pointing to the other pictures like a massive spider web, every bit as intricate and complex.

Robbie taped a picture of the deformed cross on the board. She and the other investigators needed a visual of the players: victims, suspects, crime scenes, and evidence, as much as they could fit on one board anyway. It was a better way to keep track of all the crazy twists and turns in this killing spree.

It was a bizarre case spinning way out of control, to be sure. Robbie felt like a compass needle spinning around and around, searching for true north. She didn't know where to go from here, but she had encouragement from this room full of good, experienced cops. Collectively, they would come up with something. They had to.

"Okay, everyone." Alan balanced a cup of coffee as he rested his feet on the chair in front of him. "Let's settle down and let Robbie give the briefing. We've got a lot to cover."

"Well, at least now we have some decent information on this case." Robbie pointed to the composite on the board. "First, ballistics made the match on the weapon used at the Perry homicide. It was definitely Brad's. No question."

Eric lowered his head and bit his lip. Robbie didn't like delivering that kind of news. No one in the room wanted to think that a cop's gun could be used like that. But the link was undeniable now. It was plain to see that Eric didn't want Brad's weapon associated with Wilson's murder. The case was getting rougher by the day.

"Sorry, Eric." Robbie flashed a sympathetic look his way.

Eric shrugged. "What else do we have?"

"According to Mrs. Perry's composite, the suspect is a large white male, dark black hair, and a neck as thick as a telephone pole." Robbie tapped her finger on the sketch. "This guy would stick out in any crowd, so we're hoping to field a load of tips from the news coverage. We've got twenty-four-hour coverage on the phones if anything hot should come in."

"Since the connection, whatever it is, seems to be New Life Fellowship, has anyone interviewed the congregation and support staff?" John rested his legal pad on his crossed leg. "To see if anyone remembers this guy ever showing up, or if Brad or Wilson expressed a problem with someone that has yet to be discovered?"

"I'll go with our detectives for the church interviews." Eric continued to study the floor. He hadn't looked up since the comment about Brad's gun. "It's my church. The people might be more comfortable talking with me around. I am sure of one thing, though: this guy hasn't attended any of our Sunday services. I would remember a mug like that."

"Are you sure you're up to this?" Robbie rested on the edge of a table. "This is close to home."

"This whole case is close to home. I'm up for it." Eric raised his head and caught Robbie's attention. "I'll fall apart later when the case is solved. But for now, business first. This guy's going down."

"Have you all thought about what I said before?" Tim shifted in his chair. "I still think with that cross left at the scene that these men were targeted more because of their faith than because Brad was a cop. And I don't particularly care how kooky that sounds. It's just my gut speaking."

"That's why we're looking at this like a task force. If anyone has a theory or a decent idea, please run it by us." Alan regarded Tim and smirked. "But I do think it's extremely kooky, Porter. Since you got religion, you're starting to get a little out there, if you know what I mean."

"Maybe." Tim extended his chin, taking Alan's abuse head on. "But I stick by what I said." He turned back to Robbie. "What do you think? Give me the profiler's perspective."

Robbie sighed and rose to her feet. "Tim has some valid points. I'm not going to go as far as he has with his theory, but we can't discount the fact that whoever did this absolutely hates Christians and any icon that represents God and authority. We'd be foolish to overlook that."

"I think the plain explanation is usually the best." Alan set his coffee mug on the table. "Brad stumbled across something vile, something so criminal that whoever was involved in it *had* to murder him. I think if we go too far into extravagant theories, we're going to get further behind in the case. Since most cop killings are to escape or for revenge, I don't think we have to look a lot further than that."

"It's not that extravagant of a theory, and it makes more sense than anything else we have going now." Eric hopped to his feet. "To leave Brad's cross at Wilson's murder scene is a sign we can't ignore. Brad was incredibly strong in his faith. He witnessed to everyone in the department, held Bible studies at his house. He's the reason I came to faith. He's written letters to the editor and newspaper articles. He was very high profile with his beliefs. Maybe someone took offense at that."

"And killed him because he had Bible studies at his house?" Alan shook his head. "I think you all are a little out there on this. I'm telling you, stick to the basics, and this guy will shake out."

"Well, it can't hurt to run a number of different theories," Eric said. "And at least one of those should be related to his faith, totally opposite of everything we've looked at so far."

"I like that thinking." Tim regarded Eric. "These Palm Bay detectives are on the ball."

"I figured you would since this whole nutty theory was your idea."

"And a fine one it is, Alan." Tim folded his forearms over his stomach. "And if I'm right, you gotta promise me that I get a new car, whatever comes out first on the fleet. I'm tired of driving that hippie wagon everywhere. You should see the looks I get. It's embarrassing and downright disrespectful."

"If your nutty idea proves right, you'll get the finest car in the fleet." Alan lowered his legs back to the ground. "It's a bet I'm comfortable making because you're off in left field on this."

"I'll start picking out my color now." Tim nodded.

"I'm not trying to stifle good police work here." Alan stood and scanned the team. "I just don't want us to get tunnel vision, that's all. Investigators get so locked into a theory or a suspect that they ignore evidence leading to the contrary. We need to stay fresh and open-minded."

"Alan's right." Robbie stepped to the middle of the group. "Until we have some confirmation, we'll need to run on leads from several theories. Right now, let's focus on getting those interviews done at New Life and getting this guy's mug on the news."

"Also, have we rounded up all of the security videos from the area yet?"

"Lifetex is the last one, Alan, but they're working on it," John said. "I was told they had some glitches they were trying to iron out."

Alan shook his head. "It would be nice if someday, someone could have a security system that actually works."

"I'll contact them again and see what the holdup is." John jotted down a note on his pad. "And there's something else with Lifetex."

"What's that?" Robbie asked.

"When Tim and I met with the CEO, Warren Finstead, I just got the feeling that he was holding something back. He made some statements that were kind of odd. I don't know if it has anything to do with our cases or not, but I would like a chance to follow up with him...and soon."

"No problem," Robbie said. "Follow your instincts. We have some leads that need to be cleared out, but as soon as we're finished, do whatever you like with Lifetex."

"Okay, we know what we have to do, so let's get going." Alan checked his watch. "Let's meet back here tomorrow at 8:00 a.m. We'll get done what we can tonight and pick back up in the morning."

On the way out, John and Tim grabbed a handful of lead sheets for their interviews. Alan hobbled back to his office, looking pretty rough. With just a few weeks left until retirement, he didn't need this kind of aggravation.

Robbie had assigned a number to each lead to track it on her computer program, so no information fell through the cracks. Too many major cases went unsolved because of mismanaged leads. The idea of carrying an unsolved cop murder in her case file sounded about as much fun as having her gallbladder removed—without anesthesia.

Carrying the responsibility for any case was maddening, but to not be able to give some relief to a hurting police family was unthinkable. If she had to work straight through to Christmas, this case would get solved.

Robbie gathered a mound of supplemental reports and lead sheets off the table and stacked them in a cardboard box on the floor, keeping them in one place.

"Get any sleep?" Eric picked up a tape recorder and handed it to her.

"I'm sorry, did you say something?" Robbie's frazzled mind

sputtered to come up with an answer to such a simple question. The stupor from the case, her mother, and life in general muted anything resembling an intelligent response.

"Earth to Robbie." Eric waved his hand in front of her face. "Come on, you need to snap out of it."

"It's been a tough week." Robbie dropped another manila folder in the box. "I hope we can come up with something quick. I did another case review last night just to see if we were missing anything."

"And?"

"And I really think our suspect is going to strike again, and again, and again, until he's caught."

"What makes you think that?" Eric scooted onto the edge of the table and gave her his full attention. "Why doesn't he just run out of state to get away? Why would he stay here?"

"Because he enjoys taunting us and watching us wait to see what he'll do next nearly as much as he enjoys the killing."

Eric raised his eyebrows and grimaced. She wasn't sure if he agreed or not, but he did seem to listen and consider her observations. A maturity exuded from him that she wasn't quite accustomed to from a guy his age. John and Tim displayed that kind of maturity, but both were older than Eric and much more experienced in law enforcement. She was pleased he stayed to talk with her.

"What kind of suspect looks calmly at Joan, tells her he'll see her later, then simply walks out?" she continued. "He's either completely insane, which I don't think he is, or wanted a witness to draw out the anguish. I can't think of any other reason he left her alive."

"Whatever the reason, I'm glad he did." Eric lowered his head. "It's been painful enough with Brad and Wilson gone from the church, but I can't even begin to imagine what it would be like without Joan too. This madness has to stop."

Robbie leaned against the table and smiled at him. "You can count on it."

15

Warren's body quivered at the sound of Adam's voice, and he didn't have to turn around to realize they'd been flanked. Feigning composure, Warren turned around to see Adam hovering just a few feet behind him. He moved quietly for such a large man, which unnerved Warren all the more.

Adam grinned and crossed his colossal arms. His room was supposed to be locked at night; that lock, too, was probably tampered with. While Warren was rethinking Dr. Silverstein's culpability in the officer's murder, he did know one thing for sure—Adam had left the lab that night and run toward the area where the officer was killed. Warren couldn't take chances with him.

"Adam!" Warren opened his arms, working his best smile. He flashed a look at Steve he surely wouldn't miss. Even with Steve there, they still might need help getting this gorilla back into his cage. Adam had bulked up considerably since coming to life, his arms bulging with muscles. He continued his menacing glare at them. "Great to see you, pal. How are you feeling?" Warren smacked his shoulder; it was like whacking a marble statue.

"Never better." His speech wasn't slow and deliberate anymore, and his eyes were vibrant and piercing, boring through Warren. His expression spoke more than his words ever could.

He knew.

"Adam, what are you doing out of your room?" Dr. Silverstein stepped back. "You're not supposed to be on the floor at night."

"To correct you, Doctor, I'm not supposed to be here at all. But I have you and the illustrious Warren H. Finstead to thank for that."

"What…what has happened to you?" Dr. Silverstein cocked his head back.

Steve sidestepped and used his elbow to ease his jacket over his pistol. Warren heard the leather snap as Steve raised his gun to eye level.

Smack! The pistol sailed across the room and crashed into the wall thirty feet away. Adam slapped it so quickly Warren barely saw his hand move.

Steve's arm whipped around his body, spinning him in a semicircle. He balanced himself and lobbed a haymaker toward Adam's head.

Adam caught his fist and pushed it aside, then rapid-punched Steve twice in the face, once in the stomach, and followed up with a kick to the sternum that launched him through the air and onto his back, crashing him into the wall. Steve didn't move.

Adam glanced at Steve's crumpled body, then lurched toward Warren and Dr. Silverstein. Maybe they could make it to the rear door? Adam could outrun them both with ease. It was best to talk him down and get him corralled somehow.

"Adam." Warren said slowly. He fought to not let Adam see his fear, but it had to be obvious. He raised his trembling finger to Adam's face as he eased closer. "You need to calm down and get ahold of yourself."

"You fool." Adam's hands curled into vibrating fists. "You don't need to speak to me like I'm some kind of imbecile. You would be shocked by what I know, what I've seen."

"Adam, you must listen to Mr. Finstead." Dr. Silverstein stretched out his hands, palms up. "Go back to your room, and Neal and I will find out what's gone wrong. We can help you. We'll take care of you."

Adam's chuckle morphed into a full-belly laugh as he held his hand on his stomach. "Really, you have to stop calling me that ridiculous name. I knew the original Adam. He was quite the idiot as well. I *hate* that name. My name is Morek, and neither of you have a clue about what you've unleashed."

"I know I'm in charge of this lab." Warren pointed at

Adam and then across to his room. "You need to go back to your room until—"

Adam seized Warren's throat and lifted him off the ground, the strike so hard it nearly knocked him unconscious. Warren flutter-kicked and thrashed about against the vise grip around his throat. He couldn't…breathe.

"Adam, release him. Don't do this violence." Dr. Silverstein inched closer. "We created you to bring hope into a broken world, not more cruelty. Don't you understand this?"

"You created nothing," Adam hissed as he shook Warren like a straw man. "You manipulated the material *He* made. And in doing so, you have opened a door and given us the opportunity to stamp out *His* obnoxious cretins—forever. For thousands of years, we've waited in torment and anguish, yearning for the moment we could wrap our hands around the throats of your kind and squeeze the very life out of you."

Warren wriggled frantically, his legs still suspended off the ground. He tried to scream but couldn't. Only a guttural grunt escaped. He was helpless in Adam's grip.

"Demon!" Dr. Silverstein covered his mouth. "Neal was right. There is something wrong with you. You are a child of Beelzebub. You did murder that policeman."

"And what a glorious moment it was." Adam glowed with pride. "I could feel him close by. I could smell the stench of his spirit. He was one of *them,* worshiping the *Offensive One,* bowing down and groveling to *Him* at every chance. I killed the policeman, and when we've finished, there will be none left to serve *Him*."

Dr. Silverstein backed away. "What evil have we set free?"

"You have no idea. But rest easy, dear Doctor. You won't be here to see your work come to fruition."

16

The irritating red laser beam passed twice across Neal's eye, and the automated greeting ushered him into the lab. He'd appeased Dr. Silverstein by taking a night off and going to a movie, alone, which would only strengthen the doctor's assertion that he needed to get out more and make friends.

As Neal strolled into his office he didn't see any of the therapists and assistants milling around. The office was spookily quiet for a Monday morning, and this week kicked off the countdown to the unveiling. He expected a flurry of activity with Mr. Finstead and Dr. Silverstein pacing about. The fruits of their labors were about to be harvested. Maybe people weren't coming in until later. That's what he got for taking time off.

As much as Dr. Silverstein goaded him about his life, Neal respected him more and more after working under his careful tutelage. Dr. Silverstein dared to dream the impossible and developed what many said couldn't be done. As the world's attention would soon turn to Lifetex, Neal vowed to make sure everyone knew their amazing story and how Dr. Silverstein selflessly led the effort. No more letting him pass the credit to Neal. He would make sure of it this time.

He looked around his cluttered office, still unsure of why no one was at the front of the lab. Neal hoped he hadn't missed any meetings. Unlikely. Dr. Silverstein would surely have called him on his cell phone.

Neal slipped his white lab coat on over his jeans and khaki shirt, grabbed the clipboard off his desk, and hurried to the chamber area. Sammy sprinted from one chamber to another with a speed and vigor he hadn't seen from the experiment in quite some time.

"Sammy." Neal clapped his hands, something he'd seen Dr. Silverstein do dozens of times. It was his special call for the genetically altered fleabag. Neal's calls were ignored as he heard the mongrel's toenails tap the tile floor heading away from him. He'd let Dr. Silverstein worry about the mutt.

Neal rounded the next set of chambers. The extraction table was set up outside Beta's tube, but no one was around. He'd missed a meeting for sure. He'd never leave the lab again.

The last Neal had heard, Beta would be "born" in front of

the press with the assistance of visiting scientists. That was a week to ten days out. Not only would that be good publicity, it would also be good television, or so he was told. A sort of science reality show. It didn't make a lot of sense to him, but Mr. Finstead felt it could sway public opinion to their cause.

Beta lay motionless in the placid amniotic waters of his chamber. Just a couple weeks shy of Adam, Beta and the rest of the experiments were fully matured, sharing Adam's rippled, powerful features. Neal felt silly for his strange inklings about Adam. Neal must have indeed been working too hard.

He heard someone approach from behind and turned to see Adam smiling.

"Hey, Adam." Neal faced him and held his clipboard across his stomach. "You do have a habit of sneaking up on people. Have you seen Dr. Silverstein?"

"Yes, Neal." Adam's smile broadened. "I have seen Dr. Silverstein."

Neal glanced up and down the aisle, still not aware of anyone else in the lab. Maybe they were upstairs with Mr. Finstead.

"Is he here in the lab?" Neal tried to keep his sentences short and to the point, so as not to confuse Adam. Language and context weren't the easiest things to grasp when you were two weeks old.

Adam eased around the extraction table and placed his hand on Beta's tube. Beta's body convulsed in the chamber, churning up the fluid. He opened his eyes and locked in a stare with Adam.

The conspiracy of their shared smiles knifed Neal in the heart, and his stomach lurched as he watched the two *communicate,* just as they had before. But this time Beta responded fully, gazing at Adam with eyes that screamed of life, not a catatonic stare. Neal hadn't been wrong about Adam. He needed to find Dr. Silverstein right now.

Neal back-pedaled a couple of steps and then turned to get past the table so he could sprint for the door.

"You'll never make it." Adam's deep voice carried throughout the lab in a low, menacing tone Neal had never heard before.

He froze, his body seized with fear and confusion. He turned to see Adam aiming a pistol at his head.

"One more step, and you'll see where I used to live. And trust me, Dr. Meyer, you won't like it one bit."

Neal raised his hands over his head. What happened to Adam? Where did he get a gun, for goodness' sake? This couldn't be happening.

"Where's Dr. Silverstein?" Neal asked again, quaking, not wanting to provoke the well-armed and psychotic experiment.

"Dr. Silverstein will not be in today." Adam's infuriating smirk was etched on his face, macabre and seemingly permanent, like that of a jack-o'-lantern. "He's taking a vacation, although I don't think he's enjoying himself right now."

Neal lowered his hands and alternated his gaze between Adam and Beta, who shared Adam's malevolent grin while bubbles crept to the top of the chamber. Terror engulfed Neal to the depths of his spirit, and his body trembled uncontrollably. His vision went blurry as he struggled not to pass out. He wasn't facing an experiment gone wrong or some sort of "glitch."

Neal stood now in the presence of evil.

He could see it in Adam's and Beta's faces, and he could sense the darkness in the room. Not the most scientific hypothesis he'd ever come up with, but he knew that Adam was pure, unadulterated evil as well as he knew his own name.

The other experiments squirmed about in their chambers. The lab was alive.

"Who—what are you?" Neal's voice cracked. "Why are you doing this?"

"You will call me Morek. I am no Adam, nor son of Adam." He bristled with the mention of the name.

"You're insane." Neal regretted the comment as soon as it fled his lips.

"Oh no, Neal Meyer, man of science and logic." Adam chuckled. "I'm something much better than that. I am alive—flesh, blood, and bone. We now have bodies we can enter and use as we wish, with no human spirit to contend with. The rules have changed, in our favor, and we have you and Dr. Silverstein to thank for it. We are truly *eternally* grateful."

Neal's hands flapped in front of him as if he were waving

at Adam—no, Morek. There was no way what he was saying was true. Neal remembered his mother's constant references to angels and demons and a whole other realm of existence. Suddenly she went from a lovely woman who believed in fairy tales to the most brilliant, insightful person on the planet. As he stood here before this beast, he did something he couldn't have imagined doing just thirty minutes before. It was the only thing that made sense right now. He cried out in his spirit with the most earnest prayer of his life.

God, please help me.

"Before dear Dr. Silverstein departed, he assured me that you had all of his notes and were more than capable of helping me complete my mission. Now the only question is, are you willing?" Adam trained the pistol again at his forehead.

Neal recoiled, not sure if Morek would shoot or not. "What could you possibly hope to accomplish by this?"

"Your only concern should be how to please me so I don't kill you." Morek approached Neal, lowering the pistol. "Because if you don't do exactly as I tell you, I will pluck your scrawny arms from your pathetic, weak body, as if removing petals from a flower. And I will take great pleasure in watching you bleed to death."

"I'll help you." Neal raised his hands. "Just don't hurt me. I'll do whatever you ask."

"You're not one of *them,* so you just might be allowed to live." Morek jammed the pistol into his waistband and grabbed

Neal under both armpits, hoisting him off the ground without the slightest appearance of strain. "Do you understand me?"

Neal mustered a weak yes.

Morek eased him to the ground. "I've ensured that none of the other staff will be in today or at all this week, but we must work quickly so we can start the second phase of the invasion."

Neal nodded to appease Morek, the deranged experiment gone wild. Neal wasn't about to do anything to provoke him, but what did he have planned? What did he mean by "invasion" and "second phase"? Neither term sounded good.

What have we unleashed?

If Morek had done something terrible to Dr. Silverstein, how long would he keep Neal alive? And if he was truly in the presence of evil, could he trust anything Morek told him? Neal's composure was slowly returning, but he needed to think through the possibilities. Until he had some answers, Neal would do whatever Morek wished. He didn't have much choice at this point.

"We'll need Dr. Silverstein's notes and yours, as well as the protocols."

"I have them in my office."

"You and I will have a long chat about what we're going to do next." Morek laid his meaty paw on Neal's shoulder and sunk his fingers into the base of his neck. "We're going to become quite chummy, Neal."

Horror overtook him again. How would he get out of this?

17

Robbie tossed her purse on her desk, sat down, and prepared to fire up her computer.

She'd just met with Eric again at Palm Bay PD and picked up some statements from the New Life Fellowship staff. It probably could have waited, but when he called, she saw an opportunity to see him again. She couldn't say no.

She chastised herself for getting interested in someone—especially another cop—right now. Between taking care of her mother and working a high-profile case, the timing was all wrong. But she couldn't remember a point in her life when the timing was right. There was always something else to do, some goal to meet, some degree to seek, some mountain to climb. It was endless.

"Why now?" She massaged her temples and leaned back in the chair. "I can't do this now. Eric's a nice guy, but maybe I just need to finish the case, cut the relational strings, and go back to my life." Now she was talking to herself. Everything was making her daffy. But what life would she go back to?

With a quick knock, Tim peeked his head over the cubical wall. "Robbie, we've got a big problem."

"What's up?"

"Palm Bay PD has a situation. There's a guy with a gun at a shopping plaza. He called 911 and said he killed Brad Worthington and Pastor Perry. It definitely seems like our guy. We're all heading out there to help. The situation's still very volatile. Palm Bay SWAT's on the way."

"Let's go." Robbie grabbed her purse, her pistol inside, and she, Tim, and John sprinted toward the back parking lot. Tim opened the door of his peacemobile and grabbed an MP5 submachine gun from the backseat.

"I'll drive." Tim sprinted for Robbie's car, his weapon in tow. "Give me your keys."

"Not on your life...or ours." Robbie rattled her car keys. "Besides, I don't have a life vest in this thing. Get in."

"Aaah." Tim hopped in the back and wrapped the sling of his firearm around his neck and shoulder. "You're rotten, Sanchez."

John jumped into the passenger's seat next to Robbie, who slammed the car into reverse before John could close the door.

Screeching the tires, she fishtailed the car as it pulled into traffic on Babcock Street.

The police radio crackled with activity. The Brevard County Sheriff's Department helicopter was already in the area, giving out locations of the suspect and officers on the scene.

Robbie flicked on her dash-mounted blue lights and whizzed through traffic.

"If this is our guy, he won't go down easy." John yanked his tie off and opened the top button of his shirt, preparing for whatever they would encounter.

Robbie turned onto Malabar Road and sped toward the shopping plaza. A carnival of police lights and emergency vehicles blocked off the road. The helicopter buzzed just above them. Robbie pulled up next to Eric, who was standing next to his unmarked car and slipping on his bulletproof raid vest.

Robbie rolled down her window. "Where is he?"

Eric pushed an arm through the vest and then pointed to the shopping plaza just behind the credit union. "We've got him cornered right over there. Something's not right with this guy. When the first officers arrived, he popped off some rounds over their heads. He's just standing there with his gun at his side and a crazy look on his face. I don't know what he's waiting for, but we've got SWAT and Hostage Negotiations on the way. Be careful."

"Thanks." Robbie eased through the police line, parking her car just behind six patrol cars forming a semicircle barricade around a man with his back against the shopping center wall.

More officers were on either side of the man and kept the crowds back. The suspect wore a black T-shirt and blue jeans, and was the spitting image of the composite from Joan Perry's description. A black Glock 9 mm dangled at his side. He scanned the officers back and forth with a stupid grin, like he enjoyed the show. The constant drone of the helicopter above made it difficult to hear anything.

"Put the gun on the ground and step away from it," an officer called over his patrol car PA system. "Just put the gun down and you won't be harmed."

The man's twisted grin increased, and he shook his head. This guy was built like Adonis. He was their suspect; she was sure of that. He turned in Robbie's direction and concentrated his gaze on her. He cackled like a hyena and drew a pair of sunglasses out of his shirt pocket with his free hand and slipped them on. Pushing off the wall, he stood tall and faced the army of cops, his gun hand rigid.

"Drop your weapon," the officer continued to call over the PA, his voice reverberating throughout the plaza.

The suspect glared at Robbie and saluted her with his free hand. A chill overtook her. "Watch out! He's going to—"

He raised the pistol and fired a round that struck the car next to Robbie.

An explosion of gunfire rocked the plaza as Robbie and

every officer opened fire on the maniac. The suspect stumbled backward as the rounds struck him, but he remained standing.

He raised his pistol again and sprinted toward the wall of cops. Another volley of rounds fractured the air. Tim's submachine gun burst to life next to her, and John's pistol tapped out rounds, the brass hitting the ground.

Robbie aimed at the suspect's torso and ripped more shots off. He stumbled back again, then turned and sprinted down the sidewalk.

What happened? Robbie was sure she'd hit him. Most of the officers had to have hit him. Was this guy wearing a bulletproof vest or what? She dropped her magazine and reloaded another reflexively as she and the other officers gave chase, hoping to contain him in the plaza. Why wasn't he stopping?

He staggered as he rounded the corner of the building. A Palm Bay squad car cut him off from leaving the plaza. The officers corralled him again, still keeping some distance between them but considerably closer this time.

The man's shirt showered crimson droplets onto the concrete. Their shots had hit their mark. But the maniac was still standing...with that insane smirk. His pistol down at his side, he swayed on the sidewalk, breathing heavily; a trickle of blood rolled from his lips. Cries from the horrified spectators filled the air as many of them took off.

"Just put down the gun." Robbie had her pistol on target. The others formed a ring around him. Tim slid to her side, training the machine gun on him. There was no escaping now. "Please, just stop and we'll get you an ambulance."

"Roberta Sanchez," he growled with a gargled, broken voice. "Little Robilina."

Robbie's hand trembled as she held the pistol out. Only her father had called her Little Robilina, when she performed ballet as a child. Robbie had never seen this guy in her life. How could he know that?

"Why did you kill Brad Worthington and Wilson Perry?" She wouldn't get the chance to ask him these questions again. She didn't know how much time he had. He was bleeding profusely now and barely keeping his balance. She needed to know and preserve the evidence. "You're hurt bad and probably not going to make it. Tell us why you did this while you still have the chance."

"You can't kill me, Little Robilina." He coughed and winced.

"How do you know that name?" Robbie's voice cracked as she screamed at him. "Who are you?"

"I was your Watcher, Little Robilina." His bloody smirk showed again. "I watched you dance, watched you grow, and yearned for your soul to be in torment with mine. And now I finally get to take you with me." He raised the pistol again.

A frenzied rupture of gunfire sent him stumbling backward, finally crashing to the ground. Eric sprinted over to him and kicked the gun from his hands. The suspect's body convulsed, and he squealed and loosed an unholy screech like nothing Robbie had ever heard before. The officers backed away as he continued to quake and flop on the pavement, his arms and legs flailing about.

"What's happening?" Tim stepped up, weapon still at the ready.

With one more shriek, a gust of putrid wind passed them all, and the suspect fell silent on the concrete. Officers encircled his lifeless body. One finally stepped forward and cuffed him, though it was a bit late now. A foul stench hung in the air around them like the opening of a sewer.

"What just happened here?" John knelt next to the fallen felon and checked his vitals. He glanced up at Robbie and shook his head, which was no surprise to anyone at the scene. "Who—or what—was this guy?"

"I've never seen anything like that." Eric holstered his weapon and forced his fingers through his crimson hair several times. He flashed a perplexed look at Robbie and then bent down to examine the pistol on the sidewalk. "At least we finally got him. This is Brad's gun. I'd know it anywhere."

Robilina? The silly little name her father had given her. What did this freak know about her? Had he been a stalker reading news accounts? digging into the details of her life? Now this dead suspect gave her more questions than answers.

"Robbie, something's wicked with this dude." Tim slung his MP5 over his shoulder and gazed at her with a fear she'd never seen in his eyes. "That noise from him was just flat-out unnatural, evil. I know I emptied a thirty-round magazine into the guy, not counting what everyone else did, but he kept coming. No amount of drugs or alcohol could account for that. And that nasty smell.

"John, Eric, what do you think?" Tim pinched his nose. "Am I crazy here?"

"I don't know what to think." John lowered his pistol and gazed past Robbie and the others. "That's the freakiest thing I've ever seen."

Eric stared at the perforated body of their suspect, as if he half expected him to rise again and fight some more.

"Even though this guy's dead, we need to find out who he is and do a thorough background on him." Robbie lowered her weapon as well. "Something isn't right with him, and we're gonna find out what it is."

John, Eric, Tim, and Robbie all agreed the case wasn't over yet.

"We need to get everyone back." Robbie finally holstered her pistol, her hands shaking uncontrollably. The adrenaline spike from the shooting wreaked havoc on her nervous system. The creepy comments from the suspect didn't help. She knew what was happening to her physically—her psyche was something altogether different.

She struggled not to break down right here in the middle of the scene; she didn't want to lose it in front of the guys, especially Eric. The emotion of chasing a killer, dealing with the heartache of the victims' families, reliving her father's death, and the trauma of the shooting all collided inside her. So did the realization that they had caught their man. They would make this guy for the murders and give some sense of closure to the victims' friends and loved ones.

"We need to let Alan know what's happened and contact the shooting review team." John rested his hand on Robbie's shoulder.

His controlled demeanor drew her back from her musings. Business first. She'd cry about it later. Robbie nodded.

"I'll make the contact if you'd like." John pulled his phone from his belt.

"Thanks."

"You okay?" Eric touched her elbow.

"I'll survive." Robbie glanced over at the suspect again. Patrol officers unrolled crime-scene tape around the surreal scene. The brass from the fired rounds sparkled like a thousand pennies tossed carelessly throughout the parking lot.

"Is this your first shooting?"

"No." She raised her eyebrows and glanced at Eric. "Unfortunately not."

"Me neither." Eric shook his head and looked at the ground. "I've been down this road before. I kind of know what to expect."

"The FDLE shoot team should be here soon." Robbie wrapped her arms around her stomach and squeezed, holding everything in. "There's a mess to clean up here, to be sure."

"You know, I should feel pretty great right now that this mug is off the street forever, but I just feel sick about everything. I miss Brad."

Robbie took his hand and said nothing but searched his

eyes. Kind but broken, his expression seemed as wrecked as the scene in which they were standing. She really wanted to know this guy better and vowed that she would.

Eric returned her gaze, attempting a smile. He massaged her hand with his thumb and then released it.

Robbie scanned the area. John was on his cell phone, probably with his wife, Marie, letting her know what happened before she saw it on the news. Tim leaned against the trunk of a car in the parking lot, his face worn and tired. He was crashing and would probably call his wife, Cynthia, soon too.

Two dozen officers wandered in and out of the scene, some talkative, others quiet and reflective. A cacophony of more sirens and chopper blades droned in Robbie's head.

Nothing would ever be the same.

"You've done well, Neal." Morek lingered just behind his chair. "You've learned Dr. Silverstein's methods flawlessly. It's good that you kept such superior notes and DVDs. Anyone could follow your directions, even me."

The quakes in his hands were so violent that he missed placing his pen in his pocket three times. He glanced at the clock: 3:22 a.m. The longest day of his life. He'd spent the entire time rubbing shoulders with the most evil beings he'd ever encountered.

Morek remained within arm's reach almost all the time. He hadn't harmed Neal though—not out of any sense of kindness, but rather because Morek used Neal to birth Beta and the rest of the experiments. Dr. Silverstein's gift to the world now felt much more like a curse.

Neal was keenly aware that no matter how well Morek treated him now, his days, maybe even his minutes, were numbered. Once Morek gleaned everything he needed, Neal would have no more value to him. He swallowed hard, trying to force the thought back down.

Two of the others walked by his office door. He wasn't sure what to call them now. Each came out of the chamber and embraced Morek. They spoke to each other in a language Neal didn't recognize, but each time he heard it, he wanted to cover his ears and scream as loud as possible. It was a harsh, wicked language that assaulted his spirit with every sinister syllable. But when they spoke with him, they transitioned into the queen's English. His scientific mind didn't like the conclusion, but he'd be a fool not to grasp the obvious. Evil spirits controlled his experiments. Now what to do?

After Neal and Dr. Silverstein released Morek from his chamber, he'd played them to perfection the entire time, feigning the therapy and educational process, just waiting for the right time to release the others. Neal had suspected something wasn't right with him from the beginning; he should have pushed Dr. Silverstein more. Maybe he would be alive now, and Neal wouldn't be surrounded by a multitude of malevolent mutants.

Morek leaned out of the office door and called to one of the others in his native tongue. Neal lost track of who was whom. Trying to distinguish between genetically identical beings proved to be an impossible task. Morek stood out to him only because of his civilian clothing. The rest sported blue hospital scrubs and scurried through the lab like crazy mice.

"We'll need to take a ride now. We have some supplies to get." Morek returned to his position behind Neal. "You will help me with this."

"Of course." Neal grabbed his coat as he stood. Morek didn't need to threaten him anymore. Neal would do exactly as he was told.

Neal sifted through his options, all of which would require a level of courage that had eluded him thus far. But if a way to escape presented itself, he would take it. He must. He was sick about helping this creature and his crew and needed to do something. What that something was remained an un-known…for now.

Morek strode alongside Neal to the back door. He pushed it open and held it for Neal. "If security or anyone else comes upon us, you will tell them I'm a visiting scientist. Do you understand?"

"We shouldn't have any problems." Neal pulled on his jacket. "Security is used to us coming and going at all hours of the night."

"I don't doubt that at all, Dr. Meyer." Morek followed just

a little behind Neal, which alarmed him. Neal didn't think he had any nerves left. They rounded the building and headed toward the employee parking lot.

The crisp early-morning air revived Neal some, and for the first time in recent memory, leaving the lab was a positive thing. His blue Honda Accord was parked next to Dr. Silverstein's fire red Corvette. He was a kind, gentle, and fun man. In a strange way, Neal was glad he wasn't here to see what became of his life's work.

Neal activated his keyless remote, and the doors chirped open. Morek got into the passenger's side as Neal eased into the driver's seat. "Where to?"

"A twenty-four-hour department store. We need some clothes and other supplies." Morek chuckled. "How's your credit-card limit? Good, I hope."

"We should be able to pick up what you need." Neal wasn't worried about ruining his credit. There were other things he worried about ruining, like his cranium.

Maybe being out of the lab he'd have his first chance to get help or escape. He'd bide his time and see. He was quite convinced that if Morek felt Neal was doing something wrong, he'd kill him on the spot. Morek didn't seem to care about repercussions or witnesses. The cruelty embedded in his eyes communicated that well.

Neal started the car and eased through the parking lot. The darkness shrouded his vehicle as he sped away from Lifetex.

Emotionally and physically spent, Neal surveyed his situation: Morek wasn't just an experiment gone bad; he was a thoroughly corrupt spirit of some sort. Although until today, Neal didn't believe such things existed. They were stories invented by people to explain events that they didn't have the capabilities to understand. At least that was what he'd subscribed to before he spent the day with Morek and his merry friends.

As he sat in his Honda next to evil personified, Neal realized they were like magnets with polar opposites. He was terrified and repelled by Morek, and that propelled him toward what was good, toward the God his mother told him about as a child, the God of the Bible. Hundreds of stories bubbled inside him. He didn't know if everything Mother said was true, but it was the best explanation for Morek and his crew. A sense of peace filled Neal. He only wished he'd had these ethereal thoughts before becoming host to an evil-clone convention.

He glanced at Morek, who stared straight ahead into the blackness of the morning. For the first time in this awful nightmare, he knew what he must do, even if it meant his life. He reached up and attached his seat belt, then applied gentle but steady pressure to the accelerator.

Morek glanced at him, then looked forward. The Honda picked up speed.

Through the fear and uncertainty, Neal dared to do what scared him almost as much as Morek—his spirit cried out: *Jesus, forgive me for this mess. I'm a fool, but I need Your help. Save me.* His spirit leaped, and a spike of emotion chased away the trepidation. He felt the hand of the true God upon him. Tears filled Neal's eyes. *Thank You.*

"What have you done!" Morek screamed as he shifted toward him. "I can smell the stench of your spirit. I see His seal. You belong to *Him* now."

In a flash of motion a blade rested against the side of his neck, pinching inward on his jugular. "Stop this car!"

Neal floored the accelerator. "As you wish."

Morek leaned closer, the tension of the knife pressing ever more into Neal's flesh. "Pull this car over—now!"

Neal eyed the telephone pole just off the road. He jerked the steering wheel and veered off the pavement, the small car bouncing and skipping along the dirt shoulder.

"What are you doing?" Morek lowered the blade and alternated his gaze between Neal and the pole.

"Ending this thing right now." Neal yanked the wheel and skidded sideways. Morek's side of the car crashed into the pole. The windshield exploded, and the driver's airbag smacked Neal in the face, knocking him back, almost unconscious.

The car smoldered and hissed in the darkness. Neal pulled the flaccid airbag off his chest and fumbled for the door latch, his face stinging from the punch of the airbag. He yanked the latch hard and nailed the door with his shoulder. It was stuck. He hit it repeatedly, and it finally creaked halfway open.

Neal unbuckled his seat belt, and his torso fell onto the dirt. Hand over hand, he worked to free the rest of his body. As his feet were clearing the seat, a blood-soaked hand seized his ankle.

"Aaah! No!" Neal fell flat on his back and kicked Morek's hand twice and twisted his foot, pulling out of his grip.

Neal wobbled to his feet. The car's crinkled roof shook with a fierce blow and dented upward. Morek screamed and hit it again. He was trapped in the wreckage, but not for long.

"Neal Meyer, there's nowhere you can hide from us. You are our enemy now. I will kill you with my own hands, the ones you made for me!"

The roof rocked, and the rest of the windshield blasted out, Morek's fist protruding out on the hood.

Neal limped down the road as fast as he could. He needed whatever head start he could get. He picked up his pace as Morek continued to scream.

"We will get you, Neal Meyer. You're a dead man!"

Neal might be dead sometime, but not before he let the world know what was happening. The only problem was, would anyone believe him?

18

Robbie drove into the parking lot of the medical examiner's office just off of Fiske Boulevard in Rockledge,
about fifteen miles north of Melbourne. The brick building
behind the Health Department would draw little notice from
a passerby. She'd visited there a few times since transferring up
from Miami, working with the medical examiner on several
cases.

Lifting her coffee mug out of the center console, she passed
the café con leche under her nose. It was her second cup of the
day; the first hadn't kicked in yet. Sleep had evaded her most of
the night as the violent encounter with the suspect flashed over
and over in her mind like a tape stuck on replay. And the suspect speaking her childhood name creeped her out more than
the shooting. Who was he, and how would he know that? And

what did he mean about being her "Watcher"? Was he admitting to stalking her? Too many unanswered questions still remained in this case.

Her frayed nerves couldn't take much more. Later in the afternoon, she had an appointment to give her statement on the shooting. With so many officers involved in the incident, the investigators scheduled appointments for the interviews. Tim and John's meeting was this morning.

The post-shooting statement didn't worry her. The outcome was obvious. As much as this perp sickened her, she would have gladly taken him into custody without a fight. Her job wasn't to judge; her father taught her that. He separated the person from the crime and displayed a unique ability to treat most everyone with dignity and respect, even people who probably didn't deserve it. She hoped her actions in law enforcement and life always honored his memory.

Sliding a digital photo from her now-bulging file, Robbie examined a closeup of the suspect's face. The composite artist nailed it. He matched the drawing in every detail. A nice slice of evidence to close out the case with.

She grabbed her recorder and decided to leave the rest of the file in the car. She wouldn't need it for the autopsy. She was only an observer anyway, to garner a little more information for her case. The doctor would conduct the procedure, and the crime-scene personnel would take photos of the injuries and collect any evidence.

She skipped up the three steps, and as she reached for the

double doors at the entrance, Eric opened them from the inside. While dressed in a crisp white shirt and navy tie, sharp and professional as usual, his eyes told her that he'd slept about as much as she did last night.

"Good morning," Eric said with a stilted, droning tone.

"We'll see." Robbie adjusted her jacket. "It's going to be another long day."

"Yeah, but today is different. Today we put the finishing touches on an ugly case. I'll be happy to wrap this thing up."

They walked down the hallway to the autopsy room. Robbie and Eric each grabbed a pair of rubber gloves from a box on the table next to the door. They slipped them on as they opened the double doors.

Dr. David Slattery stood next to a gurney with their suspect lying on it. A short African American, about fifty, with several gray flecks dotting the sides of his head, Dr. Slattery donned a protective mask and green scrubs. Robbie had worked with him in the past on several cases, and he was as sharp as they came.

"We have a name on this guy yet?" Dr. Slattery surveyed the suspect through his thick glasses.

"Not yet." Eric snapped his glove. "But we're working on it. We sent his prints off last night to the FBI, and we've got his picture on the news. Something should turn up soon. Somebody's got to claim him."

"Crazy days these are." Dr. Slattery shook his head. "What's wrong with people anymore that they get so nuts? Wasn't like this when I was a kid. People had a bit more respect and decency."

Dr. Slattery pulled down the sheet covering the suspect's torso. He'd been cleaned up quite a bit, the blood washed off his body for a thorough examination. His chest was dotted with bullet holes, with several more through his arms and massive legs.

"This guy was an athlete at one time." Dr. Slattery probed one of the holes near the suspect's heart with a gloved finger. "I don't think I've ever encountered a physique as muscular and fit as this. What a shame he couldn't do more with his life. Seems like such a waste."

"Pardon me if I don't get too weepy, Doc." Eric placed his fists on his hips. "This guy killed my friend and my pastor and would have gladly killed us too. The world's better off without him in it."

"I'm not defending him, just making an observation." Dr. Slattery adjusted his mask. "Tragic. The whole thing is a shame. Wish we could change the outcome."

"How many rounds do you think he took?" Robbie leaned over the gurney.

"It's hard to say right now." Dr. Slattery stepped back. "With this many wounds, we'll have to compare it with the number of rounds fired at the scene and see what we come up with."

"Well, give me your best guess." Robbie shrugged.

"All total? Between fifty and sixty, I would say." Dr. Slattery drew the sheet over the body again. "Possibly more."

"I'll be curious to see what the toxicology report shows." Robbie rested her hands in her jacket pockets. "I don't know what kind of drugs he was on, but if I hadn't seen it with my own eyes, I wouldn't have believed it."

"I'm having a tough time wrapping my head around this too." Eric stepped to the side to let the doctor pass. "I've been doing police work for a while, and this is like nothing I've ever seen before."

Robbie drew a deep breath and let loose with an exaggerated exhale. "The only good news we have is that this guy will never, ever hurt anyone again."

Eric held the door again for Robbie, this time as they entered the Applebee's restaurant on Fiske Boulevard in Rockledge. Chivalry wasn't dead with him. They'd beat the lunch crowd and found a seat right away. The waitress took their drink orders, then disappeared.

When she first started in police work, Robbie couldn't eat right after an autopsy, but that was many, many cases ago. One of the first casualties of a law-enforcement career is often the sensitivity to death. Sometimes it still got to her. Child victims dug into her soul, but for the most part, viewing death was now just business.

"So, Ms. Sanchez, does our guy meet your profile of the killer?" Eric folded the napkin onto his lap.

"Just some light lunch conversation, huh?" Robbie gazed over her menu at Eric. She'd wanted to steer the conversation away from the case as much possible, but given the circumstances, that was unlikely. The burden of the case lifted from her somewhat now that they had some answers, but the impact of this case would follow her and everyone else involved for a long time.

"At least for the first course." Eric crossed his arms on the table. "Maybe we'll move on to ballistics and wound recognition by dessert."

"Cops." Robbie chuckled. "Unfortunately, we'll have to have a name and history on this guy before we know anything for sure. I do have a lot of concerns. Who is he? What's his motive for killing Brad and Wilson Perry? Even though we've stopped him, I still need those answers. Does that make sense?"

"Perfectly." Eric nodded. "It's the cop nature. Gotta have answers."

"True." Robbie unwrapped her silverware and teased the napkin with her fork. "I have to tell you, Eric, the way that went down yesterday has got me a little…spooked."

"Yeah, that was about as crazy a scene as I've ever seen."

"It's not just the shooting and all. Do you remember what he called me?"

"I remember him saying something to you, but I was focused on his actions. I don't remember what he said."

"Well, he called me 'Little Robilina.' That was the name only my father called me when I was very young and in ballet. He knew exactly who I was and said he was my 'Watcher.' I didn't sleep at all last night. It really is freaking me out. There's no way he could know that stuff about me."

"I wish I knew what to tell you." Eric sat back in his chair. "I'm getting tired of saying 'I don't know' in this case. We need to find out who this guy is."

Robbie sighed and twirled her fork. She tried not to let Eric see that it was really upsetting her.

"Why don't we change the subject." Eric leaned forward. "What do you do for fun, Robbie the profiler?"

"What do you mean?" She scrunched up her face.

"You have a doctorate degree, and you don't understand the word *fun*?" Eric folded his menu and placed it on the table.

"I know what *fun* means." She squirmed in the wooden chair. "I'm just busy. I have my mom to look out for, a career. Just not a lot of time for fun, that's all. What do you do for fun, Eric the Palm Bay cop?" Robbie turned the conversation on him, hoping to get the microscope off her nonlife. The psych degree did come in handy every once in a while.

"I work out, play in a flag football league, read a bit, and used to be in the Bible study with Brad. Now it looks like I'm going to be taking that over. I don't know if I'm ready to lead the study, but I don't have much choice. I think Brad would want me to continue with it."

"He seemed pretty devout, really into his faith." Robbie

didn't know what else to say. Given the circumstances, a light conversation was impossible. "Everyone we interviewed said that."

"He was something special." Eric eased back in his chair. "He led me to Christ. I miss him, but I know where he's at, and it's a whole lot better than here. So it's tough to feel sorry for him. We're the ones left to suffer and struggle through it."

The waitress interrupted them, setting an iced tea in front of Eric and a soda in front of Robbie. The young brunette then took their order. Eric chose the grilled salmon with broccoli. Healthy eater, which, given his fit frame, didn't surprise her. She got the double cheeseburger with fries. She'd pay for it later, but she craved some serious grease in her system now, another toxic side effect of police work.

"So you seem pretty grounded in your faith too."

"Yeah, I suppose you could put it like that. I didn't come to faith until four years ago, after a ton of conversations with Brad. What about you? Have you worked a profile on God or the Bible?"

Robbie smirked and took a swig of her soda. "I was raised Catholic, but I'm not quite sure what I believe now. My mom and dad were both devoted like no one I've ever seen before, except for maybe Brad. With my mom's illness and these cases, I'm having a tough time seeing God in all of this craziness. But I'm not foolish enough to discount Him either."

"Fair enough." Eric tapped his fingers on the table. "Most of the time when I talk with people at work, they either say they agree with my beliefs just to shut me up or totally ignore the conversation altogether. It's refreshing to hear an honest opinion."

Robbie smiled. Handsome and smart, Eric could probably date any girl he wished. But he stayed reserved, although not shy. He was a tough read, but she didn't mind trying. She brushed her hair back, hoping not to appear schoolgirlish.

"Is your father still devout?" Eric asked.

"He passed away a while ago."

Canting his head, he coughed and thumped his broad chest with his fist. "Excuse me. That was me spitting my foot out of my mouth."

Robbie smiled and leaned back in her chair. "Don't worry about it. It was a long time ago. You didn't know."

The waitress arrived at their table with their meals in tow. She slid Robbie's burger to her and set Eric's plate in front of him. Robbie tore into her burger.

Eric bowed his head. Robbie stopped chewing for at least a sign of respect. After he finished, she launched into the second assault of her sandwich. For some reason, the late nights and stress of everything robbed her of any self-restraint. She was famished.

A long bout of silence floated between them as they ate. Robbie feared she'd shut Eric down by telling him her father had died. She didn't like the quiet.

"My father was a police officer in Miami, Metro-Dade

PD." Robbie passed a napkin across her lips. "He was killed during a bank robbery."

The blank expression on Eric's face told her she'd blindsided him. He eased his fork to his plate and gave her his full attention. "I'm sorry to hear that. It must have been hard on you."

"I haven't told anyone that." Robbie shook her head. "None of the guys I work with know. I was afraid they'd think I was some crazy chick out to avenge her father's death or something weird like that. I didn't want the hassle, and besides, everyone looks at you differently when they find something like that out."

"Thank you for trusting me with that. I'll keep it between us."

"Well, this case has brought back a lot of those memories. It's been a little strange and tough, but I'm working through it." Robbie had just blurted out the most personal piece of information that she could think of. She has a burger and fries with this guy and spills her guts. That's not what she had in mind for lunch, but she couldn't seem to stop herself. His unruffled demeanor and poise melted her normal defenses. He was just easy to talk to.

She peered at Eric. Why was she getting neurotic over a silly lunch with him? Just because they were eating together didn't mean it was heading anywhere. He did seem to be reaching out to her, though. She could read a crime scene and discern a suspect's motivations, intellect, and personality, but she couldn't determine if the guy sitting across from her was interested in dating her or not. She really needed to get out more.

Sighing, she rubbed her hand across her stomach. She shouldn't have ordered the burger, which had already begun its devilish work on her insides. Maybe she just needed rest, some time to gather her thoughts and get her life together. A nice vacation somewhere with a beach and no cell phones or pagers, no murders or craziness.

But then there was Mima. What would she do about her? And what about work? This case still needed a major cleanup before she could go anywhere, and several more demanded her attention as well. Nope. No vacation anytime in the near future. No fun on the radar screen of Robbie Sanchez's life anytime soon.

"Robbie, would you mind doing me a favor?" Eric set his fork on his plate. "You can say no if you like."

Robbie raised an eyebrow. "Ask me first, and then I'll let you know."

"Shrewd. I'll give you that." Eric smirked. "I'm going to meet with Julie Worthington later today. Would you mind going with me? I want to update her on what's happened, and I'd really like to have you there."

Not exactly the date she'd hoped for. She was thinking maybe dinner and a movie, a chance to get to know each other a little better. But she supposed she could meet with the grieving wife of a recently murdered police officer. That should be lots of fun.

Robbie nodded. "I can't stay too late. I have to get back to my mom."

"Great. Now if I can only talk you into picking up the check. We all know you FDLE types make a lot more money than we local cops."

She chuckled. "I wish my bank account reflected that myth."

19

Robbie and Eric ambled up the sidewalk and onto the front porch of Julie Worthington's home. An arrangement of purple perennials lined the brick planter to their left as they faced the door together. The flowers had yet to bloom. Robbie wondered if they would this year.

She shuffled her feet as Eric rang the doorbell. Although she met with Julie briefly at the funeral, Robbie hadn't visited her home or had much contact with her since. Eric saw to most of that, so she could focus on the case. It was past time to get to know her a little bit.

Julie opened the door with a rambunctious three-year-old bucking in her arms. "Eric, good to see you." She stepped to the left so they could enter and gave Eric a side-armed hug as he walked into the house. With a wrinkled T-shirt and blue jeans shorts, Julie bore the unkempt appearance consistent with a freshly grieving wife and mother—still pretty, only beaten down and tired.

"Julie, I don't know if you remember Robbie or not." Eric gestured to her with an open hand. "She's the lead investigator with FDLE. I wanted you to meet with her. Robbie's been the backbone of this whole case. She's quite a remarkable woman…cop."

"I remember." Julie extended her free hand, then turned to little Kaylee still on her hip. "Why don't you go play for a minute? Mommy has to talk right now." She eased her child to the floor, but Kaylee refused to leave her mother's side. Julie glanced up at Robbie and Eric while prying Kaylee from her legs. "I'm sorry. She's been like this since…well, since Brad died. She won't let me leave her sight."

Julie hobbled, dragging the little one, through the foyer and into the kitchen with the small living room off to their right. Past the living room was a hallway door, probably to the bedrooms. A brick fireplace with a mantle and pictures of the family adorning it covered one full wall, and a host of child-scribbled pictures blanketed the refrigerator door.

Dishes stacked up next to the sink; children's toys were scattered about the living room. Julie appeared to be parenting in crisis mode, managing the important things like the emotional welfare of her children first while letting other areas slide. The Worthington family was experiencing a huge, undesired learning curve.

"That's okay." Robbie squatted down and smiled at her. "We understand."

Kaylee's light brown hair and fair skin reminded Robbie of a collectible doll. Her sad expression mocked her age, though. Children that young shouldn't know this kind of loss and pain, something she probably couldn't even express in words.

Robbie reached out and brushed Kaylee's nose with a finger. She smiled for the first time and giggled, slipping behind her mother, still clinging to her leg.

"She likes you." Julie danced in a circle, trying to round up Kaylee, who spun behind her. "She doesn't normally warm up to people that quickly."

"She's a good judge of character." Eric teased at her with his finger. "That's obvious."

"She's very sweet." Robbie rose and adjusted her pistol underneath her jacket. "You have beautiful children, Mrs. Worthington."

"Julie, please. Would you like something to drink? coffee? I know Eric drinks about two gallons of iced tea a day, so we— I—have some here." She grinned at Eric, who tossed a dismissive hand her way.

"Don't listen to her. She's always giving me grief about something." Eric scanned the room. "Where's Bradley?"

"He's playing a video game in his room." Julie pointed to the hallway entrance. "He's been spending a lot of time in there lately. Doesn't want to come out for anything anymore, it seems."

"I'll go talk to him in a minute." Eric inched closer to Julie. "He comes from strong stock, and he's a good kid. We'll help him get through this."

Julie rested her weight on the kitchen counter, closed her eyes, and sighed. "He's been to the counselor you suggested twice now. Not much has happened yet. The counselor said he'll open up when he's ready. It's still too soon to expect anything meaningful."

"That makes sense." Eric propped his hands on his hips.

"So, what's happening with the case?" Julie reached down and stroked the top of Kaylee's head, wrapping her fingers in her hair. Kaylee gazed at Robbie with her radiant blue eyes. "I'm sure that's why Eric brought you by, Robbie. I'm not trying to be rude, but knowing Eric, he'd continue chattering on with anything else but the really difficult stuff for hours, trying to spare my feelings."

Robbie liked this lady. She wasn't the beat-around-the-bush kind of gal. That would serve her well in the coming difficult years, not unlike her own mother, who was the picture of strength and stamina after her father's murder—on the outside, at least.

To those around her, Isabel Sanchez had displayed a steadfast resolve and confidence, meeting every challenge and encouraging Robbie at every turn. But Robbie's room was next to her mother's, and late into the night, the sound of Mima's broken sobs permeated the thin walls of their apartment. A staggering loss that even her stoic facade couldn't conceal.

"The gun the suspect was carrying yesterday was definitely Brad's," Eric said in a gentle voice. "The fingerprints from Wilson's house have come back as his too, linking both crimes for sure. It's over, Julie. We caught him, and now he's facing his true judgment."

Julie swallowed hard and bit her lip, her face clouding over. "So who is he? What did Brad or Wilson ever do to make him hate them so much?" Her voice cracked, and she covered her mouth. She reached down and picked up Kaylee, squeezing her tight. Her body quivered, binding the raw emotion inside as much as she could.

"Those are answers we don't have—yet," Robbie said. "And we won't stop until we find out everything we can about him and his motives."

"I'm sorry." Julie rocked back and forth. "I thought when we knew for sure it was him, I would suddenly feel a sense of relief. But I don't. I'm not sure what I feel, but it isn't relief."

"It's anger, part of the five stages of grief. You have to get through the anger before you can move into acceptance. I hate to sound clinical, but it's true." Robbie stepped closer and reached for Kaylee.

The little one's lips curled into an impish smile. She opened her arms and tipped toward Robbie, who slid her hands underneath Kaylee's arms and drew her onto her hip.

"My father was a police officer, and he was killed in the line of duty. I remember it well. The recovery is a process. It takes time, but it does happen." Robbie made eye contact with Julie as she jiggled her hips, bouncing Kaylee up and down. The girl was enthralled with Robbie and beamed in her arms.

"I'll go check on Bradley." Eric hurried down the hallway.

Robbie's eyes tracked Eric as he hurried out of the room.

"He's really something special." Julie sniffed and wiped her nose with a tissue.

"I'm sure he is. And your son has good support around him—that's going to be important. He'll get through this."

"I wasn't talking about Bradley." Julie reached over and brushed a piece of hair from Kaylee's mouth and forced a smile. "Although he's more than special too."

Robbie gave her attention to Kaylee in a vain attempt to conceal her sanguine face from Julie. Eric *was* special. She didn't need to be a cop to see that. But was it so obvious that she was attracted to him that even a grieving widow could see it? She needed to tone it down a bit and get a grip.

Eric strolled out from the back bedroom with Bradley by his side, one hand on his back. "This is the lady I was telling you about. Can you say hello?"

Bradley waved and feigned a smile that did little to alleviate his somber countenance. He was certainly Brad's son.

"Bradley is my bud, and we're gonna toss the football around later when I get off work. Isn't that right?"

Bradley nodded and gazed up at Eric. He turned back to Robbie and Julie, waved again, and then disappeared back down the corridor without a word.

"I'll be back by later." Eric rubbed his hands together. "I'll wear Bradley out. When I'm done with him, he'll sleep good tonight for sure."

"They're like two kids together." Julie rolled her eyes and reached out for Kaylee. "It's hard to tell who's the adult and who's the child."

Eric wrapped an arm around Julie and pulled her close. She wiped her cheeks again. Eric looked determined to take care of her.

"I appreciate you spending time with him." Julie sighed and lowered her head. "He really needs those connections right now."

"I'm here for the long haul." Eric drew her head onto his strong shoulder. "The only good thing going is that we know it's finally over. This guy will never, ever hurt anyone again."

"Robbie, there's a strange man in the lobby asking to see you." The department secretary, Gloria Davis, pointed to the side of her head and twirled her finger. "I think he might be a little out there, if you know what I mean."

In her midsixties, Gloria sported a figure and attitude that belied her age. Always the fashionable dresser and the Miss Manners of the office, Gloria commanded a maternal respect from the agents and provided Robbie with the only other female to talk with.

"Did he say what it's about?" Robbie glanced around the

room. Eric, John, Tim, and Alan were all waiting for her briefing. She didn't need the interruption; a load of cleanup work awaited them—people still to interview, leads to track down, and evidence to sift through. Just because their prime suspect was dead didn't mean the investigation just halted. "We're right in the middle of a meeting, and I have a lot to get caught up on."

"He says it's urgent and he must speak with you now. It's about the murders you're investigating. He said he has all the information you need." Gloria scrunched up her face. "To be honest, Robbie, the man is making me a little nervous."

"I'll go with you, Robbie." Eric stood and stretched his arms above his head. "We'll see what his malfunction is, then send him on his way."

"Sorry, everyone. Why don't you all take a break and we'll reconvene in about ten minutes." Robbie hurried down the hallway with Eric trailing her. He was good backup if another crazy surfaced in the case. Eric was big and strong enough to handle just about anyone, and she appreciated that he stepped up so quickly to help her out.

Robbie and Eric stopped next to Gloria's desk, which was situated to look out the bulletproof glass into their small lobby area. A man in his midthirties perched on the black leather couch. His brown hair stuck out in different directions like a sand spur, dirt and grass stains soiled his clothes, his blue shirt hung out, and his glasses had one lens cracked and one out completely. She'd seen homicide victims who looked better.

Robbie nodded to Gloria, who pushed the security buzzer, unlocking the door. Eric held it for her as they entered the lobby.

The man hustled to his feet and rushed toward her. Robbie sidestepped him and raised her hand as a buffer. She wasn't in the mood for someone jumping on top of her. Stranger things happened in the lobby.

"Agent Sanchez?"

"Yes, and who are you?"

"Neal Meyer." The man pushed up on his nose the tangled collection of wire that masqueraded as his glasses and made a vain attempt to straighten himself up and tuck in his shirt. "We have to talk. Now. Can we go somewhere...private?" Neal stole a furtive glance around the lobby and wiped his hand up and down his face.

"Are you all right?" Eric stepped to Neal's side, sizing him up.

"No, I'm not. We don't have much time. Please. Let me in and I'll tell you who has been killing all these people." Neal dropped his hands to his sides.

"Well, I think we have a line on him," Eric said. "And he's at the county morgue right now. He won't be killing anyone else."

"Yes, but that's only one of them." Neal reached toward Robbie. "There are many."

Robbie traded glances with Eric.

"I'm not crazy." Neal's eyes darted to Robbie and then Eric. "I'm not making this up. I can prove it. I'm a scientist. I work for Lifetex in Palm Bay. " He retrieved an ID card from his back pocket and handed it to Robbie.

Robbie checked the ID. It seemed legit. "Neal Meyer, Senior Researcher, Lifetex Labs, Palm Bay." Robbie flipped over the card. It had a magnetic strip on it, probably for security. Seemed like an odd coincidence that he worked for Lifetex, the complex not too far away from Brad's murder, and was now showing up at their office. With John's concerns about the CEO holding back something, Robbie was inclined to listen a little more.

"Okay, so you work for Lifetex." Eric placed his hands on his hips. "Why is that relevant to our cases?"

"Like I've been trying to tell you, our experiments got loose and have killed several people, including the police officer down the road from our lab." Neal massaged his forehead and appeared as if he would pass out. "May God forgive us for this. I can't believe what's happened."

However strange this guy was, the fact that he worked at Lifetex did warrant a debriefing. Even though what he said was nutty and unbelievable, he spoke it with such authority and passion that he brought a ring of authenticity to an otherwise impossible, implausible tale.

"Come in and we'll talk about it." Robbie extended her hand, directing him to the door.

Neal stepped toward the door, but Eric put his hand on his chest stopping him. "I'm going to pat you down first, just to be safe."

Neal held his arms out as Eric patted his waistband and around his legs and ankles. Eric gave Robbie a thumbs-up, though his demeanor indicated that he didn't trust this guy one bit. Neither did she, but something about him intrigued her. If he turned out to be another kook, she would send him on his way. Although even kooks could sometimes provide valuable information.

They escorted Neal down a short hallway to the interview room, which wasn't much larger than a glorified closet.

"Let John, Tim, and Alan know what we're doing," Robbie whispered to Eric. "See if they can watch the interview."

Eric jogged down the hallway as Robbie led Neal into the interview room.

"Have a seat." Robbie directed him toward the chair. "Can I get you something to drink?"

"Water, please." Neal plopped down and dropped his face into his hands. "I'm dying of thirst."

"You look terrible." Robbie removed her jacket and exposed her gun and badge. "Like you've been dragged through the wringer."

"I haven't slept in over…" Neal checked his watch. "Thirty-six hours now. I'm exhausted, but I had to come here after I wrecked my car and escaped, to be safe."

"Know what?" Robbie sat on the corner of the desk and crossed her arms, looking down at Neal, hovering over his personal space. Another little psych trick to shake up suspects.

There were days she almost felt guilty about the methods they used…almost.

Eric opened the door and winked at Robbie. He handed Neal a bottle of water and then took a chair in the corner, out of camera range.

"Thank you." Neal ripped off the lid and gulped it down, water trickling down his cheeks. He rubbed the bottle along his forehead and sighed.

"We need to get back on track." Robbie clasped her hands together. "What do you have to tell us? And please be specific."

Neal looked Robbie in the eye. "Our experiments. They have a mind of their own. They've taken over the lab and control everything now."

"Whoa, back up a little bit." Robbie held one hand out to stop him, trying to calm him down, although she still wasn't holding out a lot of hope that this guy had meaningful info. "What experiments are you talking about?"

"I know this is going to sound crazy—"

"Crazi*er*, you mean," Eric said. "This is going to sound *crazier.*"

Neal shrugged. "And what I'm going to tell you is probably going to get me in real trouble, but I don't care anymore. These…things have to be stopped."

"What experiments?" Robbie checked her watch. She was already growing tired of this guy and this conversation.

"Dr. Silverstein and I have been working for a little over

two years on a human cloning and genetic manipulation program—the Genesis Project. We've kept it secret until now. Unfortunately, we were successful in our endeavors. We were able to effectively clone a human being. And not just clone him, but to alter his genome and make him physically perfect in every way. He was a pure specimen of humanity without any genetic flaws at all."

"Isn't human cloning against the law?" Eric regarded Robbie.

"Yes. There are both international and domestic laws against this type of research, but Dr. Silverstein and the owner of Lifetex, Warren Finstead, felt it was worth the risk to reach the medical breakthroughs Dr. Silverstein predicted. And so did I." Neal removed his glasses and attempted to clean his one remaining lens with his dirty shirt while fighting back tears. "I really thought this would be a wonderful thing for humankind. I thought we could really help people by curing diseases, extending life, eradicating the evil in this world. But I fear that instead of exterminating evil, we've only facilitated it, assisting its entrance into this world with nearly unstoppable human bodies."

"If what you're telling me is true—and that's a big *if*—what makes you think that your 'experiments' have any connection to our cases?" Robbie scooted closer to Neal. Time to turn up the stress on this guy because this interview was going to end very soon.

"Well, for one thing, the murderous scum told me he did it." Neal rested his elbows on his knees. "And that he enjoyed killing the police officer."

"So he told you that, huh." Eric's eyes narrowed. "What else did this thing say?"

"Lots." Neal alternated his attention between Eric and Robbie. "But it's not what he said that scares me. It's what he's doing and will continue to do if we don't stop him."

"And what's that?" Robbie asked.

"He's creating more of them. He's using Dr. Silverstein's notes, and he made me walk him through the process."

"That's nice. Mutant creatures murdering in Palm Bay, Florida." Eric shook his head. "What do these things look like?"

Neal eased back in his chair, lowering his shoulders and relaxing for the first time since they met. "Imagine an NFL linebacker with coal black hair and steel blue eyes that look through you instead of at you, armed with the strength of several men, and an intellect beyond anything we can imagine. We did our work well, detectives. Too well, I fear. Now our superexperiments are infused with evil that would make Hitler look like a Cub Scout. They are possessed, I tell you."

Robbie's heart raced, but she didn't want Neal to know that he struck a nerve with her. But there was only one problem with his statement—it was impossible. It just couldn't be.

"Give us a minute." Robbie hopped off the desk and hurried out the door. Eric followed close behind.

They huddled in the hallway far enough from the door that Neal couldn't hear their conversation. Tim, John, and Alan hurried down the hallway to join them; they'd apparently listened in because they were smiling and chuckling among themselves.

"What do you think?" Robbie kept her opinion to herself for several reasons, not the least of which was she had no idea what to think.

"I think he's insane and playing some game with us," Eric said.

"But he described our guy to a tee, and he works at Life-tex." Robbie rubbed the back of her neck. "That's more than a little strange."

"You can't be seriously considering this guy's story, can you?" Eric shook his head. "Crazed experiments running the streets, killing cops? I don't think so. He could have gotten our suspect's description from the news or something. Now he's just playing it up."

"But that doesn't explain yesterday." Robbie's tone turned ominous. "You know that wasn't like anything any of us have ever encountered."

"You got me there." Eric slid his hands into his pockets and fell back against the wall. "That guy took more rounds than humanly possible."

"Something's not right." Tim fiddled with a toothpick in his mouth. "Downright wicked that sound was. Nothing human could do that. Gives me goose pimples just thinking about it."

"Don't tell me you're falling for this garbage, Tim." Alan scowled. "The guy's a nut and needs to be shipped outta here as soon as possible. I'm tired of listening to his gibberish."

"You weren't out there, Alan." Tim crossed his arms. "You didn't see and hear what we did."

John nodded. "It was weird. And I really felt that Lifetex's CEO was hiding something. Maybe what this Neal character is describing is that something."

"John, you're the sanest guy I know. Please tell me you don't believe this junk."

"I don't know what to believe, Alan." John lowered his head. "But what if what he's saying is true? Maybe we should go out there and investigate it a little. It can't hurt."

Robbie wasn't on board with this guy yet, but too many unanswered, unbelievable questions lay just outside her reach. "Let's hear what else he has to say, then make a determination."

Alan tossed his hands in the air. "Whatever. Maybe now he'll tell us how the Martians came down and are zapping people with a death ray."

The group dispersed, lest they feel the complete wrath of Alan upon them. Robbie knew when not to push too much.

Robbie and Eric went back into the interview room while Alan, Tim, and John hustled into the small room next to it with a video monitor hooked up.

Neal stood as they entered. "So what do we do now?"

"I think we need a little more info. You know how difficult this is to believe, don't you?" Robbie rested against the wall and crossed her arms. She wanted to stay away from the words *crazy* and *insane* from now on, although they were just on the tip of her tongue, ready to escape at any moment.

"But it's true." Neal used the top of the chair to ease himself back down. "It has all been so horrible. I wouldn't make up something like this."

"So you're saying these experiments are loose. Why hasn't anyone else reported seeing these things?"

"They're not stupid. We assumed that when they matured they would have to be educated and schooled in every area of life, language, culture, and societal expectations. But not these creatures. Something happened that we didn't consider, and until now, I didn't imagine it as a variable."

"What's that?" Robbie asked.

"The void."

Eric grimaced. "The void?"

"This is going to sound even crazier, but I know my hypothesis is right. No other explanation fits the evidence."

"You can't possibly sound crazier than you do now." Eric waved his hand. "So give us everything."

"As we prepared to execute Dr. Silverstein's program for the cloning and genetic manipulations sequences, we considered every possibility. Or we thought we did."

"So what's this void?" Robbie pushed off the wall and stepped closer to Neal.

Neal rested his head back and stared at the fluorescent lights, as if in a trance. "We didn't factor in that there might be more to creating human beings than just body and mind. We didn't consider a third component—souls. Spirits infused into our bodies by an intelligent source over and above the simple genetic codes that build our physical beings. We could give our experiments everything but a soul. We couldn't manipulate that. It created a void or vacuum in our cloned humans, something that we could never fill."

"So you created soulless beings?" Robbie raised her eyebrows. "And that's who's doing the killing?" Would this tale ever end?

"Sort of. We did create soulless beings, but they're not soulless anymore." Neal adjusted his crushed spectacles. "They have spirits now, and may God forgive us for unleashing them on earth."

"What in the world are you talking about?" Eric shook his head.

"Demons." Neal stood, the agitated, frantic look he displayed in the lobby returning. "Evil spirits have inhabited our experiments and are walking around in them like extremely expensive and powerful suits. They're capable of more wickedness than the world can imagine, and they have to be stopped."

Robbie remained silent and looked at Eric, who was surprisingly quiet as well. With him being a Christian and all, she wondered what he was contemplating. The suspect had called her Robilina. How could he know that? Could Dr. Meyer be right? She shook off the thought.

The door to the interview room flew open, crashing against the wall, and Alan entered. "Why are we still entertaining this guy? He needs a ride to Mental Health Services now! He's wasted enough of our time, and his crazy story is driving me nuts."

"I'm not crazy." Neal's hands dropped to his sides, and he faced Alan head-on. "And if you send me to Mental Health Services, all you're gonna have is more murdered people and fewer answers. I helped create them; I can help stop them."

"Robbie, this is your case, but as your supervisor, I'm asking you to get rid of this guy." Alan pointed at the door with his thumb. "You can't believe what he's saying."

"I'm not sure what I believe." Robbie's feuding thoughts yanked her in opposite directions like an emotional tug of war. "But I know that what happened yesterday is beyond our natural experience and understanding, and we still don't have an ID or motive for our suspect."

"I know the motive." Neal crossed his arms and glared at Alan.

"This should be rich." Alan smirked. "Enlighten us."

"They have come into this world to kill as many Christians as they can. They don't mind killing anyone else in the process, but Morek—that's the leader's name—especially enjoys murdering Christians. He says he can 'see' them. I'm not sure what that means, but I know it's not good if you're a Christian. I've seen the other side, and I don't want any part of it."

Tim ran into the already crowded interview room, poking a finger at Alan. "I told you all it was because of their faith, but nobody listened. Ha! You owe me an apology and lunch and a new car."

"Tim, I hate to remind you that the only other person going along with your theory is insane." Alan held his hand out to Neal. "And we haven't proven a thing yet."

"We could prove it right now."

Alan turned to Neal. "How's that?"

"Let's go to Lifetex and see if I'm telling the truth or if I'm insane. If nothing's wrong, I'll go to Mental Health Services with no hesitation. But if I'm right, you all had better have a lot of cops with you because these things aren't going down without a fight."

20

Robbie squinted as the late-afternoon sun shone brilliantly along Lifetex's reflective windows. She opened the car door for Neal in Lifetex's parking lot as Alan and Tim jumped out of the backseat. Eric and John drove in a separate car but arrived just behind them. "All right, Neal, let's go inside and get a look around."

"I don't think you understand—you're going to need a *lot* more cops." Neal scanned the parking lot. "Like a SWAT team or the entire force or something."

"If you believe that I'm gonna activate our SWAT team to do battle with demon-infested killer clones from outer space, you're crazier than I thought." Alan slammed the door with more force than needed, rocking the unmarked car. He was reaching his limit with this case. "Do you really think I'm gonna make that call?"

"I guess not." Neal stared at the front of Lifetex with abject fear radiating from his face, a look difficult to fake.

"I'm not going to retire as a laughingstock, I can tell you that right now." Alan slid his coat on and adjusted his pistol. "There's going to be enough of a roast without adding this as an apple in my mouth."

"We should head back to the lab as soon as possible. Maybe then we can all find some answers." Robbie hurried toward the huge double doors of the complex.

She'd not been here before, although she'd seen the magnificent structure from Interstate 95. Hard to imagine secret research and wild experiments scurrying about inside. She now swung back closer to Alan's point of view. She was way too run-down if she was giving Neal any amount of credibility. She could dispatch Neal to Mental Health in short order and be home for a little rest. Maybe she'd check herself into Mental Health Services too, with no pager or phone, to finally get a break and a decent night's sleep. It didn't sound that bad. Then *Robilina* danced around in her head again.

As the band of detectives trailed behind her, Alan's grumbles added an even more depressing element to the event.

Neal hurried through a set of double doors at the end of the complex with determined steps. A blond woman in her forties hurried down the center stairs toward them.

"Dr. Meyer." She paused to catch her breath. "What happened to you?"

"I'm fine, Alice. Just a little…problem."

"Well, I'm so glad you're finally here." She held her hand on her chest. "We've been looking all over for you. No one has been in touch with Warren, Steve, or Dr. Silverstein for over twenty-fours hours now. Warren Finstead doesn't just go missing and not attend meetings or return calls. I've worked for him for eight years. Something's wrong. His wife has filed a missing person's report. She hasn't heard from him or Steve at all. And some of the lab staff called today, saying they were told they were laid off and the project was closed down. What's going on, Dr. Meyer? Everything seems like it's falling apart."

"I'm not sure what's happening, but these detectives will help us figure it out." He placed his hands on Alice's shoulders. "So why don't you close up your office and go home until these detectives can sort through this. I'll call you if I hear anything from them."

She shook her head and jogged back up the steps. The woman appeared nearly as frazzled as Neal.

"I didn't know Warren and Steve were missing too." Neal regarded Robbie. "Morek only alluded to Dr. Silverstein. But this is unthinkable. I didn't have the heart to tell her what has been happening."

Robbie assessed the bewildered faces of Alan, Tim, Eric, and John. Bizarre beyond belief, the pendulum swung back in

Neal's favor. The little cop voice inside her, the one she'd been suppressing since speaking with Neal, sounded the alarm.

They approached another set of doors, stopping in front of a machine that looked like an ATM. A red laser-light emitted, scanning Neal's eyes.

"Good afternoon, Dr. Meyer," the computer-generated voice said.

"I have five visitors with me."

"Please type in the security code," the voice retorted. "And have a pleasant visit at Lifetex today."

"When I type in this code, you guys need to be ready." Neal suspended his shaking hands over the keypad. "Because if they charge out, we're going to have a real problem."

"Just open the door, Neal." Alan crossed his arms, defiant. "I have a feeling we'll be just fine."

Not wanting to look foolish in front of her co-workers, Robbie didn't unholster her pistol, but she couldn't help wondering how much ammo she had with her. John and Tim didn't prepare for an assault either.

Neal punched in a code on the keypad, and the door buzzed open. They marched into a small corridor with several offices on each side, Neal lagging behind. Just past the offices, the room expanded into a massive open lab at least two stories high.

"His office has been ransacked." Neal stopped at one of the office doors and then continued toward the open lab area, his voice echoing across the hangar-sized room. "Mine too."

Neal paused at the edge of the room. "What have they done?" He gazed across a jumbled mass of tangled wires and power cords strewn about, overturned desks, reams of papers scattered like confetti, and disassembled equipment tossed aside without care. What was once a bustling medical laboratory now resembled a debris field after a successful bombing run.

"Where are the chambers?" Neal rotated around. "We had eight-foot chambers right here in the middle of the floor to incubate the experiments."

"This looks bad." Robbie touched Neal's elbow. "Like everything has been moved out."

"It's catastrophic." Neal clenched the side of his head. "They've taken the chambers, the support equipment, the computers, and our notes. Do you know what that means? If they set up somewhere else, they can replicate what we've done here. They can make more of themselves, as many as you can imagine."

"This torn-up lab doesn't prove what you're saying is true." Alan bent down and picked up a calculator off the floor. "Okay, you do work for Lifetex and this lab is messed up, but I'm still not with you on your experiments. It doesn't prove what you're claiming."

"But Dr. Silverstein, Warren Finstead, and Steve Glick are all missing. You've got to believe me. These things are evil and will kill again and again until they're stopped. Why can't you see that?"

"If these men are missing"—Alan eased into Neal's breathing space—"then the first person we have to eliminate as a suspect is you."

"Fine." Neal threw his arms up and walked away. "Do whatever you have to do. Put me in jail or the nut house, but help track down the lab equipment and these clones in the process. If you don't, get prepared for war."

John cupped his chin in his hand. "To move this amount of equipment, they would need some moving trucks. I'll make a couple of calls and see if we can track down the company. Maybe they have an address to where the equipment was taken."

"Don't tell me you're taking this seriously?"

John stepped around a clump of papers. "So far, everything Neal has told us has been verified. I don't see the harm in following this up. What if he's right? Look around, Alan. There's a lot to see here."

"He can't be right because it's impossible." Alan's voice peaked. "Demon-possessed clones wanting to kill Christians? Come on, John, use your head. I know you're religious, but don't get crazy on me here."

Tim laid his hand on Neal's back. "After the other day and now seeing this lab with everything else, I really believe what he's sayin'. And we've got to do something to stop these things. I've seen one, and that's enough for me."

"Listen to them speak to each other in their own vile, fiendish language." Neal cringed. "You'll never be the same."

"Why didn't these things kill you then?" Eric pushed a metal drawer out of his way with his foot and walked closer to Robbie.

Neal straddled a chair that was next to him. "They needed me to teach them about the process, so I walked Morek through it. He's really bright, otherworldly smart. I figured when they were done with me, they'd kill me too. But he made me drive him out to get some supplies. On the way, I started praying. It was only a silent prayer, but it was the most earnest of my life. I begged Jesus to save me. At that very second, Morek knew. It was like he could see my spirit, that God changed me, or however that works. I'm still new at this. He was getting ready to kill me too when I crashed my car into a telephone pole and ran away. I've been running and hiding until I made it to your office."

Eric stepped away from the group and opened his cell phone.

"Great! So now you're a Christian too?" Alan tossed his hands in the air. "That explains what's going on. You had a religious experience and have truly lost it."

"I didn't have a religious experience. It was a rational response to the situation. When you stand in the presence of pure evil, you will sprint to God. Trust me on that." The man looked like a battered boxer who couldn't answer the final bell.

"I just spoke with our Dispatch." Eric slapped his phone shut and returned to the circle. "Neal's car was found this morning crashed against a telephone pole just a few blocks from here. There was blood on the driver's and passenger's sides. We towed it to our impound lot."

"Told you." Tim sliced his finger at Alan like a sword. "You just don't want to believe it because it involves the spirit world and that freaks you out."

Alan worked his jaw back and forth, glaring at the group. "Okay, some, and I repeat some, of the things he's said appear to be accurate. But whose blood is really in that car? Maybe Warren Finstead's, or his bodyguard's, or Dr. Silverstein's? We really need to look at that possibility and not just take Meyer's word for it."

The detectives nodded. They did need to move ahead with the missing persons cases. They couldn't ignore the tie-in with Neal. But the vetting process of Neal Meyer was moving well in his favor.

"Something's bothering me with all this." Eric locked his cell phone on his belt pouch. "With more of these clones out there, why did that one taunt us and make us shoot him?"

"Maybe to make us think we had our suspect." Robbie pushed over a mound of paper with her foot. "Or to throw us off of Lifetex and keep us searching for a suspect long enough to move out of here and get somewhere undetected. All of Palm Bay PD was tied up on the shooting. Even if someone from Lifetex had been suspicious and called, with all that going on, no officers would have been able to respond. I mean, he looked just like our suspect. Joan Perry positively identified the picture of him."

"One of them sacrificed himself so the rest could escape." John rested on a toppled file cabinet. "In a military context, even spiritual warfare, that makes a lot of sense. I could see why they would want to stage that to buy a little time. We've pretty much shut down our investigations since then. It's really quite brilliant."

"What's really bothering me about this conversation is that all of you are talking about this like it's a viable possibility. Come on!" Alan folded his arms and scanned each detective's face. "You are all experienced cops. Does this jibe at all with anything you've ever seen before?"

Eric glowered at Alan. "But that doesn't mean it can't be true. The spiritual world and warfare are real, but none of us have ever faced it head-on like this."

"The suspect called me Robilina." Robbie's neck bristled even mentioning it. "That's a name only my father called me when I was very young. How would he know that? He said he was my Watcher. I don't get what that means, but it doesn't jibe with any of our other assessments. It's been creeping me out ever since."

"I know who the Watchers are." John stood and raised his hand, as if a schoolboy brimming with the answer. "They're in the book of Enoch—that's an extrabiblical text, not on par with Scripture but certainly an interesting read. Anyway, the Watchers were fallen angels who originally were sent to help men but sinned, and the lot of them were bound and cast into hell. Maybe *Watcher* is a term they use when a demon is assigned to a human. If God can task angels to watch over people, I don't see why Satan can't do the same with fallen angels to cause people to stumble and fall."

"See, Alan?" Tim beamed. "How could Neal just make that up and then have that thing say that to Robbie too? Neal's explanation makes the most sense."

"You're killing me, John." Alan placed his hand on John's shoulder. "You are murdering me with a slow, agonizing death. I've been in law enforcement almost thirty years now, and I've never heard such a twisted interpretation of two simple murder cases. The suspect is dead. Now we have three missing persons. That's how I see it."

"I disagree, Alan." Robbie evaluated the situation, trying to balance all the input so far. "There are too many strange coincidences and happenings to dismiss them as delusional rantings. Neal's story has merit."

John, Tim, Eric, and Neal nodded in unison. Alan stepped away, shaking his head. Robbie's mind was assaulted with every kind of theory and rumination, and she lost all confidence in rational, worldly thought. While the facts were the facts, how could she know about the other things—the spiritual side of the conflict? Was it possible that there even were demons, much less ones that would inhabit soulless bodies? The mere thought stretched the limits of her education, training, and beliefs.

She believed in God. She trusted John's opinion. He'd been through seminary and knew all that biblical stuff. His explanation of the Watcher comment made sense, but she didn't want to believe it, mainly because it scared the daylights out of her. Unseen forces lurking all around her, fighting for her soul. Goose bumps rippled down her arms and back. All of this was overwhelming.

"Look, we don't have to come up with all the answers now." John regarded Neal and then the others. "Let's track down what we can and leave the speculation for later. We have plenty to do as it is, starting with finding Dr. Silverstein, Finstead, and Glick."

Always a voice of reason, John's counsel proved wise now. There would indeed be plenty of time to debate the other issues. Although they were moving forward with Neal's information, Robbie would keep him close in case things weren't all as they appeared with him.

"We have to follow these leads." Alan glared at the rest of the agents. "It would be irresponsible not to. But I'm telling you all now, unless I put my hands on one of these things and hear it confess, I will not believe."

"Perfect." Morek hovered behind Jaris as he completed the connection on the last of the computers. The screen clicked on, and the data flowed across without interruption. The lights inside the chambers flickered to life, while the hum of the generator reverberated throughout the warehouse.

"This is a beautiful sight." Morek ran his hand across the

top of the computer. "Everything is in place and ready to go. Our victory is at hand."

"They have no idea what's coming their way." Jaris typed test commands on the screen. "And by the time they figure it out, it will be too late."

"It's a glorious day." Morek sauntered toward the amniotic, flesh-nurturing cells as they vibrated to life. He laid his hands on them. What fruit they would bear. "Assemble the twelve. It is time."

As Jaris hurried to his task, Morek surveyed his makeshift lab, converted from a normal warehouse in less than a day. It was a finer laboratory than anything those careless fools had established.

When the master first chose Morek to lead this new mission, he doubted the humans would be so reckless as to think they could actually create life. The master knew better. He always understood precisely how they'd follow his leadings, and a new theater opened up in this war.

Working on Benjamin Silverstein from the time he was a young man, the master guided him without Benjamin's remotely suspecting that he was but a pawn—a movable, usable, and replaceable unsealed spirit, open to guidance and suggestion. How remarkable. How simple.

The plan was without flaw. While Morek's companions in the spirit realm continued to lure the humans away from the Offensive One with whispers and yearnings imparted to them,

Morek would lead a new assault and crush the sealed ones on earth, forever silencing their blasphemous mouths. He would drive them underground and finally destroy them, keeping them from spreading the knowledge of the Offensive One—a two-pronged attack that wasn't even conceivable a few years before. Now the human race was doomed, spiritually and physically, and the promise He made to redeem them would never be fulfilled. What a magnificent and ecstatic mission.

With his new formidable flesh, he could reap the harvest of all the ages. His powerful body would serve him well and last a very long time, long enough to complete his task.

There were unexpected complications, though. Since entering this world, the pain of his continuous torment was stayed, if only for a short time. But a new ache replaced it, one he could scarcely endure. His flesh cried out to destroy all of them now. He could see the sealed ones, their spirits glowing as if they were already in His presence.

Controlling his impulse to slaughter them all tortured his spirit and dueled with his desire to serve his master's wishes. He simply craved to tear them apart, limb by limb, and not wait as he'd been instructed. Wait for an army large enough to wipe the abominable stain from this world once and for all. Maybe he had moved too quickly with the policeman, but he couldn't control his cravings. It didn't matter now.

"We must begin the sequence immediately," Morek called out, his comrades taking their positions. "I want the instructions followed exactly as they have been written. There will be no mistakes. They've already prepared the genetic lines for us; now we must initiate the incubation process. We moved at exactly the right time."

"Assemble before Morek." Jaris stood in front of Morek as the twelve marshaled with him. Each carried his own bag and supplies, each armed with his own mission. The others would stay back and help the cloning process unfold. But the task of the twelve couldn't wait. It was time now to act and punish the sealed ones…and *Him.*

"You know your cause and what you must do." Morek's voice carried throughout the large bay. "This will strike at the heart of the Offensive One, so make your aim true and do not stop, do not relent. Seek them out and destroy them all. Victory will finally be ours. We will snuff out every last vestige of *His* name that there is."

The twelve hurried out the door, disappearing into the night, their destinations predetermined. Morek paced the warehouse floor, his spirit tingling with expectancy for the first time in six millennia.

21

Katie Florence smacked the coin roll on the counter twice and then tore the paper wrapper open, pouring the quarters into her cash drawer. In a mere forty-five minutes, her Friday would end, and what a long, hectic day it had been. Payday Fridays usually were. Exhausted from a tiresome week, she prepared for a relaxing weekend. She might hit a movie or just chill out at her apartment later.

Katie glanced down at the picture of her parents on the counter. Working as a teller gave her interesting experiences dealing with people and provided a nice way to supplement her upcoming missions trip and, later, college. She'd felt God's call on her for missions years before at a summer camp for teens. Only now was that vision becoming a reality. She'd miss the people she worked with but knew she'd be back to see them.

As much as her parents supported her, her mother felt uneasy about her working in a bank, with robberies and all. Katie told her not to worry. She was well trained and sat behind a bulletproof glass partition. She was as safe here as working anywhere else. But parents worry; that's what they do. Katie didn't consider those things seriously and would do what she needed to do to fulfill God's direction for her life.

"Next customer, please," she said.

A supersized man stepped up to her counter, blocking her view of the door.

"How can I help you today?"

"I'd like to make a deposit." His voice was gruff and grave.

"Checking or savings?"

"Neither, Katie. I'd like to make a deposit for eternity and one that will ensure that *you* don't ever draw interest."

"What?" She tilted her head and strained to see the man better. Was he just messing with her? She didn't wear her name tag, so she was surprised he knew her name. He gawked at her with his deep blue eyes. She swallowed hard. She didn't like the way he just leered at her, making her feel uncomfortable.

He placed his oven-mitt-sized hands on the glass in front of him.

"Do you have an account here? I don't remember seeing you before."

"No. But I remember you. Good-bye, Katie."

He drew his hands back and smacked the glass, the entire partition shaking. She screamed as he struck it again. On the third smack, the bolts on the top of the glass snapped, rico-cheting in the booth.

"Aaah!" Katie stepped back out of her station, trapped against the rear counter. The three other tellers screamed as the man pushed the two-inch-thick glass onto the floor.

He drew a pistol from his coat and whipped it around until it was pointing at her. He smiled.

"Lord, help me."

The shots echoed throughout the bank.

Robbie slogged through the back door of her office, carrying a hefty load of file folders; Eric and Neal trudged behind her. After they searched the Lifetex lab, she and Eric drove Neal to his apartment and let him get a quick shower and a change of clothes. He wouldn't go back without a police escort. The man nearly suffered a nervous breakdown every time he spoke of the experiments and what happened at Lifetex. He did appear a bit more rational and coherent after he was cleaned up and found his extra pair of glasses.

They'd hit a drive-through, and each got a burger. Now it was work time again. Where did they start looking for Warren Finstead, Steve Glick, and Dr. Silverstein? They'd begin with Lifetex and work their way out. Search e-mails, any correspond-ence with friends and relatives. Add that task to all the others, and the team wasn't getting R&R anytime soon.

John drove to Melbourne Beach to meet with Warren's wife and check his house for any clues on his disappearance. Tim went to Dr. Silverstein's apartment in Melbourne and was working with the Melbourne Police Department for leads. Palm Bay detectives were searching Steve Glick's condo. Alan worked the logistics and made calls to free up some resources. The team pounded the pavement for her. She owed everyone big time, again.

Alan wanted her to put Neal through a polygraph exam right away and treat him as the prime suspect in the disappearances. In another situation, that would be the right move. After careful consideration, she didn't think that route served them best.

She didn't fully trust Neal either, but so far he was cooperative and wanted to work with them. As a matter of fact, she couldn't get away from him. He wanted to be in a room with either her or Eric at all times. The guy was truly terrified. Along with all of their other observations, Neal got the benefit of the doubt right now. If things changed, her tactics in dealing with him would change as well.

"So what do we do?" Neal took the swivel chair next to her. "Where do we go from here?"

"We've got everyone looking for Dr. Silverstein, Steve, and Mr. Finstead." Robbie turned over a page on her legal pad. "We'll keep working that angle until some leads come in."

"What about Morek and the others?" Neal stopped spinning

and faced her. "How are we going to find them? You could hold a press conference and show his picture. Would that help?"

"I don't think we're quite ready for a press conference yet." Robbie tried to imagine Alan's reaction to that suggestion. It wouldn't be pretty. "Let's work one lead at a time."

"You don't believe me about them." Neal deflated in the chair. "You think I'm crazy, like your boss."

"It's not personal, Neal." Robbie laid her notepad on her desk. Her notes thus far amounted to a novella. She couldn't imagine what it would look like when she was done. "After everything we've seen and heard, I know much of what you've said is true. I'm just not sure about your hypothesis on the evil spirits or demons. You're a scientist, an educated man. If you were in my position, wouldn't you need a bit more evidence?"

"If I hadn't lived it, I probably wouldn't believe me either." Neal's head dipped down. "For the first time in my life, I believe there is something—Someone—larger and more powerful than ourselves, controlling the world around us. I believe the things I was taught as a child about Jesus and God. And I know for a fact now that there are beings wholly committed to opposing God and everyone who follows Him."

"I wish I had your confidence there." Robbie rested her elbows on her knees. "Part of me hopes that you're proven right. The other part doesn't. It's a lot to digest."

"I was the same way." Neal ran his hands across his face and appeared comfortable for the first time since she'd met him. "When we first birthed Morek, I started noticing little things, small slivers of his personality that weren't correct. But I chose to ignore or explain them away. I was so caught up in the dream of what we were doing that I neglected the reality. Now I wish I acted sooner and with more vigor. Maybe Dr. Silverstein, Mr. Finstead, Steve, and others would still be alive today. I won't ignore or dismiss things again."

"They could still be alive." Robbie hoped to raise his spirits. "All we know for sure is that they are missing."

"I've spent time with Morek." Neal removed his glasses and cleaned them with his shirt. "I know what he would have done with them. There's no compassion or true humanity in him."

Eric stepped back into the cubicle area. "Robbie, we need to watch the news. It doesn't look good."

Robbie reached up and turned on the television mounted above their cubicles. It could be used for watching cable or interrogations in the interview room. Robbie switched to FOX News.

"In downtown Atlanta today, a gunman opened fire in a bank," the blond reporter said. "He then worked his way down the street, shooting indiscriminately at passersby. Police have been on the scene and are still engaged in a fierce gun battle with the suspect, who doesn't seem willing to give up."

The camera switched to a reporter on the street. "We're here with Amanda Debusk, a teller in the bank when the shooting went down. Amanda, can you tell us what happened?"

The brunette nodded and wiped tears from her eyes. "This

huge guy just walked up to Katie's window. He knocked the glass out—"

"Do you mean the bulletproof glass?"

"Yes. He smacked it and knocked it out. No one is supposed to be able to do that. It's security glass. It must have been broken or something. Then he just shot Katie and walked out like nothing was wrong. He didn't take any money or anything. It was like he just came in for her."

"Could he be an old boyfriend or some kind of stalker?" the reporter asked.

"No. She didn't have a boyfriend, and she spent most of her time with her church youth group. She was going to do missions work around the world. Katie's such a sweet person. Who would be so cruel? This is just so sick." The woman started crying. "Why her?"

"We have some security-video photos in right now," the reporter said. A picture flashed up on the screen of a large, black-haired man with his hands on the glass, talking with the teller. It was a good snapshot.

"Oh, God, please forgive me." Neal focused on the television and then interlocked his fingers and appeared to be praying. "He's one of them. They've moved all over now. If he's in Atlanta, they could be anywhere, everywhere."

"Also breaking news at this time," the reporter said, "prominent Christian evangelist Gilbert Larson was found slain in his home today in southern Alabama. And we're working on a report of a church shooting in Austin, Texas. We'll have more details on both of those stories coming up."

As the newscast replayed the photo of the Atlanta shooter, Eric gazed at the image on the screen. "I believe you now, Neal. Sorry I ever doubted you. That's the spitting image of the guy we shot the other day. There's no other rational explanation. It's the attack of the killer clones from hell."

"I think I'm going to be sick." Neal doubled over in his chair and covered his ears with his hands. "When will it stop?" He convulsed, and laments of his pain and despair rocked the room.

Robbie rubbed his shoulder. "I don't know if this helps you or not, but I'm on board too. I also know that you never intended for anything like this to happen. You were trying to benefit all of mankind, and your research has. These creatures have twisted what you and Dr. Silverstein tried to do. You were used. You're not responsible for that."

"That doesn't help that young lady in Atlanta or all those other people these things are going to kill. I could go on and on about the misery we've launched on this planet, and it's only going to get worse."

Eric paced the room. "Not if we take them out before they do more damage. I'm ready to take on these creatures, whatever the cost."

"So am I." Robbie rose and adjusted her holster. "We have an advantage. We know what they look like. We can put a bulletin out for them, pass the picture and description around.

These genetic freaks are strong but not indestructible. They can die. We've proven that."

Neal raised his head. "But they have access to dozens of lines of genes. Morek and his ghouls stole those lines from the lab. If they cultivate the experiments and use those genes, they'll have dozens of completely different bodies to use—men, women, Asians, African Americans, even children if they release them early. The possibilities and potential murderers are endless. If we don't find them soon, they'll have an army of undetectable demon warriors. Then what will we do?"

"We've got to find Morek and the location of his lab." Eric bounced as he spoke, like he was warming up for a football game.

"But how do we do that?" Neal asked.

"We go to the press." Robbie snatched her coat off the back of her chair. "We have to get this information out to the public as soon as possible. Somebody has to know where they've set up shop. There are only so many places a lab like that could be established."

"And will everyone think this is some kind of stunt?" Neal rose and paced the floor. "Look how long it took you all to believe me. How much harder will it be for others to get it as well?"

"We don't have a lot of choice right now, do we?" Robbie collected her legal pad and digital recorder from the desk. "We can't just do nothing and hope for the best. We have to stop them once and for all, before the body count gets any higher."

∞

Alan tilted back in his chair in the war room, comparing a photo from the bank-surveillance camera in Atlanta with the one from the autopsy of their shooting suspect. Alan had remained frozen in that position for what Robbie considered a disproportionate amount of time. Only his rhythmic nasal breathing was audible in the room.

Pictures of Brad Worthington, Wilson Perry, and now Dr. Silverstein, Steve Glick, and Warren Finstead all lined the whiteboard. A picture of their still-unnamed assailant was posted right in the middle. The victim board was running out of room.

Alan rocked back and forth as he glanced from one photo to the next. Robbie bit her lip. She'd wait to see his response, and then she'd defend her cause. Alan needed time to work through the possibilities, as she had done.

Tim and John lingered against the wall. Eric remained next to her, and Neal sat in a chair, all watching for Alan's reaction. Ultimately, everything would fall on his shoulders.

"What do you think, Alan?" Tim tapped his foot on the floor to a hurried beat. "Do we move forward or what? Time's awastin'."

Alan placed both photos on the table. He removed his glasses and pinched the bridge of his nose. "I'm getting entirely too old for this stuff. This is not how I wanted to end my career…with the case from hell, pardon the pun."

"So, what's it going to be, boss?" Tim pushed off the wall and stepped toward him. "We need to move now."

"Robbie, call the press conference." Alan covered his face with both hands, a long, sad hiss emitting from him like the last gasp of a punctured tire. "I can't believe we're doing this. The only satisfaction I have is that if it blows up in our faces, I'll be retired before the internal-affairs investigation would be complete. That will at least spare me some humiliation."

"Thanks, Alan." Robbie grabbed her legal pad and stood. With too many phone calls to make and a press conference to set up, she didn't have time to dillydally.

"Thanks for believing me." Neal remained seated. "I know this is the right thing to do."

"Don't get crazy." Alan swiveled in his chair to face them. "I'm still not sure exactly what's going on here, but you've convinced me that the experiments are involved, and if we do nothing, we have to live with that for a very long time. It's worth whatever humiliation might come." Alan held up a finger. "One suggestion, Robbie."

"Shoot." She regretted her word as soon as she spoke it.

"We might want to go easy on the whole demon-possession angle. Not because of what I believe. I'm just not sure that it won't raise a whole lot more questions than answers. Maybe play up the experiments-gone-wrong aspect and get those photos out there."

In her zeal, she didn't consider the ramifications of the whole story being brought out at a press conference. Not that

she didn't believe it wholeheartedly, but she appreciated the dif-
ficulty of communicating about the threat posed by demon-
infested clones while trying to be taken seriously. Alan might
have a point there.

22

Agent Sanchez," the reporter asked. "Do you really expect us to believe that a series of rogue experiments are responsible for the recent shooting spree and murders? Just this morning, there were more shootings in Nashville and Topeka. Are these 'experiments' responsible for those as well?"

"I know how difficult it is to understand this right now." Robbie's voice cracked. "We weren't sure ourselves until we verified the information. Now we're positive. That's also why I've asked Dr. Neal Meyer to assist in the news briefing today. He might be able to shed some light on these attacks."

Neal approached the microphone and pulled it up to speak. A squeal echoed through the FDLE briefing room. Two dozen reporters shouted questions at Neal and hopped up and down, as if barking on the floor of the stock exchange. The nationwide spate of shootings and murders had every major news network scrambling for answers—and the latest story line. Now it was time to see if they'd listen.

"Dr. Meyer," a tall male reporter for CNN called out. "Are we to understand that you were involved in a clandestine lab where human cloning was developed against national and international law?"

"Yes. We intentionally violated nearly every law and regulation regarding human cloning, and I'm prepared to accept full responsibility for my actions." Neal didn't waver as he confessed to the world. "But first, we must stop these experiments while we still can."

"Why did you embark on such a risky experiment?" the same reporter asked. "Was it for personal glory? Were you both trying to get in the record books as the first to clone successfully?"

"No. We—Dr. Benjamin Silverstein and I—both thought we were doing the world a service by seeking the answers to what ails the human condition in the form of genetic alterations and human cloning. We thought we could *create* perfect humans, with no genetic flaws or sickness and death—thus eventually, a perfect world. But I fear our good intentions were not good enough to stave off this wave of evil."

"From what Agent Sanchez told us," the reporter looked down at his notepad, "these 'experiments' are 'genetically enhanced and incredibly strong, capable of amazing feats.' It would seem, given what we're learning today, that you succeeded in your experiments. They are genetically perfect."

"There's a lot more to life than genetics." Neal lowered his head and paused as he choked up. "And something is terribly wrong with these creatures. Please be careful. You cannot reason with them or negotiate. They have killed and will kill again until they're stopped."

A dark-haired female reporter from Reuters called out. "Dr. Meyer, what evidence do you have to prove your assertions? You must admit that this is a rather fantastic story, to say the least."

"I have all my notes and the lab at Lifetex itself. The agents with the Florida Department of Law Enforcement have agreed to allow a walk-through when the time is right. And Agent Sanchez has put together a series of pictures for you."

Robbie pulled down a sheet that covered several placards with enhanced photos. Alan, Tim, John, and Eric stood to the side of her for support. A press conference could be a rough environment.

"This is the picture of a suspect involved in two murders in the Palm Bay area as well as in a shootout with the police there in which he was killed." Robbie used a laser pointer to highlight the picture. "This is the surveillance photo from the bank in Atlanta. And this is the news coverage of the shooting in Nashville."

The room erupted in flashes and murmurings. The photo lineup was compelling, and all seemed to be the same suspect.

"Also, several of the recent attacks have occurred either at the same time or close to the same time but hundreds or thousands of miles away from each other." Robbie turned off her pointer. "The Florida Department of Law Enforcement is more than convinced that these attacks are indeed being carried out by the same group of experiments outlined by Dr. Meyer. It doesn't matter if it's fantastic, only if it's true. We've determined that Dr. Meyer has provided us with accurate and verifiable evidence supporting this information."

More rumblings rose throughout the pressroom.

"Agent Sanchez?" an African American reporter called out as she waved her arm around as if swatting flies. "With the murder of popular Christian evangelist Gilbert Larson and the fact that many of these violent acts have taken place at churches, are these experiments attacking people of faith, particularly Christians?"

The million-dollar question had been asked. Robbie had hoped and prayed she wouldn't have to get into that. Not that she didn't believe it herself, but explaining the phenomena was more complicated. Most people didn't believe in the spirit world, much less in demons and angels and the God of the Bible. This woman was paying attention, though. Robbie couldn't dodge the question, and part of her didn't want to. The truth was the truth and should be treated as such.

"The experiments appear to have an underlying motivation to attack Christians, although they don't seem to mind killing anyone in their way. No one is safe until they're stopped."

A reporter in the front row raised his hand. "Pete Yanick, from *Florida Today.* Agent Sanchez, do you really expect any rational person to believe what you're telling us? Please! Cloned humans murdering people, particularly Christians? Do you understand how insane that sounds?"

Robbie leaned forward, gripped the podium, and lowered her head. How could she convince anyone of what was happening? The crushing weight of many innocent victims pressed upon her shoulders like an excruciating loadstone. But she knew the truth. And it had to be told.

"I can't tell you what to believe." Robbie glanced at Eric, who smiled at her. That helped. "But if I would have had this conversation with anyone three days ago, I wouldn't have believed it myself. I've seen the evidence. I've witnessed what's occurring, and I know in my heart that if we do not stop them, they will kill again and again. So believe what you want. But if you see this man anywhere"—Robbie used the laser pointer again on the suspect—"please call your local police department right away."

Neal stepped back up to the podium. "Also, I think it's important to note that they have the technology to reproduce, and at an astounding rate. We have to find where they've set up the new lab. If not, they will continue to replicate and we won't be able to stop them."

"Please help us get this information out there now to save lives." Robbie waved at the reporters as she backed away from the podium. "Thank you."

A throng of reporters sprinted out of the room while some lagged behind, shaking their heads. Robbie had no idea how many, if any, of the reporters actually believed what they heard, or if they would report it as she hoped. Or if she would be labeled as the latest kook. Only time would tell. They could label her however they wanted as long as Morek's picture got out. It was nice that at least they all looked the same, for now. But if what Neal said was true, that could change quickly. Robbie shuddered at the thought.

"You did well." Robbie placed her hand on Neal's shoulder. "We'll get some leads in off of this. Until then, we have to remain strong. I think Dr. Silverstein would have wanted it that way."

"Any word on him yet?" Neal asked.

Robbie shook her head. "But as soon as we have something, I'll let you know. I promise. It had to be hard for you today."

Neal wiped his palms on his khaki pants. "It's funny. As educated and learned as we are, neither Dr. Silverstein nor I factored in a soul. He would have said, 'How can you test something like a soul?' A mind, yes. A body, yes. But a soul? No. I think even he would change his opinion now."

Eric, John, Tim, and Alan huddled with them.

"Good job, you two." Alan placed his hands on his hips and gave a conciliatory nod. "Now comes the hard part. Every news agency will want to follow up on this, but we're done with press conferences until we get a line on these…things."

"You mean the demon-possessed killer clones you didn't believe in until now?" Tim grinned.

"Keep it up, Porter, and I'll make sure you drive your hippie wagon until *you* retire."

"I say we try to catch one of these things and make it talk in that freaky speak. That should be enough to weird anybody out and convince the whole world." Tim lowered his body like he was preparing for a tackle. "Maybe we can ask it spiritual questions and throw holy water on it and make it tell us the truth or something. Imagine what we could do with one of them."

"It wouldn't do any good." John shook his head and tossed an arm around his partner. "Since being cast out of heaven, these fallen angels or demons have been in a place of torment for thousands of years. Anything we could do to them can't begin to compare with the agony they've already experienced. And we know their master is the father of lies, so nothing they would ever say can be trusted. They're thoroughly corrupt, depraved beings."

"Yeah, but it's fun to think about." Tim straightened up and tucked his shirt in. "Although, after our experience with the walking dead from the other day, I don't think I want to test my theories. I'm gonna need therapy after this case."

"Trust me, you don't want to be anywhere near them, dead or alive." Neal quivered. "They might be technically alive, but they carry the stench of death. I'm going to have nightmares for a very long time just thinking about it."

"I just want you all to know, for the sake of this absurd conversation, I'm still not on board with the killer-demon-clones theory." Alan held out a hand. "I don't think I'll ever be there."

"You all right, Alan?" Eric asked. "You look like you need some rest."

"I'm not doing so well." Alan brushed his hand across his forehead, his normally pale skin now the color of curdled milk. "I just got word that there were two more shootings—one in Minnesota and one in Arkansas—that they believe are related to our case. I'm on my way now to brief Governor Maclartey. We've got to find these things. This insanity must be stopped now."

Morek paced between the chambers as he had watched Benjamin Silverstein do a hundred times before. Of course, he watched from another realm, a firmer reality to which he was more accustomed. Standing right next to Silverstein, he had monitored the old fool beaming with pride at *his* creations. How laughable. Morek's master fed Silverstein's spirit a constant dose of strong, positive feelings. Small murmurs into the ears of his soul. So easy was it to affirm him, coddle him, until Morek's body lay fresh and strong, ready for the taking.

Now he was the one gazing at his own masterpieces. Twenty-one more vessels readied for war, each different than before. A cornucopia of flesh tones, sizes, races, and genders, careful camouflage in a wanting world. An army too numerous to count waiting on the other side to cross over and slip into the finely hewn sinews of their new forms.

Morek trembled in place, clenching his fists, his mind alive with thoughts and dreams of violence against the sealed ones. He yearned to sprint from the lab and maul the first one he could lay his hands upon. His spirit whirled as he fought to soothe his raging temper, a disadvantage of being in a human body.

With all the possibilities available to Morek, he was finding it more difficult to control himself. Soon it wouldn't matter. Enough of his brothers would be with him that he could join in the attacks. But his mission came first. Gritting his teeth, he regained composure.

Morek stood in front of a dark-skinned body. The girl was maybe twelve years old by human standards, and she'd soon be loosed to wreak untold havoc upon them. Their own weaknesses would be used against them. They'd only see a little girl approaching. Before they could react, it would be over. Another vanquished in a matter of seconds. The plan was flawless, and the humans were loath to do anything to stop them.

Morek raised a fist to the heavens, growling. "You won't stop us now. Not even by *Your* own rules. Always the follower of rules, *You* will be wounded by them."

His flesh felt good, powerful. How long had it been since he'd walked the earth with men? He did enjoy every minute of this, but there was much more pleasure to come.

It was time to toy with Little Robilina.

23

Robbie accelerated through the late-afternoon traffic on Babcock Street, weaving in and out, trying to get home in time to help Kathy fix Mima's dinner. She might as well move Kathy in with them for as much as she was using her. Kathy was working enough overtime now to earn a summer cruise, that was for sure. And maybe a mad shopping spree for them both. A girl could dream.

Her cell phone rang. She looked at the number, and it read *Private. Blocked.* She flipped open the phone. "Agent Sanchez."

"Hello, Robilina," the gravelly, malevolent voice said. "How nice to finally speak with you. It's been a while since I've seen you."

A wave of chills rolled down her spine, and a lump the size of a softball formed in her throat. "Porter, if this is you, it's not at all funny."

"You know this isn't your partner," the graven voice said.

"You looked very nice on TV today. Quite professional. Daddy would be so proud. I can't wait to see you again. We will have such a fun time."

"Who is this, and how did you get my number?"

"You know who this is. You're just too frightened to admit it. I can feel your fear. I can smell it. I thrive on it."

Robbie pulled off the road, her car jiggling as it took the ruts hard. She couldn't concentrate on the road and the creep at the same time.

"Neal looked much better too. Tell him I said hello and I'm going to see him again real soon."

"Morek."

"It's so nice that we're getting to know each other on a first-name basis. I think that's quite appropriate. Especially since I've known you your entire life."

"So you say." Robbie switched the phone to her right hand.

"Oh, you don't believe me? Always the skeptic, Little Robilina. I was there when you sprained your ankle in dance class, when you had the measles, when your mother sang 'Crocodile Rock' to you so you could sleep, and when your father was shot in the back and left to die like an animal. He's in torment with my master as we speak."

"Liar!" Robbie gritted her teeth and squeezed the phone. "John said you would lie. And I trust him before I'll ever listen to a word you say."

"We have something special planned for John Russell and Tim Porter, and your precious Eric. They're all *sealed ones*...and as good as dead. But fare thee well; they will depart in hideous, painful ways, I promise you."

"Over my dead body." Robbie pounded the steering wheel. "You'll have to go through me to get to them."

"Oh, don't worry, Little Robilina. You'll be dying with them. As your Watcher, I've yearned for the day I could wrap my hands around your throat and snuff out your miserable little life. Now that you and I are in the same world, my wonderful dream can come true. We will defeat you and wipe out your blight forever."

"You're forgetting something really important, genius."

"Do tell."

"You can die too. I watched your wormy friend eat it the other day. And I'm gonna watch you die and send you back to hell where you belong. Why don't you tell me your location, and we can end this now?"

"Always Daddy's little tough girl, weren't you? There will be plenty of time for that. I just want you to remember that we are coming, and you and your little troop of detectives can't do a thing to stop us. Sleep tight, Robilina. Just be sure to look under the bed before nappy time."

The line went dead.

Robbie crashed her head against the backrest. Her nerves frayed and her body quaking, she called out, "God, if You're there, please help us. Whatever happens to me is fine, but please let us stop Morek. He's as evil as they come. We need Your help... *I* need Your help."

∞

"We need to stay on our guard." Robbie unlocked the front door of Lifetex with the passkey she'd been given. "Morek might have just been messing with me, but we can't be sure. He knew all of our names. He knows what's going on."

"With the heat turning up on him, I don't think he'll come after us individually." Eric held the door for Neal. "But we can't take any chances. I don't like the idea of this thing toying with you, Robbie. You have to stay safe."

Alan, John, and Tim had been apprised of her phone call from beyond. Alan tried to downplay it, but she could tell he was worried. So was she. Who knew what else this demon was privy to?

Lifetex emanated anything but life right now. The echo of the empty footsteps down the hall and throughout the office complex played like a requiem for a dream lost. The entire operation had closed down, everyone laid off. Even the children's hospital relocated to a facility in Baltimore. Neal still had access to the building but only to assist law enforcement.

Crime-scene techs had swept the lab, searching for blood or any other trace evidence of Dr. Silverstein, Warren Finstead, and Steve Glick. Nothing. Just like the rest of their investigation. Three more names added to the nightmare that was Robbie's case.

Robbie massaged her temples as they walked into Neal's former office. Every thought that revolved around this case seemed to induce physical pain. Last night, sleep was as elusive as Morek had been. His dreadful voice haunted her all night.

She actually liked being at work now. At least more people were around. She hadn't been afraid of the dark since childhood, but the idea of Morek or some other evil being standing in her room—watching her—destroyed any measure of comfort. And worst of all, she believed him in one real sense—he was indeed coming for them. She slept with her pistol on the dresser next to her. This case was changing her by the minute.

Despite the insanity and the breakneck pace, one positive thing had sprung to life—Robbie had truly started to pray. Sure, she had prayed occasionally, when things got tough or when she needed something. But they were the rote prayers she'd memorized as a child. While there was a certain comfort in them, she often wondered if there was more, something deeper.

She observed John's faith, Tim's recent conversion, and now what she knew of Eric. Something was different with them. Faith meant more to these men than an occasional prayer or ethereal thought when convenient. It permeated every aspect of their lives—much as she had seen with her father, even though he hadn't been as vocal as John, Tim, and Eric. They all were confident that they had a relationship with God.

Now, as evil stalked her like a crazed hunter, she marveled at the petty concerns she had occasionally brought to God. For the first time in her life, she understood what people meant when they talked about fervent prayer. Now she cried out to God with more than just memorized mumblings and a laundry list of complaints and wants. She called out to the Lord from the depth of her being—an experience that was truly foreign to her, but one she was growing to rely on in a short amount of time.

"The place is destroyed. I doubt that I have anything left." Neal crouched down in his office and grabbed a clump of papers tossed carelessly on the floor. Sifting through the mess, he made an attempt to reorder them, to establish a sense of stability in the madness of the room. An impossible task.

"When this is all done, we'll help you get back on your feet." Eric leaned against the doorjamb with his hands in his pockets. "You're a follower of Christ now. We'll do everything we can to help you. The Palm Bay guys won't forget how you came forward to help us too. You've shown a lot of courage and integrity."

The bundle tumbled from Neal's hand and dropped to the floor, mixing in with the other debris. Neal turned to Eric. "I don't know what to do now. My whole world has been turned upside down. Everything I thought I knew has been called into question and found wanting."

Eric's cell phone chirped. He stepped into the hallway. "Detective Casey. How long ago?… Where are they now?… Oh boy, this isn't good… Thanks for the call… I'll be on my way in a minute." He returned to the room and sighed. "You might want to sit down, Neal."

Neal eased into his chair and leaned his elbows on his knees.

"It's about Dr. Silverstein, isn't it?"

"One of our patrol officers just found three bodies in a wooded area about a mile from here. Although we can't be sure right now, it looks like it's Dr. Silverstein, Steve Glick, and Warren Finstead. I'm really sorry, Neal."

"No!" Neal wrapped his arms around his stomach and lowered his head. "Please don't let it be true. Please, God, no."

Eric eased next to Robbie. "I'm going to head down there and secure the scene. Palm Bay PD will work it and attach our case to yours. You've got enough going, and we already know who did it." Eric turned to Neal. "I'm truly sorry."

Neal wept and Robbie fought to keep her composure. She hated hearing people cry. The suffering of the injured and afflicted never sat well with her. Neal's broken laments echoed throughout the empty Lifetex complex.

Neal sniffled and wiped his nose on his sleeve. "I'm sorry. I knew in my heart what had happened, but to hear it out loud…it's just so unfair."

"We understand, Neal." Eric laid a hand on his shoulder and squatted down. "I've cried recently over lost friends too. Do what you gotta do."

"He just didn't deserve this. He was such a fine man, a brilliant mind. And all he had to share it with was me and… Sammy?" Neal slapped his forehead. "Where's Sammy?"

"Who's Sammy?" Robbie asked.

"He was our first successful clone experiment, a little mongrel Yorkie. Dr. Silverstein just loved the mutt. It was the closest thing to family he had. I haven't seen him since I was here with Morek. Sammy took off running. Everything's been so crazy, I haven't had a chance to even think about him."

"Well, he'll turn up." Eric glanced at his watch. "I need to get to the scene."

"I'll touch base with you later." Robbie yearned for the time when touching base with Eric didn't have anything to do with a dead body and worldwide mayhem. "I'll stay here with Neal awhile."

"I've got to find that mutt," Neal said. "It's the least I can do for Dr. Silverstein."

"I understand. I'll walk the property with you if you want, but I only have a short amount of time."

Neal stood and rubbed his chin. "It shouldn't be that hard. He subscribed to that pet-locator service, the Internet thing with the locator chips in the animals. A little obsessive for an animal, if you ask me, but he did love that thing."

He walked over to his laptop, which had been toppled over in the corner of his office. Pulling it from the debris, he brushed the top off, eased into his chair, and set the computer on his legs. "Hey, at least this still works and the wireless Internet connections are still set up here."

Logging onto the Internet, he typed in the address. "I remember him using this Pet-Be-Found Web site. I know he used this system, but I can't figure out his password." Neal typed in several more. "I thought it would be *Einstein,* like everything else. I even tried *Adam,* yuck. But I had to try."

"Why don't you call Pet-Be-Found and explain what happened?" Robbie peered over his shoulder, reading the screen. "I'm sure they'd help out."

"They'll think I'm playing some game." Neal lifted the laptop up and stood facing Robbie. "And I'm not very good on the phone."

"I'll call them." Robbie flipped open her phone. People tended to listen better when speaking to a cop. "What's the number?"

Neal read it off the site, and Robbie dialed.

"Pet-Be-Found, how can I help you?" the operator said in a chipper voice.

"I'm Agent Roberta Sanchez with the Florida Department of Law Enforcement. I'm working a violent-crime case, and we're unable to locate the victim's pet. He subscribed to your service, and we were hoping you could help us out. We would really like to find his dog. It would be very important to him."

"Let me see what I can do. Hold, please."

Robbie nodded to Neal, who smiled. Maybe she could help him feel a little better.

"Okay, I got the approval from my supervisor, so let's see if we can find that pet. Whose name is on the account?"

"Benjamin Silverstein."

"In what city is his account held?"

"Palm Bay, Florida."

"Okay, give me a second. I'm in his file now," the operator said. "Which account are you interested in?"

"Which account? What do you mean? He had a Yorkie. That's all I know of."

"Well, they're not listed by breed with us but by number. So do you know the animal's account number?"

"No. Just tell me what you have, and we'll figure out the rest."

"He has more than one account set up with us. Which one are you looking for?"

"How many does he have?"

"Give me a second. Wow! Mr. Silverstein is quite the animal lover. Let me see…twenty-two."

"Twenty-two?" Robbie held the phone to her chest and smiled for the first time in a couple of weeks. She beamed at Neal. "Dr. Silverstein has twenty-two accounts."

He grinned and clapped his hands.

Robbie's day was definitely improving.

24

Merritt Island, Florida

Robbie raised the digital camcorder and zoomed in on the enormous warehouse on the west side of the Merritt Island Airport, about twenty miles north of Melbourne. The small, single-runway commuter airport boasted several tourist flights for around Kennedy Space Center, which was a mere ten miles to the north.

A flight school and several shipping businesses were nestled next to Morris Shipping Inc. The company had just moved in, the deal for the rental space brokered over the phone and fax. No personal contact at all. Tim was checking the electric company records. If what Robbie suspected was going on there, they were draining some serious kilowatts to keep the chambers and computers up and running. The airport was closed at night and offered much privacy, a perfect location for Morek and his goons to set up shop.

The behemoth corrugated-metal warehouse had a loading dock in the back and a transport van parked just outside one of the roll-down doors. Three more bay doors covered that side of the building.

"What's Pet-Be-Found telling us?" Robbie snapped off a series of photos and a video streamer. The more intelligence they possessed about the layout, the better. Everyone would be interested in seeing this.

"Looks like we have seven or eight devilish dots on scene, best as I can tell." Eric reclined in Robbie's backseat as he monitored the laptop. He turned the screen her way so she could look for herself. "When they get real close together, it's difficult to count them. I think the metal roof interferes as well. But it's enough to know they're here. Pet-Be-Found tracked them down just like the other twelve, who are being rounded up as we speak."

"I don't understand why Dr. Silverstein didn't say anything to me about loading all of the experiments with locator chips." Neal slumped down in the front seat with Robbie. Surveillance techniques didn't appear to be Neal's strong suit, but he was doing his best. "I thought he shared everything with me."

"Maybe deep down he had his own reservations about what he was doing." Eric shifted the laptop back around. "Maybe he just wanted to have a method to track them if some were lost or stolen, or if something went wrong."

"Well, I think we're there," Neal mumbled.

"John and Alan are assembling the team now." Robbie eased the camera down into her lap. "I just hope that we can keep the element of surprise."

"You mean, *pray* we have the element of surprise." Eric smirked.

"Okay, pray. But what if these things know we're coming?" Robbie shifted her hips to see Eric better. "What if they can still communicate with the other side and know our every move? What if we're walking into one big trap?"

"These things are powerful but not *all*-powerful. They know a lot, but they're not *all*-knowing. We will pray that the One who is truly all-powerful and all-knowing will blind their eyes to our plans." Eric set the laptop on the seat next to him. "It's the only true hope we have."

"I never thought I would say this on a case, but can we pray right now?" Robbie's composed tone veiled the fear that fluttered just beneath her calm veneer. "I don't think I can go to another cop funeral anytime soon, and we've got three dozen officers preparing to hit this with all they have."

"I would be honored to pray with you, Ms. Roberta Sanchez." Eric slid his hand over to hers.

"Hey, what about me?" Neal raised his eyebrows. "I'm in this too."

"Let's do it." Eric nodded. "Dear heavenly Father, we need You now more than even we can imagine. Our enemy is strong and vicious and is a committed enemy of Yours. Please protect our people as we set forward to take them down, and blind the eyes of our enemy, that they would not see us coming. Give us Your wisdom. Strengthen us. Send Your Spirit ahead of us. Give us victory, Lord. In Your name. Amen."

Morek stalked around the chambers, surveying the waiting vessels of destruction, although they were not quite matured. His senses told him something wasn't quite right. He opened and closed his fist in front of his face, the novelty of his new body wearing off faster than expected.

For so long he'd yearned for the freedom the flesh gave him so that he might seek out and destroy the sealed ones. Now that very same flesh imprisoned him like a straitjacket instead of the suit of armor he'd envisioned, one that only death could loose.

His communication with the other side had all but ceased, limited to small flickers of hazy commands here and there, muted voices from his realm trying to connect, a consideration he'd minimized before entering this wretched body. Now, like the humans, he was trapped in a world of limitations, unable to pass through the chasms like before, powerless to skim the ruminations of mortal minds. He'd been cut off from the spirit dominion and from his master. Even his ability to sense or see the sealed ones seemed blunted, not nearly as strong as it was when he first took on this meaty form.

Bits of information had come to him with the release of the others. Little to nothing since then. He sensed his master trying to contact him, his flesh-clogged ears unable to hear his voice but his spirit tingling. Something was afoot; forces were moving, but what? Where? Should he release more warriors a little early and receive messages from his master? Or was the Offense One playing games with him, tempting him to move too quickly and prove him unworthy of his position?

Morek understood now how his schemes succeeded with such effectiveness before. His power and knowledge limited by his entombment in muscle and bone gave him a fresh perspective on his spiritual weapons, a lesson he'd surely use in the future. But for now, he needed to think clearly.

The low, constant drone of the generators was the only sound he could hear. Something was indeed happening, and his greatest fear seized him with a death grip—the Offensive One was moving against him.

25

Robbie scanned the horde of police officers the likes of which she'd never seen on a police operation. SWAT teams from the county and local municipalities huddled in the parking lot of the Brevard County Sheriff's Department substation on Merritt Island. Brass from the agencies stood along the back as well.

The sea of cops ebbed and flowed throughout the parking lot as the metallic sounds of weapons being loaded, checked, and holstered added to the murmurings of the task they were about to undertake. Most officers were decked out in typical SWAT gear—the Kevlar ballistic helmet, Level 4 body armor to stop rifle rounds, elbow and knee pads, face coverings, and attitude. Lots of attitude.

John and Tim passed out photos of the airport layout and of Morek to the crowd. Aerial snapshots of the building covered a placard up front as well as a diagram of the warehouse interior, at least what it looked like before its latest occupants moved in.

Robbie's head ached, the memory of their last encounter with a cloned being still fresh in her mind. It took dozens of police officers to kill just one in the shootout. How much more difficult would it be to corral eight? How many of these officers might not go home tonight? As disturbing as her thoughts were, it was more troubling to wonder what would happen if they didn't move now. How many more innocent lives would be taken by these beasts?

Cops were cops, and they would do what cops do—put themselves on the line to save others. But knowing it was their job to do this didn't allay Robbie's fears. She closed her eyes and lowered her head.

God, I don't know how this is all going to end, but I'm asking You to protect these men and women. I really need You.

Robbie raised her head and stepped up on a chair so everyone could see her. "Thank you all for coming today. Most of you have been briefed by your respective agencies, and you've all seen the news accounts, so you know what we're up against today."

She held up an enlarged photo of Morek. "This is him, and fortunately, right now we know what they all look like. So don't be freaked out if you see several suspects that look exactly the same—because they are clones, perfect replicas of each other."

"So you're saying these creatures look human but aren't?" a burly blond deputy asked as he slipped a wad of chewing tobacco into his mouth. "So do we arrest them, or just shoot them? What are our rules of engagement? Will we have to face a grand jury investigation if we pop some caps at them?"

"Shoot to kill." Robbie lowered the placard. "You all know what happened in Palm Bay last week. These things will not go quietly. And, please, understand that these creatures have extraordinary strength and speed and cunning. Do not underestimate them. They have no problem killing at all."

"Are these the same things responsible for the Palm Bay officer's death?" the deputy asked and then spit a brown streamer on the pavement.

"Yes," Robbie said.

"That's all we need to know." The deputy racked his shotgun.

"You all know your assignments." Robbie stepped down from the chair. "Each team has an area of responsibility. FDLE will breach the front door. After that, everyone has to move quickly."

"How will you take out that door?" a deputy asked. "There's a lot of open space between the buildings and near the tarmac. You don't want to leave a lot of officers out in the open trying to breach a possibly fortified door. It's a huge kill zone."

"We've got that covered." Tim smirked and crossed his arms. "It's called Operation Beetle Bash."

Robbie parked her car on the side of the hangar approximately two hundred yards south of Morek's warehouse. Darkness rolled toward them from the eastern sky, chasing away a spectacular sunset of brilliant orange and blue streaks. She watched the light vanish for at least one more night, all from the comfort of her presurveillance position.

Waiting for the cover of darkness, Robbie worked her plan over and over. She didn't know how much Morek and the others would be able to detect their coming. Robbie could be leading some of the best people she'd ever known into a slaughter. Surprise was their only hope and edge. It had been the most difficult decision she'd made in her law-enforcement career. But there was no time to fret the decision now; they were on the move.

A pizza delivery van pulled up to the front door of the warehouse. Even though they were cloned human beings, they still had to feed their flesh. The horde proved to have voracious appetites with a fondness for pizza. Since moving in, a dozen pizzas had been delivered every morning, noon, and night, just the mistake she'd exploit.

Eric positioned himself in the front seat next to her. Wearing his raid vest and a ballistic Kevlar helmet, he kept the notebook computer on his lap, intently watching the dots moving around on screen.

"Are they all there?" she asked. "Can we account for every one of them?"

"I'm not sure." Eric scanned the screen. "Some of them are so close together it's hard to tell, but there's a large group in there."

"Well, it's dinnertime, so I'm guessing we'll see them collect in one place to eat." Robbie pulled her hat down tight and adjusted her gun belt. "And that's when we move."

"You cops are very sneaky." Neal hung his hands on Robbie's seat. "I wouldn't have thought to do that."

"Just stay in the car." Eric still focused on the laptop. "We'll come get you when we need you."

"Robbie, we can't afford to mess this up." Alan sat in back next to Neal. His arms were crossed, and the near-permanent scowl was on his face.

She gave him credit, though. At least he was going on the operation and not sitting back in the safety of the office, waiting to hear what happened. Alan wasn't like that. He'd never send cops in to do what he wouldn't do himself—even if it meant going after not-so-human murderous clones.

The front door opened and the delivery man, a detective with Palm Bay PD, gave them the pizzas and collected the money. He scanned the area and hopped back into the van, slowly pulling away.

Robbie handpicked the detective to be the delivery agent. Eric informed her he wasn't a Christian, a fact he was quite sure of. She didn't want to take the chance of these guys taking him out just for fun before the operation got going.

"Okay," the detective called over his pack set radio. "Dinner's on, and I've cleared the scene."

"Nice job." Eric picked up a handheld radio from the seat next to him. "Now you can set up with your team." He switched on the radio to pick up the microtransmitter they had slipped into one of the pizza boxes. You could never have too much intelligence.

A foreign, raspy, hissing language filled the air, an eerie reminder of what was in store for them.

"What in the world is that?" Alan shifted in his seat.

"It's them." Neal squirmed, his chin quivering. "It's their wicked native tongue. Imagine listening to that for about twelve hours straight. That alone can make you mad."

Alan shook his head, and a perplexed look covered his face. "Well, we don't want to wait too long. They might find the microphones and be on to us. Let's get this thing going."

"They're all moving to a spot just east of the warehouse's center." Eric regarded Robbie. "Nice call, Agent Sanchez. Looks like human nature is consistent even with the inhuman."

"All units," Robbie said, "it's go time. Tim, John, release the Beetle. And may God be with us all."

Eric raised his eyebrows. "Nice touch."

"I'm working on it." Robbie smiled.

Alan unhooked his seat belt and positioned himself for the assault. Eric laid the laptop on the floor and slung his modified M-16 around his shoulder. They'd need all the firepower they could get. Checking her gear one last time, Robbie adjusted her pistol. *Lord, help us. We're moving.*

A distant buzz, like the approach of a giant bumblebee, and a set of headlights rolled off the runway as the yellow Beetle accelerated toward the front door of the warehouse.

Only Tim Porter would be crazy enough not only to come up with the idea for the breach, but to volunteer to execute it.

She couldn't decide if Tim was the most insane officer she'd ever worked with or if John was, since he'd agreed to go with him. John wouldn't let his partner do such a risky thing alone. As far as she was concerned, they were both nuts—and the best cops she'd ever known.

The VW Beetle quaked and vibrated as it sputtered past their position. John waved at them with his crash helmet on. Robbie pulled in behind them, a little farther back. Three other vehicles rounded the corner from the other direction, all converging on the front door.

A puff of smoke burped from the tailpipe of the little Bug as it rambled ahead. Tim approached the door at an angle, cutting back at the last second to hit the door head-on. A clash of metal on metal tore through the night as the VW Bug pierced the door, disappearing into the blackness behind it.

Robbie skidded to a stop just outside the opening where the door used to be. She hopped out and sprinted through the gaping hole with her flashlight in one hand and pistol in the other, Eric right behind her.

Pop. Pop. Pop. Tim and John were already under fire as they stepped behind the Beetle in the center of the warehouse. Another salvo of rounds ripped through the torn metal next to Robbie's head, sending sparks flying.

She ducked into the building and ran toward the Beetle. Tim's VW battering ram lay smoldering in the center of the warehouse floor. Rows of tubes were to Robbie's left, and the cauldron of half-humans were gathered to her right, just past the Beetle.

The clones turned back to back and gathered in a semicircle, each armed with an assault rifle. They unleashed a barrage of automatic fire at the oncoming force.

A loud burst came from Robbie's right as Eric sighted in on an armed assailant bearing down on them. More gunfire erupted as the chaotic scene grew. The second team hit the rear door, and officers filed through the breach, weapons raised, rushing into the depot.

Several of the clones backed up and fired indiscriminately throughout the building. They were being forced into a corner of the complex.

Robbie fired three shots at the same clone Eric had. She couldn't tell if she'd hit him. She sprinted behind the VW and used it for cover. Robbie, Tim, John, and Eric were pinned down there. She'd lost track of Alan and everyone else. The pounding of the rounds echoing off metal walls throbbed in her ears.

A clone stood just feet away and blasted an AK-47 with a drum magazine into the Beetle, a plume of smoke pouring out of the engine compartment.

Tim rose over the hood and cut loose with a blast from his 12-gauge shotgun, knocking the beast off his feet.

Eric curled around the trunk and fractured the air with his M-16, the flash pouring from the muzzle like lightning.

"I'm hit! I'm hit!" an officer screamed. "Officer down!"

Robbie didn't know who it was or even where the voice came from. Smoke from all the gunshots filled the air. A clone separated from the others and sprinted toward a side door.

"Stop him!" The relentless gunfire muted her shouts. "One's trying to escape!"

"I've got him!" Eric sprinted across an open portion of the floor after the fleeing suspect. Tim and John laid down cover fire. Eric was going after him alone. He needed backup. Robbie raced around the trunk of the car and gave chase with Eric.

"Stop!" Eric trained his rifle on the suspect, who bounded toward to the door with the speed of a cheetah, boggling Robbie's mind. These creatures were everything they were built to be.

Eric cut loose with another burst from the M-16 and knocked the clone off his feet and into the corrugated metal wall. The rest of the rounds ripped through the metal around him, showering the suspect with sparks as he tumbled to the floor.

"Show me your hands!" Eric crouched as he approached the downed suspect, rifle on him. "Get 'em up now."

The clone rolled onto his side and held his hands in the air. "Help me, please. I'm hurt bad. I don't want to die. I don't want to go back there. Please don't send me there again."

"Roll over onto your stomach and extend your arms." Eric leaned into his rifle, targeting the head. "I'll cuff you and then get you medical attention. But don't mess with me, or I'll send you back to hell."

"Okay, okay. Just help me." The clone complied with Eric's command.

"Cover me." Eric lowered his rifle and brushed it to his side.

Robbie stepped up, focusing her pistol at the mutant's head. The screams and the firefight were dying down but still sporadic. Each clone was content to go down fighting.

Eric dropped his knee into the small of the suspect's back, grabbed his wrist, and bent his thick arm back. He slapped on one cuff, then went for the other arm.

The clone flipped over and tossed Eric through the air, crashing him into the wall on his way to the ground.

Robbie fired her pistol, but he moved so quickly the round skipped off the concrete floor. In a flash, he slapped the pistol out of her hands and seized her by the throat, yanking her off her feet. Grabbing his wrist with both of her hands, she dangled two feet above the ground.

His eyes narrowed, and she saw only hate and rage and violence—all focused on her. He squeezed tighter, and she felt herself losing consciousness.

"Nooo!" Eric scrambled to his feet and leaped through the air. He tackled the clone from behind, knocking them all to the floor.

Smack! The clone's backhand was fast and vicious, knocking Eric away. Robbie crawled toward the pistol that lay just feet from her. The clone snatched her ankle and dragged her toward him as he stood.

Robbie took her free foot and launched it between his legs.

"Aaah!" He let go and doubled over. At least that part was human. Robbie crawled low across the concrete, snatched her pistol, and raised it.

Eric dove between the clone and Robbie and punched him twice in the face, which knocked him backward. Then Eric lunged at him again, but the clone front-kicked him in the gut, dropping him to the ground. The clone jumped to pick up Eric's M-16, still lying next to the wall.

"Watch out, Eric!"

The clone spun around and bore down on Robbie.

Pop. Pop. Pop.

The clone staggered sideways, dropped the rifle, and fell down, ambushed by shots coming at him from the side.

Alan emerged from the shadows, smoke rolling from his pistol as he continued to cover the suspect. He ran over and kicked the M-16 away from him. "Are you two all right?"

Eric wobbled over to them, holding his stomach and sucking wind. Robbie scrambled to her feet and jogged over, sliding an arm underneath Eric's to hold him up.

"Whatever you do, don't try to cuff him." Eric spewed out a ragged exhale, a trickle of blood leaking from his mouth as he leaned on Robbie.

"Wasn't planning on it," Alan growled.

Robbie moved closer. At least two shots had struck the clone in the head, but he was still moving and conscious, breathing hard and alternating his glance between them.

"You haven't seen the last of us." He grimaced. "We will watch you grow old and die—and your children and their children. We will tempt and lure and destroy them, and there's nothing you can do to stop us."

"Not us," Eric said. "Someone else has won that war, and He paid that debt for us. You're doomed, and there's nothing you can do about it. You failed. You can't stamp out the message of redemption—ever."

The creature hissed and spit at them. Everyone stepped back. He smirked as the blood flowed freely down his face. His body convulsed, and he issued a wail like a multitude of tortured voices crying out in unison.

Alan backed farther away and looked at Robbie. "What's he doing? What's going on?"

With another ungodly screech, his body seized up, and a rush of nauseating wind passed between them. Several more sinister death cries echoed from other parts of the building.

Tim and John jogged around the corner, weapons at the ready. "Everyone okay?"

"I think so." Robbie squeezed Eric tight. He was unsteady on his feet but was nevertheless alive.

"Did you hear it, Alan?" Tim asked. "Did you hear that wicked sound or what?"

Alan stood transfixed on the clone's lifeless body, his hand shaking with the weapon still in it.

"Alan! Did you hear it?"

Alan nodded at Tim hard enough to cause whiplash. "I

thought you all were crazy, but what we just saw isn't normal. No human could do that."

Robbie and Eric hobbled toward the center of the warehouse. The floor looked as if it were made of gold with the number of spent ammo casings on the ground. Ambulance sirens reverberated through the night. Two officers lying on the floor received treatment from SWAT team medics.

Robbie met with the sheriff's office commander. "How many officers are down?"

"Looks like six with gunshot wounds of some type, but I think they're all going to make it. Several others with minor injuries." He shook his head. "With all the rounds spent, I don't know how more of us weren't hurt. The Big Man upstairs had to be looking out for us. That was the craziest thing I've ever seen."

Robbie propped Eric up and surveyed the scene. "Big Man upstairs" seemed too tame for what she just witnessed. "Hand of God" fit the situation better. "How many suspects?"

"We're counting them now." He slid his MP5 machine gun to the side and loosened his ballistic helmet, which had a gouge from a round in it. "They split up when we hit the place, so they're spread out all over the warehouse. It's not going to be a pretty scene to clean up, that's for sure."

Robbie nodded. "We'll be here for a few days sorting this out, but it sure beats the alternative."

"Roger that." He turned and walked toward his men. "Get the perimeter secured. Crime Scene's gonna clean this mess up."

Robbie eased Eric into a chair.

"I think I broke a couple of ribs." Eric groaned and rubbed his hand on his side.

"I'll get one of the medics to check you out." Robbie rested her hand on his shoulder.

"Let 'em look at the others first." Eric waved at her. "I've broken ribs before. I'll survive."

Robbie walked over to the rows of chambers. The one closest to her had been shattered in the gunfight, the gooey liquid oozing onto the floor. The body lay in a clump at the bottom of the chamber. In any other situation, she would try to administer aid. Even though it looked like a teenage boy, she didn't want to get anywhere near that thing. What if one of the demons had already inhabited it?

Alan stood next to Robbie and gazed in wonder at the rows of chambers before them. "That nut was telling the truth the whole time. They really did try to pull this off."

"They didn't try; they succeeded." Robbie loosened her vest to finally draw a deep, lung-saturating gulp of air. "Now what do we do with their creations?"

"Get Neal in here." Alan danced around the nasty puddle of goo on the floor.

Robbie followed Alan around the chambers to get a better look at the macabre collection of young men and women of different races and sizes, a cross section of humanity. Their hearts beat and their lungs pumped, but the spark that made them human was missing.

Neal jogged into the lab and hurried toward Alan. "So this is how far they got. If this group would have been birthed, only the Lord knows what would have happened." Neal walked over to the control panel of the smashed chamber.

The hum of the generator pulsed, keeping the rest of the mutated flesh alive.

Alan regarded Neal. "Can you shut this thing down?"

"Absolutely and with pleasure." Neal punched in a series of commands on the control panel. "The Genesis Project is officially over."

"You did good, Robbie." Alan crossed his arms. "We'll never know how many lives you saved by putting this together. I'm sorry I was such a hard sell, but it all seemed so…unbelievable. Clones? Demons? The rational mind just can't handle all that at one time."

"I know what you mean. Everything I thought I knew about life has been called into question on this. I have a lot of soul searching to do." She shook her head. "I just wish we could have stopped them sooner."

"Me too." Alan rubbed the back of his neck. "If it makes you feel any better, I have a lot of soul searching to do as well. Just don't tell John or Tim. They'll be all over me with that Jesus stuff."

"Deal." Robbie put an arm around him. "I just hope the others can be tracked down now before anyone else is killed. If Dr. Silverstein hadn't implanted the locators on them, we'd all be in a lot of trouble."

Dozens of officers gathered around as Neal flipped switches in sequence on the control panel. The generators halted, the bubbles from the oxygen tanks ceased flowing, and a deafening silence permeated the warehouse for the first time since they'd arrived.

Wounded officers were being carted out by ambulance crews as the lights dimmed and went out in the lab.

The SWAT commander approached Robbie. "We have a final count on those things—seven total."

"Seven!" Robbie shook her head. "There should be eight. Where's the other one? Could he have escaped during the entry?"

"It's possible." He shrugged. "But not probable. We had snipers set up on the perimeter since the operation started, and no one was observed leaving. To be safe, we'll sweep the airport and see what we come up with."

"I don't like this." Robbie jogged to the car, grabbed the laptop from the backseat, and set it on the trunk. The Web page was still loaded. Eric eased up behind her as she did a hasty count on the screen. Only seven small dots on the map. She widened the view to the entire airport. Nothing. She widened the search area again to most of Merritt Island. Nothing again.

She expanded the view to all of Brevard County. A lone light blinked in the south-county area—Palm Bay. She highlighted it, zooming in. The light pulsed just off of Babcock Street at the Vining's Apartments—her complex.

"Oh no!" Robbie screamed. "Please, no."

She flipped open her cell phone. The number rang and rang and rang.

"Please, God, no."

26

Kathy Henderson picked up the phone, hoping the ringing didn't disturb Isabel. "Sanchez residence."

"Grab Mima and get out of the house now!"

"Robbie, is that you?" Kathy almost didn't recognize the voice. "What's wrong?"

"Get my mom and leave now as fast as you can. You're both in danger. Please run now."

"Okay, Robbie. Okay. But your mom's not dressed. I was just getting her—"

"I don't care if she's naked. Both of you need to run now! Someone's coming—"

Crack! The front door bowed in and the trim split.

"Ah! Robbie someone's—"

The door shattered, pieces flying in all directions. A huge stranger stepped in the doorway, grinning at her.

Kathy screamed, then dropped the phone and backed away.

"Hello, Kathryn," he growled as he stalked into the room toward her. "It's so very nice to meet you and the lovely Isabel."

"No!" Kathy sprinted into Isabel's room and slammed the door. She fumbled with the lock until she felt it click.

A fist spiked through the center of the door, launching splinters throughout the room just above her head. Kathy back-pedaled to Isabel's bed.

"Hello, ladies." The sicko peered through the hole. Who was this maniac?

Isabel sat up and looked at Kathy and then toward the door with the consistently confused gaze that dominated her days.

Kathy darted to the window, yanked it open, and pushed out the screen. "Help, call the police!" she screamed into the empty darkness. A second-story jump would kill Isabel for sure. But she couldn't leave her.

The door blasted off its hinges. She had to get help. Throwing one leg out the window, she straddled the sill. The nut marched at her and lifted his shirt, drawing a pistol. He zeroed in on her head.

She arched back and felt her body tumble out the window just as the shot fractured the air. Smacking the ground hard, Kathy bounced on the grass. Pain pierced her shoulder, and the wind was knocked out of her. Her collarbone must be broken. Maybe her back too. She couldn't…breathe.

The man peeked out the window and pointed the weapon at her again.

Pop. Pop. Two more rounds dug up chunks of earth next to Kathy's head as she rolled away. She staggered to her feet and hobbled through the empty parking lot. The psycho slammed the window shut.

"Help," she squeaked out, the air still not returning to her lungs. "Someone please help me." What would that psycho do to Isabel?

Nausea turned Kathy's stomach as she went to get help.

"Kathy!" Robbie looked at the phone as she screamed into it. "Kathy!"

She turned to Eric. "We've got to get to Palm Bay. He's there. I know it. Morek's slipped away and is at my apartment."

Eric snatched his microphone off the dashboard. "Dispatch, send every officer you have to the Vining's Apartments. One of these creatures is there. Hurry! I'm on my way."

Eric spun the car tires on the tarmac as he peeled a half circle and rocketed toward Palm Bay, still a good twenty miles away. They'd never get there in time.

"Go! Go!" Robbie pounded her fist on the dashboard. This couldn't be happening. *Please, God, don't let this happen!* "Can this thing move any faster?"

"I'm doing the best I can." Eric winced and grabbed his

ribs as they skidded around the corner and onto Courtney Parkway.

A trail of red and blues closed the gap between their cars as John, Tim, Alan, and others joined in the pursuit. With their hideout destroyed and Neal shutting down the current experiments forever, Morek would be left here on earth alone. Even if he escaped again, it would take him years, if ever, to replicate the lab and research. All the while, every law enforcement agency in the state would be pursuing him. He could have gone to Robbie's apartment for only one reason—revenge.

Her cell phone chirped, and she glanced down. It was her home number. She flipped open the phone. "Kathy, are you okay?"

"She's just fine, Robilina." His wicked whisper ripped and tore at her nerves. "But I'm a little worried about your mother. She doesn't seem to be doing so well." Mima screamed in the background.

"You evil scumbag, if you harm—"

"You'll what, arrest me? send me to jail? For where I've been, that would be like paradise. You are so out of your league, little one."

"Even better than that. I'll send you back to hell where you belong."

"Oh, Robilina, you poor, self-deluded child. You don't understand that no matter what happens, we win."

"Then what do you want? You must want something, or you would have killed her already."

"You are perceptive, Robilina."

"What do you want?"

"*You!*"

Eric skidded to a stop in the apartment complex, awash in pulsating blue and red lights. Four patrol cars were visible, their rotating lights still running. Others cut off entry and exit points throughout the complex. Palm Bay PD locked down the area tight. The spotlight from the helicopter cut across the complex as it passed overhead. Robbie hopped out and sprinted to one of the ambulances.

"Robbie, I'm so sorry." Kathy held out a hand from the gurney, her neck secured in a brace and her body strapped down. Tears poured down her face. "I should have taken her with me. I should have made her jump."

"You did the right thing." Robbie took her arm and squeezed it with both hands. "There's nothing else you could do with him. I understand."

"He's in there with your mother." Kathy's body quivered. "I'm so scared. He's crazy, Robbie."

"We'll take it from here." Robbie checked out her apartment window coverings, which had been drawn shut.

Alan slid his car to a stop, and John and Tim jumped out of their car, still geared up from the raid at the warehouse. They jogged toward her.

"Who's in charge here?" Alan called out.

"I am." A tall, thin sergeant snaked his way between several cars and met with Alan, who flashed a badge at him.

"Alan Cohen, FDLE special agent. We have the scene now."

"You can keep it too. It's a real mess up there." The young sergeant shook his head, laid a map of the area on the trunk of his car, and oriented it to their position. "This is going to be another fiasco. I just don't want any of my guys or your people getting hurt."

"I'm with you there." Alan broke out a notebook. "What do we know so far?"

"Just that he's taken the old woman hostage and says he'll only negotiate with Robbie." He turned toward her. "I'm assuming that's you. Anyway, we've got the apartment surrounded, so he's not going anywhere. He opened the drapes twice and stood behind the woman with a gun to her head, using her as a shield. Even if our SWAT snipers get here in time, he seems shrewd enough not to give them a shot."

"He's too devious for that." Robbie slipped her raid vest off and let it tumble to the asphalt. "I'm going to call in."

"Robbie." Alan reached out and took her wrist. "You're too close to this. We need to get SWAT on scene and the hostage negotiators too. Then maybe we can talk him out."

"How can we negotiate with that?" Robbie pointed to the apartment window. "You saw what these things are. There's only one thing we can give him that he wants."

"And what's that?" Alan asked.

Robbie's cell phone buzzed. She glanced at the number, surprised it had taken him that long to call. She flipped up the phone. "You know you're surrounded and there's nowhere you can go."

"Who says I want to go anywhere?" Morek growled. "Your mother and I are having lots of fun, catching up on old times. We're just waiting for you."

"Well, I'm here now. What do you want me to do?" Robbie gazed up at the window.

Morek drew back the blinds, hovering just behind her mother, whose face showed her oblivious to the chaos around her…thankfully. He lifted his gun high enough for everyone to see and let the drapes fall back into place. He was sending her a message. She got it, in no uncertain terms.

"Come up and join the party," he said.

"If I do, will you promise to let my mother go?" She swallowed hard. Not that a promise from the embodiment of evil meant much to her, but she had to try. It might also make him think she was being sucked into his plan and might actually believe something that his filthy, lying tongue would say.

"You are all I want…for now. Your dithering old mother is nearly gone as it is. Hardly any fun at all. She doesn't seem to appreciate the true joy of this situation. But you, my dear, are a different story. You and I have a very special date together. Because of you, our plan has been delayed—"

"You mean foiled and destroyed." Robbie wasn't giving him that. "We stopped you and your demon friends forever."

"You only slowed down this process." Morek's voice irritated her. "My master can foretell these things. More humans will follow this path until they succeed again. This is only the beginning. Do you have any idea how many people are trying to clone humans as we speak? It will never stop. We will never stop."

"We'll see about that." Robbie brushed her hand through her tangled hair. "Everyone will know what happened. Your evil delivery system will be banished forever. You've tipped your hand, and we burned you with it."

"You're such a fool," Morek hissed. "Where money and power go, so goes the will of men. We've guided the hearts of humans for thousands of years and know well what keeps them coming back for more. Even a hint of physical perfection, eternal life on their own terms, and the witless wonders will run to my master and never look back. We are the future and will return again and again. So get used to the sound of my voice."

"I don't know much about you or your kind." Robbie squeezed the phone. "But I'm a real fast learner. And from what I do know, you chose the wrong team to mess with on your way back to hell."

Morek ripped into a tirade of profanity. Mima screamed again. He was punishing her. "We'll see who's heading to hell. If you don't come to me in five minutes, I will rip your mother into little tiny pieces and enjoy every moment of it."

"Okay! Okay!" Robbie had pushed too far and she knew

it. But how far was too far with Morek? "I'll do whatever you want me to. Just don't hurt her!"

If she was to stand any chance, she needed to think like him. But how do you think like pure evil?

"Come to the door." Morek's cool tone returned. "And knock, please, before you come in. I wouldn't want to be surprised by anything. You never know what could happen then. And you'd better be alone, for your mother's sake. Our little transaction shouldn't take long."

"I'll be there in five minutes. Then you need to release my mother." Robbie closed the phone and turned to Alan. "He wants me to go in."

"That's not happening." Alan crossed his arms and scowled. "We're not putting any agent in there with *it*, much less you. No deal."

"She's my mother and I'm going. I don't have any choice. He'll kill her if I don't."

"Robbie, think about it." Alan rested both hands on her shoulders and locked eyes with her. "He's going to kill her anyway. He'll kill both of you if he gets the chance. He's a maniac—"

"Demon-possessed clone." Tim held up a finger. "We need to get the terminology right and call these things what they really are. Evil beings."

"He is what he is." Alan stepped away and spit on the ground. "One thing we do know is that he has no problem with killing and likes doing it a lot. There's no way I'm letting you go."

"Robbie, he's right. You can't go in." Eric staggered back against a car, his face pale and covered with sweat, as if he might pass out at any time. The fight at the airport was taking its toll on him now. "You know he only wants to kill you, to take you with him. I won't allow it. SWAT's not going to make it in time, so I say we roll the dice, rush him, and take him out now."

"But I can't stand by and allow him to torture and kill my mother. He's using her as a shield. If we kick the door down and go after him, Mima and goodness knows how many others will be killed. And if I don't go up there, who wants to listen to my mother shriek in pain as he tortures her? Just raise your hands." She gazed into the long, silent faces of her friends.

"Robbie, I'm your boss…and your friend." Alan's shoulders slumped. "I can't in good conscience send you in there to die. I know this sounds harsh, but your mother is a very old and sick woman now and probably doesn't have much longer to live. You have a long, long life ahead of you. You can't forfeit that. It won't help anyone."

"She is sick, but she's also my mother. She might not be able to recognize me in her mind, but her heart knows." Robbie stabbed a finger at her chest. "Her soul is alive and real and every bit as valuable as the day she was born. She would have given her life for me anytime. If I have to, I'll go down with her, but I will not abandon my mother to this evil—ever! So unless you plan on physically stopping me, you'd better come up with a plan now, because we only have about two minutes left."

John stepped forward. "What if we do both?"

"Let's hear it, Russell," Alan barked. "And be quick."

"Send Robbie in but with a plan and a purpose." John held his hands out. "She gets Morek to separate far enough away from Mrs. Sanchez; then we come in and finish this thing once and for all."

"That works for me." Tim punched his fist into his hand. "Let's take this guy out—now. He's really rubbing me wrong."

Alan checked his watch and then passed his hand across his shiny bald head. "We don't have enough time, and the equipment isn't here to wire up Robbie. How will we know when to move in?"

"You call me," Eric said. "Give me your cell phone."

Robbie handed it to him, and he punched in a series of numbers.

"All you have to do now is hit Send." Eric pulled his cell phone from his pocket. "I'll have mine set on vibrate. We'll be outside the door. When we come in, you get your mother on the ground. We'll do the rest."

"What if the call doesn't go through?" Alan asked. "What if you get another call, and we move too soon? What if he kills Robbie as soon as she walks in the door? This is too impromptu. I don't like it all. Way too many variables."

"None of us like it." John adjusted his gun belt. "But we're running out of time and options."

"That's the plan." Robbie clapped her hands together. "And I like it, mainly because it's the only chance we have. If it goes bad, I'll just scream. You guys do what you've got to do then. Other than that, we'll let BellSouth take up the slack. We need to move now."

Tim opened Alan's back car door and pulled out a long black bag. "After our first little encounter, I took the liberty of upping my firepower a bit." He pulled a 12-gauge pump shotgun from the bag and racked the chamber. "I figure if a 12-gauge slug will down a buffalo, it'll drop one of these things. I'll be aiming for a head shot, Robbie. Just get clear of him. I won't miss."

"I know, big guy. You're the best shot I know. I trust you." Robbie tapped her foot as she kept track of the time. "Okay, we need to move."

"Not yet." John waved everyone closer. "Too much hanging in the balance here. We have to pray."

"Good deal." Eric wrapped his arm around Robbie's shoulder and flinched as he drew her close. He was in a lot of pain.

Everyone stared at Alan.

"What are you looking at me for? Pray! Pray now; pray a lot. Yell if you have to. Just get it done."

"Heavenly Father, we need You more than ever." John laid his hand on Robbie's shoulder as well. "Put Your protection around Robbie and her mother. Guide their steps. Surround them with angels. And do a miracle here and get Morek away from Mrs. Sanchez and send him back to the abyss where he belongs. We need You, Lord."

"Amen."

Eric grabbed Robbie's hand and held it close to his chest, slipping the phone in it and squeezing it tight. "Robbie Sanchez, you come out of that apartment, do you understand me? We have a lot to talk about and do together. So I don't want any excuses, like, 'I'm sorry I got myself killed.' That's just not going to cut it."

"I'll make it out." She bit her lip and hoped her fib passed the test. There was no way this crazy plan would work. But if it did, she promised right then that she would drop her guard and excuses and allow herself to fall for Detective Eric Casey. She smirked. "Come on. Where's your faith? We're going to do this."

"One more thing, Robbie." John cut between them. "Remember, this creature is a born liar. Whatever he says or does cannot be trusted, and he'll take every advantage of any situation to take you out. I don't have time to give you my whole spiel. Just trust Jesus, Robbie. He's our only hope."

"Thanks, John. You're a good friend." Robbie hugged him and opened the phone, dialing her number.

"Hello, Robilina."

"I'm coming up."

"Just remind your friends not to try anything foolish or there will be a bloodletting like you've never seen before."

"Everyone understands. You're in control, and we'll do whatever it takes to get my mother out."

"Good girl. Now come to me." He hung up.

Robbie punched in Eric's number on her phone again to prepared it for the call. She dropped it in her shirt pocket with the top of the phone open, ready to go. She hustled to the stairs, keeping an eye on the window above.

Tim, John, Eric, and Alan slipped around the cars and worked their way through the shadows to the entrance of the breezeway and stairwell, staying out of sight of Morek's position. Tim shouldered his shotgun at the low-ready position at the front of the team and nodded to her as she passed.

Scanning the faces of her friends and co-workers, who in less than a minute would burst in to face down evil personified, she saw something she'd never seen before. Their expressions couldn't lie; they were terrified for her.

Breaching the breezeway, she jogged up the stairs, stomping each footstep hard and loud to announce her coming and to cover the sound of the team moving behind her. She felt the open phone in her pocket, Eric's number still programmed in. She could push the Send button through her shirt if she needed to.

This was the craziest plan she'd ever been involved in, but it had to work, at least well enough to get Mima out. Whatever happened after that didn't concern her. Robbie's and her mother's lives teetered on the cusp of two worlds. She hoped and prayed to stay in this one.

She stopped at her door. What if this was the last door she ever walked through? Was she ready for that? *Jesus, forgive me for letting life get in the way of knowing You. Right now, we really need You. I need You. Guide me. I'm Yours.*

She knocked.

"Come in. It's open."

Robbie turned the knob and pushed it open but didn't enter. Standing in the living room nearly fifteen feet away, Morek loomed behind her mother, his arm draped around her neck, his pistol poised against the side of her head. Mima looked indignant and bewildered. Morek's eyes flickered with the flame of rage.

"*Tranquila de la estancia,* Mima." Robbie needed her to be calm if this was going to work. She held her arms out so Morek could see them. She walked into the room. "Everything's going to be okay now."

"Close and lock the door." Morek's monotone order disturbed her more than if he were ranting and raving. It was cool and calculated. She kept reminding herself that he wasn't crazy—he was wicked.

She reached behind her and pushed the door closed, locking it. Knowing Tim, the cheesy lock on her door wouldn't stop his powerful foot. She must trust her friends now…and God. She had nothing else.

"You're such a beautiful young woman." Morek hid his mouth behind Mima's head.

Staring at Morek face to face evoked a torrent of emotions from the other clone's shooting. The same creepy, disturbed face taunted her with his eyes.

"You can let Mima go now and do whatever you want with me." Robbie scanned the room for some cover close to her. Nothing. She was exposed in the middle of the living room. She sidestepped toward the couch. Maybe that would help if it went bad.

"You've changed, dear one." Morek's eyes murdered her a thousand times. "Something is different about you. You've become one of them. You've become a *sealed one*, haven't you? That makes this all the sweeter."

Robbie's hands trembled as she glared into Morek's sinister gaze. He knew she trusted God now, and she froze, wondering how to answer him. She considered lying to him or just not answering at all. But with one foot in this world and one in the next, she didn't want her last act to be a denial of what she knew was true. She nodded. "I do trust Him."

Morek constricted his grip around Mima's neck and lifted her onto her tiptoes. She grabbed his forearm instinctively. "She's so fragile now, you know. The life sucked out of her by an unloving, uncaring God. Isn't it cruel that a supposedly benevolent Being would allow your mother to suffer so? This is the One you've chosen to follow? Whatever else you are, Robilina, you are not a foolish woman. It doesn't make any sense for you to follow this Being."

"Just let her go, and I'll do whatever you want." Robbie

was stuck. He wasn't budging. If the guys busted in now, Mima would be caught in the crossfire. She couldn't bear that.

He's a liar. I have to beat him at his own game. But how?

"All I really want, Robilina, is for you to follow my master." He grinned and forced the pistol against Mima's head. "If you will do that one little thing, both you and your mother will walk out of here unharmed. I give you my word. Simply swear allegiance to the true king, and I will spare you. My master is the master of this world, and he will give you everything your heart desires."

"How would I do that?" Robbie worked for a sincere look. She didn't know if she pulled it off. Could this demon read her thoughts right now?

"Simply renounce the Offensive One." His eyes locked with hers. "Look to the heavens and reject Him. You won't regret it, Robilina. Your father followed my master."

Robbie quaked, as she knew the lie as soon as he spoke it, and she yearned to run across the carpet and slap his wicked face. Whatever else confused her in life, she knew who her father served. She struggled for composure. *God, help me here.*

"I don't think I know what you mean." Robbie kept her hands out, but they began to shake. "Who is this Offensive One? This is all so new to me."

Morek gritted his teeth and growled. "*Jesus* is the *Offensive One.* Now bow down to my master or die." Morek shifted the pistol from Mima's head and aimed it so Robbie could stare down the barrel.

Lord, help us.

Mima chuckled and covered her mouth with a hand, stealing Morek's attention. She then broke into full laughter. Mima stared straight at Robbie, her countenance like she'd not seen in years. "Roberta, don't you see them? They're everywhere."

"Mima?" Robbie's hands dropped to her sides. Her mother seemed to be talking to her in a coherent way. This wasn't possible.

Morek loosened his grip, perplexed. The pistol lowered to his side.

"Oh, Roberta, they are magnificent." Mima's eyes searched around the room again as she beamed. "You have nothing to fear, my child. They are here with us, to help us. Their swords are bright and beautiful. The light…it's so wonderful, so glorious. The music—"

"Nooo!" Morek stepped back from Mima with a frenzied scan of the room, waving the pistol around as if swatting at flies with it. "*He*'s sent them. They've come to stop me. *He*'s interfering again."

Robbie eased her hand toward her pocket as the surreal scene played out. Her mother locked in a stare again with her. "Do not fear, sweet Roberta. Papi is here too."

"Shut up, woman!"

Robbie sensed fear in him for the first time. Something was indeed in the room with them. He shuffled back several more steps, gun aimed at Robbie now. "Both of you, be quiet."

Robbie pressed the Send button and then held her hands high over her head, hoping to keep Morek's concentration on her.

"Where are they?" Morek screamed as he swung the pistol back toward Mima. "Tell me where they are!"

"All around us, condemned one." Mima stood tall, elegant, beautiful, and restored. She faced Morek without a hint of fear. "Your time is at hand. They've come for you as well."

Crash! The door splintered open as Tim sprinted forward, shotgun raised at eye level. John, Eric, and Alan trailed him.

Morek's and Tim's weapons exploded at the same time. Robbie dove and rolled on the carpet. Another hail of rounds came from the group. Morek stumbled back against the wall, sliding down. The thunder of gunfire rumbled through the apartment.

Her mother collapsed, clutching her chest.

"Mima!" Robbie crawled to her and pulled her into her bosom. A crimson stain mushroomed through the center of her mother's nightgown, a round having pierced her chest.

"Roberta, don't cry." Mima brushed Robbie's face with her hand. Her hand trembled, but her smile increased as she gazed upon Robbie with a comprehension that had disappeared long ago. "*He* is waiting. It's so beautiful…"

"No! Please, God, no. Please!"

Eric knelt next to her and laid a hand on her shoulder. "I'm so sorry, Robbie."

Morek's death throes echoed throughout the apartment, and the foul stench of his wicked being spilled over with his passing.

Tim stood over the lifeless, Lifetex-generated body with his shotgun still trained on the beast. There would be no chancing it with him.

Robbie wept as she squeezed her mother. John, Alan, and Eric sat with her on the floor as she raised her laments skyward.

27

Dr. Meyer," a male reporter called from the crowd as he waved his hand above the others.

Robbie and Eric hung in the back behind Neal. It had been a tough two weeks, but she had good friends helping her through it, and they'd all promised to support Neal during his trials and difficulties ahead. How much could one man endure? The guilt he felt was palpable, but so was his resolve. With firsthand knowledge others could only dream of, he'd determined to take his tragedy and educate as many as would listen. He was a man with a redefined mission. He pointed to the reporter.

"To what do you attribute the violent nature of your cloned experiments?" he asked. "Do you think you made a mistake when replicating the human brain? Maybe some sort of damage was incurred during the process?"

"No. We didn't make any mistakes in our genetic manipulations. Actually, we got that part right." Neal adjusted the mic, a dash of sweat forming on his forehead. He still wasn't used to public speaking, but he was finding his legs. "Where we made our mistake was in not factoring in all of the variables."

"Could you be more specific?"

"We manipulated the genetic material quite well and used the already existing DNA to reconstruct magnificent flesh structures, or bodies. Their minds were superior, and their physical forms outstanding, without peer." Neal paused, lowering his head. "But there's so much more to human beings than just DNA, muscles, and tissue. We have spirits—something none of us can control, much less create. There's a void in each of us that has to be filled by one spirit or another. Our souls come from God and God alone, and no one can manipulate that."

"In an earlier interview, you said that demons had taken control of the cloned experiments." The reporter snickered and shook his head. "What exactly did you mean by that? You can't possibly mean real demons, can you?"

"I meant exactly what I said." Neal pushed up his glasses. "Evil does exist, and so do evil spirits. They did indeed inhabit the bodies of our experiments. I don't know exactly how that happened, but I know it did. It explains why they were so vicious and why the majority of their victims were Christians."

"C'mon, Dr. Meyer. You're a man of science. You don't really expect anyone to believe that, do you?"

"You can believe anything you like." Neal rested his hands on the podium. "I am a scientist, and as a scientist, I cannot dismiss my observations. I've documented them carefully, and I know what I saw and heard. I will tell it to anyone who will listen. Evil exists and seeks to destroy all of what God has created. Dr. Silverstein and I helped facilitate that evil, even if unknowingly and unwillingly. I won't make that mistake again. I owe that to Dr. Silverstein and everyone else who was hurt by this. It is my duty."

"Is that what you're going to say when you testify before Congress?" another reporter called out.

"That's exactly what I'm going to tell them and the United Nations panel as well." Neal nodded. "We made many beneficial advances with our research that can and will improve the lives of people all around the world. I don't want to stop that. But when we tried to create life and control it—that's when we went too far. There must be recognized limits on this technology." Neal leaned forward as more flashes lit up the room.

"They're going to rip him apart and paint him as a nut." Eric crossed his arms. "They'll eat him alive and work very hard to discredit what he's telling them."

"Maybe." Robbie moved closer to Eric, her shoulder resting against his.

Since Mima's death, Robbie experienced more emotional ups and downs than she thought possible. She grieved for her mother but at the same time rejoiced because she was sure where Mima was—a place of beauty, no pain or suffering, and in the presence of God. Eric spent a lot of time with her, explaining the realities of heaven. Though the pangs of loss still overwhelmed her at times, she felt a gentle, healing power in her life like she'd never known before.

"But I think he'll win over a few. He's a committed man, armed with the Truth."

"Has he won you over?" Eric smiled. "What do you believe now?"

"I don't understand everything. For that matter, I don't understand much of anything. But I'm a follower of Jesus now, and I've made some promises that I'm obligated to keep."

"Then I'm just as obligated to help you find answers, Ms. Roberta Sanchez." Eric lowered his hand and brushed hers. She opened it and took hold of his. "If you don't mind, of course."

Mind? Prayers were already being answered for her.

"Okay. Everyone settle down now." Tim clanked his fork against the glass, drawing the group's attention. Robbie wasn't sure why he voted himself emcee for the night, but it did seem natural. He was the loudest and chattiest of them all.

Tim's wife, Cynthia, sat next to him. John and his wife, Marie, were beside them. The guest of honor, Alan Cohen, sat at the head of the table, posed like the fatherly boss he was. The group crammed into the back room of Paisano's Fine Italian

Restaurant for Alan's special dinner. After thirty years of faithful service, Special Agent in Charge Alan Cohen was retiring from the Florida Department of Law Enforcement, and the least he deserved was a decent dinner.

Robbie invited Eric to join them, and she was more than pleased when he agreed. The whole crew was there to wish their boss well in his new life, away from the insanity of the police world. Could he survive a life without the constant danger and stress of police work? Time would tell.

For the first time in recent memory, Robbie wore a full-length dress and her hair was styled in something other than a ponytail. With her mother's passing, Robbie had taken inventory of her life to see how she'd really let herself go, consumed with the difficulties and pressures that come with being a primary caregiver. Even with Mima gone, she still felt guilty about taking some time for herself. Her life would take a while to reclaim, and she'd have to be patient.

Alan had only wanted an informal gathering of the crew, not some large bash, but since she hadn't dressed up in a long, long time, she took advantage of the situation.

"Everyone raise your glass to Special Agent in Charge Alan Cohen, the best boss anyone could ask for." Tim lifted his drink high.

"Here, here." The crowd followed.

"We've got a little gift for you, boss." Tim nodded to John, who placed his cloth napkin on the table, took a bag from the floor, and pulled out a plaque.

John rose and cleared his throat. "In appreciation for all of the late nights, crazy chases, and all your aged wisdom, we, the agents from the Melbourne office of the Florida Department of Law Enforcement, wish to thank you for your supreme service and great patience with your adopted children. May you out-live all the people you've put on death row. From John Russell, Tim Porter, and Robbie Sanchez."

Alan shook John's hand to another round of applause. "Well, I don't know what to say."

"We're not quite done yet." Tim pulled a straw farmer's hat from the bag and plopped it on Alan's head. "Since we know you won't be catching any more bad guys in your retirement, we thought we'd get you some proper attire. You'll need this for all the gardening you'll probably be doing."

John handed him a rake. "This will help you stay busy."

"Wow." Alan's droopy, ridiculous hat hung down on his head. "I'm really going to miss all the kindness I've received through the years from you all."

"Speech! Speech!"

"Well, I do have a few things to say." Alan leaned on his rake like Eddie Albert in the *Green Acres* television show. "First, I didn't think that walking away would be so hard. We've found missing children together, rescued abducted teens, caught killers, and fought with demon-infested clones. That's for you, Tim." Alan paused as they all clapped. "You all are the bravest, most decent police officers I've ever had the privilege of serving with, and I'm going to really miss each of you. We've shared some of the most fun, rewarding, and downright frightening times of my life together. And I wouldn't trade those memories for anything. Thank you all."

"Are you goin' soft, boss?" Tim clapped. "You're starting to sound like you're on Oprah's couch."

"Maybe a little." He shrugged and tipped his hat back. "I think it's the hat. Anyway, now it's my turn to give gifts." Alan pulled a bag from underneath the table.

"It's your party." John held Marie's hand on the table. "You're not supposed to give the gifts."

"Give an old curmudgeon his due." Alan pulled a box from the bag. "Agent John Russell. I've worked with you longer than anyone else in my career, and you are one of the finest cops, and men, I've ever known. A bit hyperreligious maybe, but a good fellow just the same."

Alan handed him his gift. "I thought long and hard about what to get you. I finally thought of the perfect gift, so here it is." Alan handed John a slim package.

John ripped it open. It was a school picture of Dylan Jacobs, the missing boy John located after six years.

"I spoke with his mother, and she wanted you to have this, to remind you and all of us why we do what we do. You're a great cop, John. Don't ever forget that. It's been a pleasure."

John stood and embraced Alan. "Thanks. I really appreciate it. It's been an honor working with you too."

"And now for Timothy Porter." Alan handed him a box.

Tim opened it, smiled for a moment, and then he frowned.

"I take back all the nice things I said about you, Alan." Tim held up his toy 1968 replica Beetle, painted yellow in meticulous detail to match the ride he sacrificed in the warehouse. "You're a bad man. I never thought I'd see this thing again."

"I was curious why you were so eager to volunteer to ram the door at the warehouse." Alan leaned his rake against the wall. "Some guys will do anything to get a new car."

"I'd have driven that ugly thing off a bridge, if I thought I could get rid of it."

"Look in the rest of the box," Alan said.

Tim pulled out a pamphlet from Dr. Walter Simmons's Higher Learning Method seminar.

"Because of you, this man is no longer deceiving and murdering young people. You stopped him cold in his tracks and saved your daughter in the process. This gift is to remind you of that, lest you ever feel that your work doesn't impact others. Tim Porter, you are possibly the bravest, if not the craziest, cop I've ever known." Alan rested his hand on Tim's thick shoulder. "And I will miss you a lot, my friend."

"Now you're getting me all Oprahed out." Tim's eyes watered as he seized Alan's hand and shook it hard. "You're the best boss I've ever had. And I mean that."

"Now that leaves you, dear Roberta." Alan lifted a bag onto the table. "I thought long and hard about what I could give to you. You've had a rough few weeks, and I know it's probably not getting any easier. So I got you the one gift I knew you wouldn't go out and get for yourself."

Robbie looked around. She had no clue where he was going with this. The man was unpredictable, to be sure.

He handed her a folded slip of paper. She took it and laid it down on the table.

"Open it." Eric nudged her with his elbow.

Robbie rolled her eyes and opened the paper. "What's this?"

"It's a vacation request, signed and approved." Alan removed his straw hat and placed it on the table. "You probably don't know what one looks like because you haven't taken a vacation since you've worked for the agency. So, Roberta Sanchez, I'm giving you the gift of time off…and you *will* use it. My last act as supervisor of the Melbourne FDLE office was to sign your month-long vacation request. Use it in good health, and please get a life outside of this job. While I'm looking at you all at the end of my career, the only thing I really value and will miss are the people and the relationships. It's you, my friends and co-workers, who have provided me with more joy and pleasure than I ever thought possible. Thank you all."

The group stood and applauded, then made their rounds, each taking a turn to hug Alan.

Robbie hung back. John and Tim had worked longer with Alan, and she let them say their farewells first.

Alan turned his attention to Robbie and Eric. He took her by the shoulders. "Robbie, you are such an amazing police officer and young woman. If I had a daughter, I'd want her to be just like you. Take care, and please don't let this job eat you alive."

"Thanks, Alan." Robbie nodded. "I'll take it to heart."

"And you, Eric." Alan shook his hand. "You're young and strong, but you must remember that age and treachery beats youth and skill every time."

"Okay…" Eric shrugged, obviously not quite sure why Alan said that.

"You need to remember that because if you break our Robbie's heart, I'm going to have to hunt you down and kill you."

Eric chuckled and looked around.

John and Tim stared him down as well, neither laughing along. Maybe they weren't kidding. It was like having a group of twisted, dysfunctional big brothers…with guns.

"I will treat Robbie with all the honor and respect that you could ask for." Eric took her hand. "I give you my word."

"I hope so." Tim slapped Eric on the back. "Because we know where you live."

28

Robbie lowered the flowers into the metal vase embedded in the ledge of the marble headstone at the family plot of Jorge and Isabel Sanchez. The gravestones were now fixed together on a solid concrete slab, just as her parents had been joined together in life.

The marble and etching were first rate; Robbie made sure of that. Her father purchased the plot just a few years before his death. Robbie always wondered if it was an omen, a strange foretelling of a catastrophic future event. Her father always spoke of their family being together forever. When Robbie had asked him why he didn't buy a plot for her next to them, he just laughed and said, "Because, sweetheart, someday you'll have a family of your own. And I pray that you're as happy as your mother and I have been." She prayed for that too…now. What a difference a few long weeks could make.

The sky was overcast and glum, not unlike her feelings in this moment. She'd spent the morning driving down from Melbourne, contemplating her life, or the lack thereof. Since she was a little girl, she'd wanted what her parents had, to feel loved and secure.

She crouched next to the graves, hoping somehow that being closer to the ground would help her feel closer to them spiritually. In just a few weeks, her entire life had been upheaved and scattered like ashes tossed into the wind. She'd lost her mother, relived her father's murder in vivid, agonizing detail, and come face to face with evil forces beyond her comprehension. But through the worst time she'd ever known, glimmers of hope peeked over the horizon like the first callings of the morning sun across the gloomy night sky.

Up until this point, her droning existence consisted of one attempt after another to achieve and conquer the next challenge at work, to stay so busy she never had to deal with the pain and yearnings of her own heart. It was easy to make excuses about finishing degrees and taking care of Mima and working more and more. Truth was, she'd mastered the art of avoidance in her own life—to her own detriment. Now she searched for something to take the place of all the "things" she'd filled her life with.

Neal's words rang so full of truth. Robbie had felt empty

and hollow, like one of the Lifetex clones, with a void in her soul. She'd tried to fill herself with everything but the right thing. Now she was set to know the purpose for which she was created. Her spirit was no longer void and had finally tasted peace. She reflected on the promises she'd made, those she intended to keep. She would continue to soul search, continue to face her past, and ultimately, was determined to discover the God who showed up on this case.

"Thank You, God, for giving me time with Mima again, even if it was only a few seconds. I'll never forget what You did for her, for us. I don't understand many things about You, but I want to try."

"*Adiós*, Mima and Papi. I'll come back soon." She kissed the tips of her fingers and touched the top of each headstone.

For all the heartache of losing both parents, she wouldn't forget the memories of her family and the life they gave her. By most accounts, she started out way ahead of the game. Now, she hoped she could give her children the gift of the solid home she'd known. Another thing she promised to fulfill.

Standing up, she brushed her hands along her jeans. The summer breeze swirled around her. Seasons were changing fast. Nothing remained the same forever, not now anyway. She turned to Eric, who leaned against her car, arms crossed and waiting.

He told her he'd wait as long as necessary for her to recover from her loss. And he'd be there through the transition. He wanted to share with her everything he knew about God and what he knew about himself. He, too, was ready for something new in his life.

She meandered across the small grass strip back to the car and scanned the expansive memorial park.

"Are you sure you don't need more time?" Eric pushed off the car. "I've got all week."

"I've taken enough time already." She took his hand and rubbed it with hers. "It's time for me—for us—to move on." Leaning forward, she kissed him.

Thanks to Alan's forced vacation, Robbie didn't have to be back at work for three more weeks. She'd use this time wisely.

"Do you want to take I-95 back?"

"No. Let's take U.S. 1 and see the coast." Robbie gazed out toward the Atlantic horizon. "I haven't driven up there in years."

"As you wish."

Robbie Sanchez and Eric Casey drove out of Graceland Memorial Parks and turned east into a future of hope and new beginnings.

DISCUSSION QUESTIONS

1. How does Robbie deal with the emptiness in her life? Why did she wait so long to address her own spiritual void?

2. Dr. Silverstein and Dr. Meyer violated—for the greater good—laws regarding human cloning. Is it ever permissible to violate the laws of the land? If so, when?

3. Scientific ethical boundaries are stretched to the limits in *The Void.* Should there be moral limits on scientific research? Where are those boundaries, and who determines them?

4. If scientists ever successfully clone human beings, will these creations have a soul like ours? Will it be possible for them to be saved and redeemed by Christ as well?

5. As Isabel's life hangs in the balance, Alan suggests that because of her mother's illness and age, Robbie's life wasn't worth risking. Does a person's age or infirmity diminish the value of his or her life? Did Robbie make the right decision to trade her life for her mother's? Why or why not?

6. Do you believe that demons are actively engaged in spiritual warfare today? If so, in what ways does the warfare manifest itself?

7. Morek referred to Christians as the "sealed ones." Would a Christian's spirit appear differently in the heavenly realm from a nonbeliever's? Explain.

8. As Robbie and Eric's relationship blossomed, what attracted Robbie to him? What qualities do you feel are important in a potential spouse?

9. Jorge and Isabel Sanchez modeled a healthy, loving marriage to serve as an example for their daughter, Robbie. Have you ever had friends or family who did the same? In what ways were they a good example? What qualities are key to maintaining a godly marriage?

10. Robbie allowed the busyness of life to interfere with her relationship with God. Can you relate to that? If so, in what ways?

11. What theme(s) did you take away from this book? Did it challenge you personally? If so, in what areas?

Thank you for joining me on this literary journey. I would love to hear your thoughts about *The Void* as well as my other novels. Please feel free to contact me at my Web site: www.copwriter.com.

—Mark Mynheir

Other Novels in the Truth Chaser Series:

Rolling Thunder

John Russell is the Florida Department of Law Enforcement Agent assigned to the missing Dylan Jacobs's case. But while he's tracking down clues in his professional life, a murderer is hot on his trail—his own flesh and blood. John's father relentlessly seeks something John refuses to offer: forgiveness. Forced to face the source of his paralyzing fear of thunder and his stolen childhood, can John find the missing boy without his personal life completely unraveling?

From the Belly of the Dragon

People associated with him have been killed, but Dr. Walter Simmons is a successful man. His books and tapes incorporate psychological principles with New Age, feel-good spiritualism and are a hit on college campuses. But when his top students join him for an intensive "training" program, they are actually joining a dangerous cult. FDLE Agent Tim Porter's daughter, Ruby, is lured in like the rest, the heights of a dream plummeting her to the depths of a living nightmare. To what lengths can Tim and his wife go to rescue Ruby from the belly of the dragon?

Available in bookstores and from online retailers.

MULTNOMAH BOOKS
www.mpbooks.com